CRITICAL ACCLAIM FOR ROBERT B. PARKER

'Parker writes old-time, stripped-to-the-bone, hard-boiled school of Chandler... His novels are funny, smart and highly entertaining... There's no writer I'd rather take on an aeroplane' – *Sunday Telegraph*

'Parker packs more meaning into a whispered "yeah" than most writers can pack into a page'
– *Sunday Times*

'Why Robert Parker's not better known in Britain is a mystery. His best series featuring Boston-based PI Spenser is a triumph of style and substance'
– *Daily Mirror*

'Robert B. Parker is one of the greats of the American hard-boiled genre'
– *Guardian*

'Nobody does it better than Parker' – *Sunday Times*

'Parker's sentences flow with as much wit, grace and assurance as ever, and Stone is a complex and consistently interesting new protagonist'
– *Newsday*

'If Robert B. Parker doesn't blow it, in the new series he set up in *Night Passage* and continues with *Trouble in Paradise*, he could go places and take the kind of risks that wouldn't be seemly in his popular Spenser stories'
– *New York Times*

ALSO BY ROBERT B. PARKER

THE SPENSER NOVELS

The Godwulf Manuscript
God Save the Child
Mortal Stakes
Promised Land
The Judas Goat
Looking for Rachel Wallace
Early Autumn
A Savage Place
Ceremony
The Widening Gyre
Valediction
A Catskill Eagle
Taming a Sea-Horse
Pale Kings and Princes
Crimson Joy
Playmates
Stardust
Pastime
Double Deuce
Paper Doll
Walking Shadow
Thin Air
Chance
Small Vices*
Sudden Mischief*
Hush Money*
Hugger Mugger*

Potshot*
Widow's Walk*
Back Story*
Bad Business*
Cold Service*
School Days*
Dream Girl (aka Hundred-Dollar Baby)*
Now & Then*
Rough Weather
The Professional
Painted Ladies
Sixkill
Lullaby (by Ace Atkins)
Wonderland (by Ace Atkins)*
Silent Night (by Helen Brann)*
Cheap Shot (by Ace Atkins)*
Kickback (by Ace Atkins)*
Slow Burn (by Ace Atkins)*
Little White Lies (by Ace Atkins)*
Old Black Magic (by Ace Atkins)*
Angel Eyes (by Ace Atkins)*
Someone to Watch Over Me (by Ace Atkins)*

THE JESSE STONE MYSTERIES

Night Passage*
Trouble in Paradise*
Death in Paradise*
Stone Cold*

Split Image
Fool Me Twice (by Michael Brandman)
Killing the Blues (by Michael Brandman)

*Available from No Exit Press

ROBERT B. PARKER'S

BROKEN TRUST

THE NEW SPENSER NOVEL

by MIKE LUPICA

NO EXIT PRESS

First published in the UK in 2023 by No Exit Press,
an imprint of Bedford Square Publishers Ltd,
London, UK

noexit.co.uk
@noexitpress

ISBN
978-1-915798-22-0 (Hardback)
978-1-915798-23-7 (eBook)

2 4 6 8 10 9 7 5 3 1

Typeset in 11.1 on 13.85pt Minion Pro
by Avocet Typeset, Bideford, Devon, EX39 2BP
Printed and bound in Great Britain by
TJ Books Limited, Padstow, Cornwall

MIX
Paper from
responsible sources
FSC® C013056

This book is for my friend James Patterson

Spenser's BOSTON

to Susan's home and office,
Linnaean Street, Cambridge

Charles River Dam Bridge

CHARLES STREET

Charles River

Massachusetts
General Hospital

ESPLANADE

Longfellow Bridge

CAMBRIDGE STREET

ESPLANADE

STORROW DRIVE

State House

to State Police,
Boston Post Road

BEACON HILL ■ The Paramount

■ Hatch Shell

to Fenway Park

BEACON STREET

Boston Common

CHARLES STREET

The Taj Boston
(formerly the Ritz-Carlton)

Public Garden

MARLBOROUGH STREET

BERKELEY STREET

ARLINGTON STREET

■ Swan Boats

Four Seasons Hotel
and Bristol Lounge

COMMONWEALTH AVENUE

Jacob Wirth ■

BOYLSTON STREET ■ Spenser's office

Davio's

Boston
Public Library

Copley
Square

Old Boston Police
Headquarters

STUART STREET

TREMONT STREET

to Boston Police Headquarters,
Roxbury

■ Grill 23

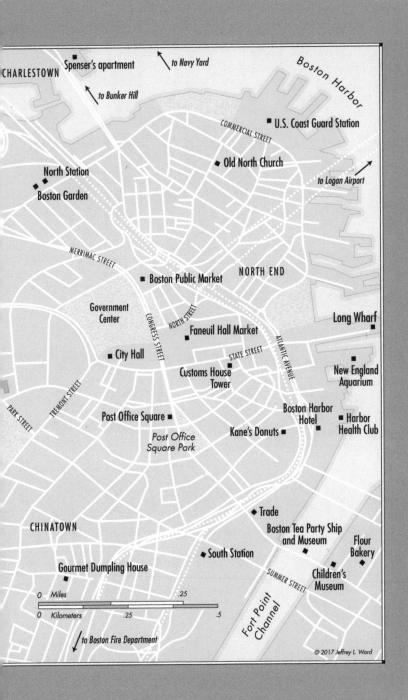

1

I was sitting at my desk drinking my third cup of coffee of the morning. I was doing this guilt-free, having read that two to five cups a day not only prevented a long list of diseases, but also helped you live a longer, if more caffeinated, life. But then you can always find somewhere on the Internet that tells you what you want to hear, about almost anything.

I was certain that if I looked long enough, I could find a site promising a reasonably priced way for me to look like Bradley Cooper.

By now I had already made short work of the second Boston Kreme I'd picked up at the Dunkin' just down Boylston from my office, the one near the Public Library. Two blocks down, two blocks back. But I had walked briskly, telling myself it was exercise, even if the prize had been the donuts, which didn't extend your life, just made it more worth living.

Dunkin' Donuts had long since rebranded and was just calling itself Dunkin' now. I had considered doing something similar, but knew it was too late for that. And when it came to branding yourself with just one name, I had frankly been way ahead of the game.

Carol Sloane's voice was coming out of the tiny speaker near the Keurig machine and I was methodically making my way through the print edition of *The Globe*, as I still did every morning, front to back, section by section, saving sports for last. The man who owned *The Globe* also owned the Red Sox. The paper was having a far better September than his baseball team was.

But then just about everybody was. It had reached the point where I was no longer certain that the two guys who were supposed to be our top starting pitchers were actually still right-handed.

'Maybe you should think about finding a new hobby,' Hawk had said the other day after listening to me bitching again about the local nine.

'I've got too much time invested in them,' I said. 'It's the same reason I'm still with you.'

'You're with me,' Hawk said, 'because I don't have no bad years.'

We had just finished moving the last of my furniture that we could carry ourselves into my new apartment, which just happened to be a few doors down from the one I'd been burned out of a few years ago. It was the event that had prompted my move away from Marlborough Street and all the way to the Charleston Navy Yard.

At the time Susan Silverman, trying to mitigate my loss, had said that while it had been the equivalent of a forced eviction, it might have been time for a change, even though she knew better than anyone that I liked change about as much as I liked TikTok.

'Most people do move sooner or later,' Susan said.

'The Red Sox haven't,' I said.

She had promised that I would embrace the new place once I was in it, and proceeded to move in and decorate it like an invading ground force. And eventually I had grown both fond and familiar with my new surroundings, the neighborhood, the proximity to the Navy Yard, even the younger vibe over there, as if I were the one who was young and had moved to Boston all over again.

But recently I'd done some work for a man named Kevin Boles, who owned great big chunks of property in Back Bay, getting Boles's son out of a jam with Tony Marcus that involved substantial gambling losses that Tony had decided required more than just money in payment. Tony wanted real estate favors from Kevin Boles, specifically involving a particular building he hoped to use for a new escort service on Charles Street now that COVID was over and the sex trade was booming again.

Boles had come to me and I had gone to Tony, reminding him that he owed me a favor. Tony told me that he didn't owe me shit and get the fuck out of his office. But being as transactional as he'd always been, an accommodation had been reached and he got the building he wanted. Kevin Boles considered it a small price to pay to get his son clear of Tony, and even after he'd generously settled up with me, he said that he was the one who now owed me a favor.

About a week later he'd called and told me that an apartment on Marlborough near the corner of Arlington had opened up, having remembered me mentioning that I'd lived on the same part of that street before what I called the Great Boston Fire. Boles said that the apartment hadn't yet gone on the market, and asked if I might be interested in moving back to the old neighborhood. I surprised myself at how quickly I said that I was. He said he could give me a break on the rent. I told him that wasn't necessary. He insisted. A month away from the end of my lease in Charlestown, I signed the lease that day, put down a deposit, and just like that Daddy was home.

'Do you know how much I've missed walking to work?' I said to Susan the first time we stepped into the empty apartment.

'At this point, people in outer space know that.'

She asked me just how much Kevin Boles had paid for my services, and how much of a break he was giving me on the rent. I told her. At which point she had smiled, wickedly. Susan has a lot of smiles, most of which make me feel light-headed and oxygen-deprived when directed at me.

This one, I knew from experience, was going to cost me money.

'I know that look,' I said.

'What look is that?' she asked innocently.

'The one where you can't wait for the stores to open.'

She'd kissed me then and said, 'Don't you worry your pretty little head about it.'

The new apartment, about the same size as the old one, didn't actually feel like home yet. But I was getting there. Pearl the Wonder Dog had already settled in quite nicely when she and

Susan would be there for sleepovers. Pearl hadn't come right out and said how much she liked it that she could walk to work with me, too, when Susan would leave her with me. It was more something I had intuited.

Now I just needed work, as there hadn't been any since I'd saved Kevin Boles's son.

'If you can walk to work but there ain't no work,' Hawk had said, 'answer me something: What's the fucking point?'

I was pondering that, and whether I should walk back down to Dunkin' for more donuts before I got too close to lunch, when there was a knock on my door and the wife of the sixth-richest man in America came walking in.

2

Laura Crain was a friend of Susan's from a couple charity boards they both served on in Boston, one of which – the Jimmy Fund – was as famous a charity as there was in the city, aligned with the Dana-Farber Cancer Institute, and deeply connected to the Red Sox all the way back to when Ted Williams had first gotten involved.

Susan and Laura Crain shared a Pure Barre class a couple times a week and would meet occasionally for lunch. I knew that Susan liked her very much, as rich and famous as Laura and her husband were, and not just in Boston.

Laura had met Andrew Crain when they were both students at Harvard. Laura was an English major. He was a full-fledged, card-carrying Division of Science nerd, along with his best friend, Ethan Lowe. I knew the general outline of their shared biography, because by now most people in America knew it. Five years after Lowe and Andrew Crain graduated, working out of a small rented lab in Dorchester, they had invented a synthetic form of lithium that had reimagined the world of batteries forever.

Susan had mentioned in passing a few weeks earlier that I might be hearing from her friend Laura about a problem she was having, one she'd shared in confidence with Susan.

'Are you treating her now?'

'Not professionally. Just hearing her out as a friend and offering advice when she's asked for it.'

'And she has a problem that you can't solve?' I said. 'What is it, the melting of the ice caps?'

'She'll tell you when the two of you meet,' Susan said, 'if she doesn't lose her nerve.'

'Couldn't she buy some nerve?' I'd asked. 'I assume she can afford it.'

'Let's just wait and see,' Susan said. 'She should be the one to tell you what's happening in her life. But I told *her* that if anybody could help her, it's my cutie.'

Now Laura Crain sat across my desk from me. Tall. Honey-colored hair hanging to her shoulders. Blazer, white jeans that fit her the way God intended jeans to fit women with legs as long as hers, ankle boots. Whatever her actual age was, I had already decided she looked younger. She reminded me of a slightly younger version of Julia Roberts, not that I would ever say that to Julia.

A knockout by any measure. It was something I knew I couldn't verbalise without sounding as if I were objectifying her, and being on my way to Weinstein Island.

But Andrew Crain, I could see, hadn't just gotten stupidly rich. He had even gotten the girl.

'So you're Spenser,' she said, crossing one long leg over the other.

'I am he,' I said.

I had come around the desk to greet her when she'd arrived. In the post-pandemic world I'd first asked if she wanted to shake hands before extending mine. She'd said she'd risk it if I would.

'People often say "I am him,"' I said. 'But that's ignoring the fact that "he" is actually supposed to be a predicate nominative renaming the subject.'

She smiled. It was, by any measure, a high-wattage dazzler, if not of Susan quality, at least in the conversation. Susan had prepared me for how lovely Laura Crain was. I was certain I would be cross-questioned later about just *how* lovely *I* thought she was.

'Susan told me about you,' she said.

I ducked my head in false modesty.

'The rugged good looks?' I said. 'Or devilish charm?'

She shook her head slowly from side to side, as if in the presence of a precocious child.

Which, all things considered, she was.

'She actually told me how hard you'd try, almost immediately, to show me what a literate detective you are,' she said. 'And that if I didn't acknowledge that fact you might get the bends.'

'I can also diagram some sentences if you want,' I said.

'Maybe when we know each other better.'

Now I smiled at her.

'Want to can the small talk?'

'I'd be willing to pay you,' she said.

I asked if she wanted coffee. She said thank you, but she'd pass, she was trying to quit caffeine. I told her I didn't want to live in that world. She managed to contain her laughter, but I sensed it was difficult for her.

'Might I offer just one last tiny bit of small talk?' she said.

'Okay, but *just* one.'

'You really are as big as Susan said you were.'

'Well, sure, but I come by it naturally.'

We sat there in silence for a few moments, as if each of us were waiting for the other to make the next move. It often went this way with potential clients, like an awkward first date, and just how much they wanted to drop their guard.

'So how can I help you, Mrs Crain?'

'Please. *Laura*.'

'So how can I help you, Laura.'

Her blue eyes were so pale as to be as clear as glass.

'That's the thing,' she said. 'You probably can't.'

3

It was always best to let them tell it their own way, at their own pace, editing their own narrative as they went along. Editing just how much of their own truth they wanted to share with a complete stranger.

There was another long silence now as she stared down at hands as lovely as the rest of her, as if suddenly remembering they were there. The nails were clear, no color to them. A single gold wedding band, no other jewelry of any kind. She clasped her hands tightly now in her lap.

When she looked up again she said, 'Susan said I could trust you, even if you choose not to take me on as a client.'

I smiled at her now. Not my big one. She was clearly having a hard time with all of this, and hitting her with my big smile, what I thought of as the Whopper, might cause her to lose control. Or, at the very least, her train of thought.

'I have to be honest, Laura,' I said. 'The only thing that might dissuade me from taking you on as a client is if you put a cigarette out in one of my eyes.'

Now she laughed, even if the sound seemed to die somewhere between us and land on the paper plate where the donuts had been.

I wanted to get up and make myself another cup of coffee, but we finally seemed to be getting somewhere. In moments like these I tried to pretend I was Susan, who had once told me that people in her line of work who talked too much with patients or interrupted too frequently should perhaps think about finding another profession.

'It's my husband,' she said.

I waited for her to elaborate. She did not, at least not right away. Maybe she thought telling me would be as easy as it had been for her to tell Susan, whatever she had told Susan.

Either way, she'd get to wherever we were going when she did and I had no desire to speed up the process.

'We love each other very much,' she said finally.

'I think I've seen you referred to as the planet's power couple,' I said, 'now that Bill and Melinda…' I shrugged helplessly, with palms up, a gesture that seemed to take in their breakup and divorce, and the whole damn thing.

'So sad about them,' she said. 'I thought they'd be together forever.' She shrugged. 'But I guess that's what people always say when it ends for people like them.'

'Not just people like them.'

'But they're both still friends of ours. Melinda and I are making another Africa trip next spring, as a matter of fact.'

She made it sound as simple as a donut run.

I wanted to ask her if the alimony that Bill Gates had to pay in his divorce might have enabled her own husband to move up on the money list, but knew better. It was only the two of us in my office. Hardly a challenge for me to read the room. I could already see how hard this was for her.

And Susan had made me promise, if Laura Crain did indeed end up here, that I would do my best to behave.

'When you say your husband, are you referring to your marriage?' I said. 'Are the two of you having problems?'

'Oh, no,' she said. 'That most certainly *isn't* the problem that brought me here, Mr Spenser. Oh, God, no. No two people could love each other more than we do.'

I knew two others. But telling her that wasn't going to do either one of us any good.

All I had so far was her husband. I remembered a story now about a well-known novelist spitballing possible movie ideas with a producer. Finally the producer, excited, said, 'I've got it. World War Two!'

'What about World War Two?' the novelist had asked.

And the producer said, 'Hey, you're the writer.'

Her husband was the problem.

I was the detective.

'He's in some kind of trouble,' she said, 'and it's making the most kind and gentle man I've ever known suddenly behave erratically, almost like he's having some kind of breakdown. He routinely flies off the handle into these fits of rage over nothing at all, or what seems like nothing at all to me, even though that's never been his nature, all the way back to when I first met him in college.' She sighed. 'And there are these awful nightmares, sometimes waking him up screaming.'

'You're his wife, you must have some idea about what's bothering him. Some sort of indication. Or have at least asked.'

She shook her head.

'I did ask, repeatedly, until I finally gave up,' she said. 'He just said he's going through some things, but will work them out himself. At one point I even suggested that he see Susan. That only made him erupt again. He screamed at me that he didn't need a shrink, and stormed out of the room.'

'Has he thought about seeing someone besides a friend of yours?'

'He won't even consider it. It's why I'm the one seeing you.'

I waited now, the way I knew Susan would have. It had occurred to both of us, on multiple occasions, that our chosen professions possessed remarkable similarities, especially in the sometimes artful way we had to draw out our clients. Susan's work just didn't involve her having to shoot people from time to time, or punch their lights out.

I waited as long as I could before finally saying, 'You sound as if you're in pain yourself.'

'It's why I'm here,' she said. 'I want you to see if you can find out what kind of trouble my husband might be in, whether it's personal or professional, before he loses his fucking mind.'

Her language was like a glass shattering.

She paused then.

'And maybe loses his company.'

4

Susan and I were having dinner at Bistro du Midi on Boylston Street, at an upstairs table with a panoramic view of the Public Garden, a view of which I never grew tired, from any possible angle. Boston's version of Central Park, just in miniature.

'I take it you're taking the case,' she said.

'Not until I can figure out a way in.'

She reaches under the table and gives my thigh a squeeze. 'And here I thought you'd finally gotten the hang of that.'

'Do they teach you to talk like that at Harvard?'

'No, big boy. That's all you.'

She'd let me choose the restaurant tonight, as she and Pearl were having a sleepover. Susan had patiently explained to Pearl before we left the apartment that we would walk her in the park when we returned.

'What if all that walking after dinner tires me out to the extent that it dims my ardor for you when we're finally in bed?' I'd asked her.

'It is my belief that not even a missile attack while the two of us are looking at the swan boats could do that.'

'Want to know why I picked this place?'

'Because we could walk to it?' She gave my thigh another squeeze. 'I sleep with a detective, remember?'

'You lucky duck.'

Susan smiled, this one full of mischief and promise. 'You did say *duck*, right?'

I liked to dress up when we went out to dinner, though not as much as she did. Tonight I was wearing my new Brooks Brothers blazer, purchased about fifty yards from my office at the mother ship. Gray slacks, tattersall shirt open at the collar, perfect maroon pocket square, tasseled Ralph Lauren loafers, no socks. It was as much sartorial game as I could muster short of a tuxedo, or my one good suit.

I still looked like a bouncer sitting across from Susan Silverman.

She had taken even longer than usual getting herself ready tonight, to the point where we were nearly late for our reservation, which wouldn't have been the first time. It was all because of what she called 'The Process': Lengthy shower after a day of seeing patients, then blowing out the hair just right, something that could occasionally take longer than the opera. At that point she was really just warming up. Then came makeup, and reviewing the jewelry options she'd given herself in her overnight bag. Eventually the only jewelry tonight turned out to be a necklace of cultured pearls I'd purchased for her at Tiffany, spending some of Kevin Boles's money. She was wearing the necklace with a simple and elegant navy blue dress, just short enough to show off her sensational legs as we made our way across the park to the restaurant. There was just the faintest scent of what I was pretty sure was a new perfume.

The other Spenser, Edmund the poet, had once written of sovereign beauty.

That was Susan Silverman, in total.

Once our drinks had been delivered, a Kir Royale of just the perfect shade for her and a Tito's martini with a twist for me, she raised her glass and I raised mine, as we toasted each other.

She saw me staring at her, and smiling to myself, before I reached for my glass.

'Something you'd like to share?'

'Nothing you haven't heard before.'

'Love talk, I hope.'

'Yup,' I said.

'Give it to me,' she said. 'I can handle it.'

'Not only can't I believe you love me,' I said. 'I still can't believe you talked to me.'

'Back at you.'

Now we both drank, in no rush to even look at the menu.

'I know you've been waiting to talk about Laura Crain,' she said.

'You probably know most of it.'

'First I want to hear what she told you, and what you think,' Susan said.

She took a sip of Kir. Though 'sip' might have been a rather generous assessment. Generally when Susan was working on an adult beverage she reminded me of a hummingbird pecking at sugar water.

I, however, took a much healthier swallow of my martini. It was icy cold and merely wonderful. But then it had always been my experience that even a bad martini was better than none.

'I'll take all the help I can get with this,' I said.

She sighed.

'I'm sure she's already conveyed to you what she thinks about her husband's recent behavior, and how alarmed she is by it, Suze.'

'That he's acting like a total wingnut? She has.'

'Ah, yes, Dr Silverman,' I said, stroking an imaginary beard and affecting a bad German accent. 'Would wingnut be from the structionalist school, or functionalist?'

'Swampscott High School.'

She took another small sip. I sometimes wondered what the point of ordering the drink even was. It was like watching her attack a salad, half a lettuce leaf at a time.

'She told me he's starting to act even more secretive and paranoid lately,' I said.

'On a good day, from what I gather.'

'But she says when he's out in public, or making an appearance somewhere, he still comes across like a lovable sitcom dad. It's one of the reasons he's as popular around the world as his friend Bill

22

Gates. You know he's just as generous. If a good cause anywhere needs money, he's the first to raise a hand. The past decade or so, he's focused most of his money and energy on supporting women's rights, especially in countries known for oppressing women. Iran. The United Arab Emirates. Mostly Saudi Arabia, my God, the most gender-segregated country on the planet. He *hates* them.'

'He sure doesn't need oil from the bastards,' I said.

'No,' Susan said. 'He does not.'

'Now his wife really is convinced the guy's on the verge of some kind of breakdown, at what would be a very bad time.'

'Is there ever really a good time for a nervous breakdown?' Susan asked.

I'd finished my martini. I caught our waiter's eye and discreetly pointed at my glass.

'I'm talking about a bad time professionally, at least according to Laura,' Susan said. 'Because of the merger. Even you've heard about the merger, right, even though it hasn't been covered in the Sports section of *The Globe*?'

Crain's company was on the verge of merging with an electric-car company from Canada called Prise, a French word that basically meant plug-in. Prise had quickly and quietly moved up into second in the market behind Tesla and ahead of the Germans, and was looking to expand in both the US and Europe.

'Hawk told me,' I told Susan. 'He gives me information like that on a need-to-know basis.'

Susan smiled. 'I think that's wise.'

'But in the grand scheme of things, what does it matter if that merger doesn't happen somehow?' I said. 'They're already rich as shit.'

'But just remember,' Susan said. 'If money could buy happiness, I'd be out of business.'

'I've heard that it can't,' I said, 'but consider it to be irresponsible gossip.'

'On top of everything else,' Susan said, 'as I'm sure Laura told you, Andrew is giving even more money away than usual, in an almost manic way.'

'Even in his world, I don't see how that could be considered a bad thing.'

'In mine,' she said, 'we contextualise things whenever possible. And in this context, his wife does think it's a bad thing, no matter who it benefits. He's acting out and she doesn't know why.'

'Is she worried that he's going to give it all away before he's through?' I asked. 'Didn't the guy who owned The North Face give it all away to fight climate change?'

'Patagonia,' Susan said.

I grinned. 'He wanted to fight Patagonia?'

She took a real sip now.

'You're an idiot sometimes.'

'But I'm your idiot.'

I ordered the sweet corn soup and then duck breast with baby kale and figs as my main course. Susan ordered the arugula and endive salad and king salmon. Salmon was often her go-to entrée, no matter where we were dining. Tonight she had studied the menu the way she would have studied for a final in Counseling Psychology once, finally putting it down and saying, 'I've made my decision.'

'Salmon?' I'd said.

'Aren't you funny.'

'Kind of,' I said.

I politely asked then if she thought we should order pommes frites on the side, this being a French restaurant and all.

'Rhetorical question?' she said.

'*Oui.*'

We passed on dessert and then walked back home to walk Pearl. When she had finished her nighty ablutions and we were all on our way back to Marlborough Street, Susan and I had returned to talking about Andrew Crain, whom his wife wanted me to investigate without him knowing he was being investigated.

'I have a bad feeling about this, Suze,' I said. 'It's why I haven't officially said yes to her yet.'

'Which parts? Or all of it?'

'All of it,' I said. 'She wants me to find out what's tormenting the sixth-richest man in America without him knowing that she's hired me to do just that.'

'When you put it that way,' she said, 'it does sound like a hairball. But aren't those your specialty?'

'Only one of them,' I said, and when we were back upstairs I showed her a few more. With undimmed ardor.

When she had shown me a few specialties of her own, she fell back on her pillow, flushed and sated and out of breath and somehow glowing at the same time while I tried to get my own breathing under control.

'*Ooh la la,*' Susan said.

5

Because of my move, Hawk and I had taken to running along the Charles again, usually at least three times a week, alternating with track work at Harvard.

My knees felt better than they had in years, even though I had relented to getting an occasional cortisone shot. I knew I was keeping up with Hawk only because he was letting me – something which he took endless pleasure in reminding me – but I felt that I was more than holding my own lately, even when we dialed it up to five miles the way we had today.

We had crossed over the Fiedler Footbridge, run down to the Mass Ave Bridge and then over to the Cambridge side, heading along Memorial Drive before finally turning back, the view even better from the Cambridge side, taking in all of Back Bay.

Hawk wore a BLACK MAMBA T-shirt, black Lululemon running

tights that looked as if they had been applied to his legs with a lacquer brush, and Adidas running shoes that I was certain had cost him more than my first car. I had dressed down because I didn't know any other way when working out, decked out in a Harvard sweatshirt with the sleeves cut to my shoulders and baggy gray sweatpants and old New Balance gray shoes that I was sure were going to once again catch the fashion curve any day.

When we were finished we sat on a bench before heading back over the footbridge, drinking from the water bottles we'd both Velcroed to our upper arms. My breath had slowly returned to normal. It was different with Hawk. It always was. He was neither sweating nor breathing hard, giving no sign that we'd just run as far and as hard as we had, especially at the finish, when he'd delighted in running away from me the way Michael Johnson had famously run away from everybody in the 200 in the Olympics once.

Hawk, in fact, did not look as if he'd just done anything more strenuous than retie his laces.

We had not yet decided whether we wanted to have breakfast at Mike's on Washington Street or Victoria's on Mass Ave after showering at the apartment. While we waited to make the call, Hawk was explaining to me exactly how Andrew Crain and Ethan Lowe had won the lottery with their invention after they'd left Harvard.

'Think of it this way,' Hawk said. 'Crain be Gates. Lowe be Paul Allen, he should rest in peace.'

He proceeded to give me a brief but detailed tutorial on lithium and its uses and most of all its value, especially in the age of the electric car, all of it delivered as only Hawk could, in his spectacular street patois, as if he were the second lead in *The Wire* telling you how to split the atom.

'So am I your Gates?' I said.

'First among equals? Fuck no. I got no equals.'

He leaned back and let the sun hit his face, smiling as he did, looking neither young nor old, looking serene and completely comfortable in his own skin and his own impressive self, looking the same as he always had to me, which meant looking like Hawk.

'Okay, you can be Gates and I'll be Allen.'

'You gonna keep interrupting, or you want me to explain this shit to you in a way even you can understand?'

'I promise to shut up now.'

He snorted. 'When pigs fly.'

He turned and leaned an arm over the back of the bench. 'You understand why the world needs lithium, right?'

'Batteries?'

He nodded. 'Lithium-ion currently be going at a compound rate 'bout thirty per cent. And that don't even figure in what the number might go to over the next ten years on account of all the cheap Teslas gonna be on the road 'fore long. I was reading something the other day, *The Times*, all about how lithium *is* gonna make electric cars more affordable, and how this one lithium mine, up to Quebec, basically feels like it walked into a way to just start printing money.'

I watched and listened, fascinated, not surprised by the intelligence and curiosity, they'd always been there, even in his leg-breaking days. I was just knocked back all over again at how well versed he was about so many different things.

'Them lithium-ion batteries, just them, they charge faster, last longer, and have a higher power density for a longer life.'

'I could use something like that,' I said.

Hawk grinned. 'Be called Viagra, leastways for old white men like you.'

I grinned. 'But you digress.'

'Yowza,' Hawk said. 'So all of a sudden these two nerds come up with a way to make they own. Nobody knows how they do it, but they do it. And now this country don't have to go beggin' to Chile or Argentina or Australia or Quee-bec for lithium. Or fucking Bolivia.'

'And Crain and Lowe are the ones printing money and saying they're going to use a boatload of it to save the planet.'

'Or at least give the planet one of them extreme makeovers.'

'And while all that is going on they're supposed to live happily ever after, Crain especially,' I said, 'because he out-kicked his coverage with his significant other.'

'Look who's talkin'.'

'Only now his wife is worried that he's having a nervous breakdown, even if only she knows it yet.'

'And she don't know why.'

'And wants us to find out why, lippity lop, if I decide to take the case.'

'*If* you decide?' Hawk said. 'You know you gonna take it.'

He theatrically raised his eyebrows then. 'And did I hear you say *us*?' he said, now sounding as if he belonged in *The Crown*, making the transition as effortlessly as he always did.

'Indeed you did, old boy.'

'Yo, Jeeves?' Hawk said. 'Who you callin' "boy"?'

6

I had called Laura Crain first thing the next morning and told her I was taking her case. I asked if her husband's business partner shared her concerns. She said that he did. I asked if he would be willing to meet with me. She said she could check, and called back later and said that Ethan Lowe would be more than willing to meet with me, as early as today.

The old John Hancock Tower was now officially 200 Clarendon Street. So it had been rebranded, too. But if you lived in Boston you still thought of it as the Hancock. It was still the tallest building in the city, and in New England, whatever people wanted to call it.

Lith, Inc. was located on the forty-ninth and fiftieth floors. These were where their business offices were headquartered. The factories where their product was produced were scattered around the country. The site closest to Boston was right off 495 in Lowell. I had seen photographs of it. The buildings looked quite modern, and not at all as if they were helping to change the world, with LITH in huge block letters on the side of the largest one.

Ethan Lowe didn't want to meet at the office. When I called he asked if I knew where the Friendly Toast breakfast place was on Stanhope, saying it was just a short walk from the Hancock. I told him I knew exactly where it was.

'I can walk there from my office, too,' I said, making no attempt to hide the pride in my voice.

I was waiting for him when he walked in. I had gone to the Internet to remind myself what he looked like. He turned out to be taller than I expected him to be, even realising that guessing someone's height by merely looking at a head shot was like trying to guess their weight at the same time.

He wore a black crewneck sweater and khaki pants and white Federer sneakers I recognised because Susan had a pair just like them. He was mostly bald in that way that had become fashionable, just a fringe of blonde-gray hair. He wore wire-rimmed glasses, was quite tan and whippet-thin, yet somehow his sweater looked one size too small.

I got up when he got to the table I had managed to score for us. He grinned as we shook hands. 'Laura told me to just find someone who looked like he could lick any sonofabitch in the house.'

'John L. Sullivan said that,' I said.

'I happen to know he was born in the same section of Roxbury I was,' Lowe said.

'Ward Bond played him in *Gentleman Jim*,' I said. 'In glorious black-and-white.'

'I've always thought the world looked better in black-and-white,' Lowe said.

'You seem to have done just fine in this one.'

'I have these bursts of nostalgia,' he said. 'But I'm not crazy.'

He ordered a cold brew.

'Thank you for meeting with me,' I said. 'I'm sure this must be awkward for you.'

'It is,' he said. 'But since we're both here, you already know how difficult it is to say no to Laura Crain.'

'I held out a whole day.'

'Wow,' Lowe said. 'Now I'm sure you *can* lick any sonofabitch in the house.'

His cold brew was delivered. The waiter topped off my hot coffee. I didn't like iced coffee. Susan said it was a generational thing and I just told her to go ahead and add it to the list. She said the list would eventually be longer than the phone book used to be.

When the waiter was gone Lowe said, 'It goes without saying that this meeting never took place.'

'What meeting?' I said.

'But as I'm sure Laura told you, I'm as concerned about Andrew as she is. As is Claire.'

'Claire?'

'Laura didn't mention her? She's the woman we call the other Mrs Andrew Crain. Claire Megill. His executive assistant. He met her in California when he hired her to work for us, and she eventually fast-tracked her way here, and to the office outside his. Andrew and I joke all the time that if the company plane ever went down with us on it, Claire could take over without missing a beat. She's truly like Andrew's other brain.'

'Maybe I should talk to her, too.'

'She may share our concerns, but I'm not sure how forthcoming she'd be with a stranger,' Lowe said. 'I myself don't see meeting with you as a breach of loyalty, but rather an act of loyalty toward my partner. She would. She just wants to write this all off to stress.'

'Involving the sale?'

'Just the accumulated stress of having been Andrew Crain, all the way back to when we hit it as big as we did. She thinks it's just finally caught up with him. That he's going through a phase.' He put air quotes around the last word. 'Claire sees what she wants to see. And what she's always seen with Andrew is an honest-to-Christ American hero.'

'See no evil, even now?'

'And hear no evil, even when he's acting out the way he has been lately.'

'Is she married?'

You poke at things when the opportunity presents itself, nibbling at the edges. We seemed to have gotten off-point with Claire Megill, but perhaps not.

'Claire was married briefly, a long time ago. She never talks about it, other than to say that the only good that came out of it was her son. Cameron. He's a junior at Cal Poly. Andrew is quite fond of him. I have no doubt that Andrew will find a place for him at Lith when he graduates. He's already worked summers for us as an intern.'

'I need to ask this,' I said. 'But is there a chance that his relationship with Ms Megill might be more than professional. It wouldn't be the first time something like that has happened in an executive suite.'

'I'd be shocked,' Lowe said. 'As loyal as he is to Claire and she to him, Andrew is even more connected, more reliant, on his wife. I tell him all the time that he's the most married man in America.'

I saw the waiter go by with a blueberry muffin the size of a football, and wanted to tackle him from behind, if I thought I could catch the muffin before it hit the floor.

'I've done some reading on both you and Andrew,' I said. 'It appears that he's the first among equals.'

'Sixty-forty,' he said. 'It was that way from the start, because he did most of the science. My role was more entrepreneurial.'

He took off his glasses, pulled a small cloth out of his pocket, cleaned them carefully, put them back on. Everything about him was meticulous, with even the smallest movements.

'What if he woke up one day and decided he didn't just want to spin off the software company, but cash out of Lith, too?'

'At that point,' Lowe said, 'there wouldn't be a goddamn thing I could do to stop him. Somebody else would own his share, and I'd probably be thinking about selling mine, maybe to the same person, though the list of people who would have the kind of money it would take would be a short one.' He shrugged. 'Ownership of our company would make the fucking earth move, I know that.'

'What would you do if that happened?'

He took his phone out of his pocket, looked at it, frowned, put it away. I liked him better for not keeping it on the table in front of him while we'd been talking.

'Him selling, or both of us selling?'

'Either way.'

He looked at me and grinned. 'How did we get here from talking about Andrew's behavior?'

I shrugged then. 'I have a short attention span.'

'Somehow, Mr Spenser, I doubt that. We've only known each other a few minutes, but I have a good sense of people. You need one from what I guess you could call my perch. And my sense already is that people who underestimate you probably end up getting carried off the field on a stretcher.'

I drank more coffee. It was very good coffee.

'So what do you really think is going on with your partner? You're the one who's known him even longer than his wife has, from what I've read.'

'I guess that's true,' Lowe said. 'He spent his first couple years at Harvard just worshipping Laura from afar. So technically I have known him longer.'

'So the two of you have been in each other's lives, passionately joined, for more than two decades.'

'Just not continuously,' he said.

'I'm not sure what that means.'

32

'It means,' Lowe said, 'that I lost track of him for a couple years after college. But then pretty much everybody did.'

7

I knew how much easier research was now because of technology, and had been since the first www.com. But there was a part of me that still missed going to the Boston Public Library when I needed to look things up regarding a case or a client.

Additionally I missed calling a friend like Wayne Cosgrove, the columnist who had become editor of *The Globe*, and asking him to go into the magical place I thought of as 'the clips' when I needed information.

I'd mentioned this to Susan on the phone this morning.

'Please tell me this isn't going to be another occasion when you wax poetic about microfilm,' she said.

'Those were the days.'

'If you miss them that much, you can always Google them,' she said.

Instead I spent the morning and then into the afternoon intensely Googling Andrew Crain, even though when I thought of it that way I always imagined inappropriate touching.

A lot of it I already knew, not just about his invention and the formation of his company, but about his passion for saving the oceans and supporting the right political candidates and nearly buying one of the big pharmaceutical companies during COVID, because he believed he and Ethan Lowe could somehow speed up the vaccine process.

He and Lowe had started charter schools from Africa to Serbia. There was no telling how much of his own personal wealth Crain had directed to Ukraine by now, in support of its president and its army.

All in all it was a modern American success story, another one out of the tech world, this one originating in Boston the way Mark Zuckerberg's had with Facebook.

Just like that, another nerd ruled.

When it happened, I always pictured another angel getting its wings.

Two nerds in this instance, Crain and his partner.

Looks-wise, Andrew Crain reminded me of a grown-up version of Harry Potter, just with red hair and not black. Tall, skinny, round and oversized Harry glasses. Even now, more than twenty years after Harvard, he still looked as if he were late for class.

There was just one gap in his history, the one Ethan Lowe had mentioned over coffee, the two years after graduation and before Crain and Lowe went into business together, when Andrew was completely off the grid.

His story, one that had never changed, a story he repeated almost word for word every time he told it, was that he had strapped on a backpack and gone off to find himself. His parents, both dead by then, had left him enough money, or so he said, to finance a search for meaning in his life from Boston to the Himalayas and back.

He sounded like Larry Darrell in *The Razor's Edge*. Maugham's character had been traumatised by World War I. I wondered what might possibly have traumatised Andrew Crain, who'd found not only meaning in his life when he had come back to civilization, but the pot of gold at the end of the rainbow along with it.

'I got my head out of books,' he told Diane Sawyer in an old interview I'd watched, 'and tried to understand the world as a way of trying to understand myself.'

Laura Crain had sat with him for that interview. She'd smiled and said to Sawyer, 'He didn't call, he didn't write.'

'All part of my master plan to win your heart,' he said, 'just praying that my absence would make it grow fonder.'

'Well,' his wife said, 'mission accomplished.'

'She was out of my league then,' Crain said, 'and still is now.'

Somehow the two of them were genuine enough and clearly loved each other enough that watching a sit-down like this didn't cause a sugar high, even seeing it all this time later.

At breakfast I'd asked Lowe if he'd ever pressed Crain on at least some of the places he'd gone and things he'd done.

'He has always been light on specifics,' Lowe said. 'In the end he just makes the whole thing actually sound like a religious experience. When it was over he said he knew the person he wanted to be. And, better yet, knew the one he didn't want to be.'

When he did come back he and Lowe did a modern-day version of Alexander Graham Bell telling Watson to get his ass into his office, just with secondary cell construction, and the rest was history.

Both of them had apparently lived quite happily ever after until Andrew Crain had started to act as if he had a screw loose.

I was finally getting ready to leave the office when Susan called and said that we were having dinner tomorrow night with Andrew and Laura Crain.

'You're welcome,' she said.

8

I had a long-standing date to meet Martin Quirk at the Street Bar at The Newbury, which was previously The Taj, and before that had been the Ritz since around the time the *Mayflower* landed. If you had been around long enough, and Quirk and I both had, the place would always be the Old Ritz. The bar inside, right off the Arlington Street entrance, was still the best in the city and one of the best anywhere.

'I can walk here from my new apartment,' I told Quirk when I arrived.

'So I heard.'

'Who told you?'

'Everybody,' he said.

He was now assistant superintendent of the Boston Police Department. He'd been captain before that and homicide detective before that. Cop-wise, at least in this city, he was the equivalent of Tom Brady. When I'd told him that one time he said, 'I never left to wear a fucking pirate helmet in Florida.'

Quirk never aged, the way Hawk never seemed to. More gray to the hair these days, more lines around the eyes, well earned, he liked to point out. He wore a tweed jacket despite unseasonably warm weather this week, blue button-down shirt with the Brooks Brothers roll to the collar, navy knit tie. Big hands, thick fingers. Having known him as long as I had, I was aware that he knew how to use them when a situation presented itself.

He rarely changed expression. And was not someone you ever wanted to needlessly antagonise. I'd once seen him put a small-town southern cop who'd falsely arrested me against a wall and say, 'You want to fuck with me, dick breath?' After that you could have cleaned away the officer in question with a mop.

All in all, Quirk was Quirk the way Hawk was Hawk.

We both ordered martinis. I had my usual lemon peel with mine. Quirk told the waiter he could skip the fruit in his. We had the table situated squarely in front of the picture window, looking across at the Public Garden.

'This going to be social,' he said, 'or do you want something from me?'

'Fellowship?'

'Join a book club.'

It had been months since we'd seen each other. I asked him how Frank Belson was, once Quirk's top sergeant, now a lieutenant, working for a homicide captain, Glass, whom Belson privately called Nurse Ratched.

36

'He asked me to thank you for not making any work for him lately,' Quirk said.

'Ah, but the night is young.'

I told him about Andrew Crain and his wife and everything else I'd learned about him over the past couple days. When I finished I said, 'Any advice?'

'Yeah,' Quirk said. 'Run.'

'I was hoping for somewhat more positive reinforcement than that.'

He might have smiled just slightly. Or, and more likely, there had just been an involuntary twitch to his lips. But there was no real change of expression, his cop eyes never leaving me.

'Oh, shit,' he said finally. 'You were serious with that part about the positive reinforcement.'

We both watched a young woman in tight faded jeans walk past the window, in the direction of Newbury Street. She was young and pretty and had buds in her ears and I wasn't sure, watching her until she disappeared across the street, how she'd managed to get into the jeans. And didn't care.

When I turned back toward Quirk he said, 'Doesn't make either one of us a bad person.'

We both drank. I told him that the only way I could approach this case was as a cold case, and asked how he handled things when he'd open a file on an open unsolved.

'You look at what you already know,' Quirk said, 'but that doesn't get you anywhere, you'd know that if you ever opened up the file before. If it did get you anywhere, the goddamn case wouldn't be unsolved.'

'What I mostly know about this guy is what everybody seems to know, that he's a prince among men.'

I told him that it was Susan's professional opinion that Crain was exhibiting signs of buried guilt.

'How's Susan doing, by the way?' Quirk said. 'Obviously she's still with you.'

'If a thing loves, it is infinite,' I said.

37

'Should I write that down?' Quirk said.

The crowd in the bar began to increase, as did the noise level. A lot had changed at this hotel over time. Just not the dimensions of this room, and the general look of it. The furniture was obviously new. Green chairs at the bar. Blue chairs once you stepped down into the area where we were. A green wraparound sofa in the middle of everything. And the vast and unchanging view of the park across the street.

'Maybe this guy is just having a midlife crisis,' Quirk said. 'Apropos of no bad shit in his past. He wouldn't be the first, no matter how much money he's got in the bank.'

'But maybe something from his past has reached out and grabbed him by the balls.'

'Is that a line of poetry from Blake, too?'

'You knew that was Blake before?'

'There's a lot of layers to me,' Quirk said. 'I thought you, being an ace detective, would have picked up on that by now.'

I waved for another martini. Quirk put his hand over his own glass. 'I'm driving,' he said. 'I know, I know, you can walk.'

'All I've really got is those two years when he went to find himself and it sounds like nobody could find *him*,' I said.

'Can you ask him where he went and what he did at dinner?' Quirk said.

'If I do, I need to be artful about it, so as not to make him think it's some kind of cross-examination.'

Quirk took another sip, put his glass down, and then shook his head.

'Artful?' he said. 'Shit, I was afraid of that.'

9

Susan had a meeting for the Margaret Fuller Neighborhood House, located over on Cherry Street in Cambridge. After that she and a few of her fellow board members were having dinner at Harvest.

So I was cooking for one. I had spent a lot of my adult life cooking for one, even after Susan and I were together. I liked cooking, the passion for it being something I had inherited from my father and from my uncles. Tonight I was keeping things relatively simple, a lemon-pepper chicken dish that had become one of my favorites, pasta primavera on the side, featuring the vegetables I'd picked up the day before at the Copley Square Market.

I'd prepared the same dish for Susan a couple weeks earlier. When she'd tasted it she demanded to know what exotic marinade I'd used.

'Newman's Own,' I'd said.

I was listening to Diana Krall and having a civilised glass of chardonnay and thinking about chopping up the vegetables when Mattie Sullivan called from Los Angeles.

She had been there since the start of the summer, working with Zebulon Sixkill, who now had his own detective agency Out There. Mattie had postponed taking the police exam, at least for now, after visiting Z. I suspected she was a goner from the first time she'd walked up and down Abbot Kinney in Venice. Now she was living in Z's spare room and helping him out at work, effectively having turned in a cop badge she hadn't yet earned, at least for now.

She was even dating a young actor from some Netflix series that she had tried in vain to describe to me, about an alien and his human sidekick and time travel, until I begged her to stop. She said he played the sidekick, for what it was worth.

Having her with Z was like having two grown-up children living together.

'You can't believe what I did today,' she said.

'Found USC without using Waze?'

'Went to Bunda for the first time.'

'Bunda?'

'It's in West Hollywood. The best full-body workout in LA. Hottest exercise place in town. Z knows somebody there.'

'Come home now.'

She laughed. 'Keanu Reeves was there.'

'OMG!' I said.

She asked what I was working on. I told her.

'Susan and I are having dinner with him and his wife tomorrow night,' I said, 'at which point I will artfully try to gather information.'

'You?' Mattie said. 'Artful? You're so fucked.'

'Quirk basically said the same thing,' I said. 'See that, if you'd stayed and taken the exam you'd be on your way to making detective.'

'Can't lie,' she said. 'I really like it here, Spenser.'

'Almost everybody does until their show gets canceled.'

'I've been to a bunch of Dodger games to watch Mookie Betts. It's practically like I was the player to be named later after the Sox traded him here.'

She pronounced it 'Sawx,' as always. You can take the girl out of Boston.

'Okay, that's it, I'm hanging up on you,' I said. 'You know Mookie is the name that must not be spoken.'

'You need help on the case I can always fly back,' she said. 'It actually sounds like fun.'

'Trust me, kid, it's not.'

'Let me ask you something,' Mattie said. 'What if you find out that your very own Bill Gates has some deep, dark secret that

40

could wreck his life, and stop him from fixing all the things in the world he's trying to fix?'

'The best way to explain it is in a way you will completely understand,' I told her. 'I have no fucking idea.'

She told me how much she missed me then, and Susan and Boston and Pearl and Hawk, just a little less than she expected when it was seventy-five and sunny every freaking day. I told her weather wasn't everything.

'Yeah?' Mattie said. 'Ask Mookie.'

I did not watch the Sox game while I ate dinner tonight. The Mookie-less Sox. I switched the music over to Sarah Vaughan and Clifford Brown. I had read somewhere that it was her favorite album. I also knew it had been released the year before Clifford Brown had died in an automobile accident on his way to a gig in Chicago.

My mind was so often filled with random information like this. I knew that Mookie Betts's real name was Markus Lynn Betts, because his parents wanted him to have the initials 'MLB.' I knew that Elvis and Babe Ruth had died on the same date, August 16. I knew that a man named Percy Spencer – Spencer with a c – had invented the microwave when he was working at Raytheon, in Burlington, Mass.

I had switched from wine to Bushmills by now, sitting at my kitchen table and studying some of the notes I'd taken. I knew more today about Andrew Crain than I'd known the day before. So that was progress. Wasn't that progress?

I finished my first Bushmills and poured myself another as Sarah and Clifford Brown eased their way into 'You're Not the Kind.'

After a while I put the notes away and went to stand at my picture window, the draperies Susan had ordered still not having been delivered, late the way things still so often were in the post-COVID world. The view from my living room was different than it had been at the old place. But then so was I. When I'd first lived a couple buildings over, I didn't have Z in my life. Or Mattie. Now

I had both of them, even if they were three thousand miles away. Mattie said she'd be back. Maybe for a visit, I thought. But my instinct was that she wanted to live there now.

Bunda, I thought.

Tip of the iceberg.

So often in the past, or so it seemed to me, I had taken on new clients who had come to me because they found themselves at risk. Or in danger. Or some loved one was. Just not always. Once Paul Giacomin, who I'd treated like a son the way I now treated Z like a son, had shown up at my office with a young woman who wanted me to find out how her mother had died back in the seventies, a bank robbery gone wrong. I had eventually discovered that the woman wasn't her mother at all, and that she was in fact the granddaughter of a mobster. None of which I had shared with her in the end, because I didn't think the knowing would improve a single day of the rest of her life.

How much did Andrew Crain's wife need to know about him, if I uncovered something bad he had buried in his past?

How much did *I* want to know?

Gabriel García Márquez had written about public lives, private lives, secret lives.

What would it be like if my Bill Gates, as Mattie had called him, had some kind of a secret life once?

I was nursing the second Bushmills and considering a third. This was a good time of the night for whiskey, alone in the new apartment except for Sarah and Clifford Brown's trumpet.

Sometimes I wondered about the value of the kind of work I did, and had done for a long time, and done well, in a modern world where everybody seemed to know everything, *about* everybody.

Now there were things that Laura Crain did not know about her husband, things I was intuiting, with little to go on, at least so far, that she might not want to know. But in her mind, it was her husband who was now at risk, which is how she had ended up at my office.

Sarah had circled back now to 'September Song,' the song with which she and Cliff Brown had started the album and was now ending it.

'I played me a waiting game...'

I finished the last of my Irish whiskey then and rinsed my glass and took one last look at the Public Garden, at least for tonight. It was still here and so was I.

It was just Mookie who wasn't coming back.

10

We ate at Davio's on Arlington Street. Susan had picked it, but not until she had made me promise that we would eventually venture out of the neighborhood again when dining out.

'Come and get me, copper,' I growled.

'Bogie?'

'Cagney. *White Heat*. You can't tell the difference?'

'God, no.'

Laura Crain said that Davio's was actually on the short list of Boston restaurants her husband liked, and that they had a car bringing them from Brookline so as not to have to worry about driving home after a few drinks.

'I just like being able to walk here again from my apartment,' I said when we were all seated.

'Sigh,' Susan said.

'She thinks I've become too territorial,' I said to the Crains.

'Somewhat like a wolf,' Susan said.

Andrew Crain looked less geeky than he did in photographs and on television. Gone at last were the long bangs hanging down to his eyes. His hair was much neater tonight. And as skinny as he still was, I could see from the way his long-sleeved polo shirt

43

fit him that he was in good shape, as if he'd gotten with a personal trainer and stayed with one.

He didn't take off his Red Sox cap until he was seated.

'Don't take it off on my account,' I said.

He grinned. 'It's more a way to avoid too much eye contact on my way into a room like this than a pledge of allegiance.'

When our first round of drinks had been delivered – Crain had surprised me by ordering a jalapeño tequila – his wife raised her glass in a toast.

'To Susan,' she said.

'Any particular reason,' I said, 'other than her extreme wonderfulness?'

'For finally making this night happen,' she said.

I had told Susan that Armando, the maître d', would almost certainly give us one of their small, private dining rooms if I asked him. But Laura said the main room would be just fine, that even as recognizable as her husband was, he generally didn't cause a stir when they did dine out.

Andrew Crain hung back on the conversation at the table, but did not appear bored by it. It was almost as if he were eavesdropping on the rest of us from the next table. And he did pose questions about Susan's work, finally asking her if she'd ever envisioned herself in a committed relationship with someone in my line of work.

Susan smiled at him now. 'I'd actually hoped to run away with someone like you, Andrew.'

'Hey, wait a second,' I said.

Crain laughed along with the rest of us.

'I was just joking, honey buns,' Susan said to me.

As our entrées were being delivered, he asked where I had grown up.

'Wyoming,' I said. 'Laramie. I was raised by my father and uncles after my mother died.'

'I spent some time in Laramie after college, working on a road crew one summer,' he said.

He had opened the door, if only a crack.

'Hopefully not a crew from the Albany County Jail,' I said.

Crain laughed again. 'No, nothing as colorful as that. They were just doing some work on Interstate 80 when I was passing through, and I managed to sign on.'

'Eighty was the road I took out of town when the time came,' I said.

'I took the same road,' Crain said. 'But I was hitchhiking.'

'Part of that period when you talked about going off to find yourself,' I said.

'I see you've done your homework,' Crain said.

'He's always liked being the smartest boy in class,' Susan said.

'Got me out of Wyoming,' I said.

I saw a sudden shift in Andrew Crain's attention then, to a young couple a few tables away, on the Arlington Street side of the restaurant, against the wall. There is rarely a slow night at Davio's, here or at their sister place at the Seaport. But not all of the tables in the main room were full tonight, and neither was the bar, so it wasn't as loud as it could sometimes be at high tide.

I followed Crain's eyes to the young couple. The guy was leaning forward, hand on his date's arm, face red. His face, not hers.

He was making no attempt to keep his voice down.

'You don't get to decide when we leave,' he said, leaning closer to her. '*I* decide.'

I heard Laura Crain ask her husband how he liked his halibut. But he appeared not to hear. He was focused on these two strangers having a very bad moment, one becoming an increasingly public event. The woman was quite pretty, but you could see the tension on her face from where we all sat, how pale she looked.

'Please lower your voice,' she said.

'Why? Am I embarrassing you again?'

'I want to leave,' she said now.

'We leave when I say we leave.'

45

'Andrew, what's the matter?' Laura said at our table, seeing the tension on her husband's face, all of us feeling it.

'He's a bully,' Crain said, not looking at his wife, still looking at the couple. 'You know I hate bullies.'

I looked at Susan, saw the concern in her eyes.

The young woman got up, shaking her arm loose. 'You're hurting me,' I heard her say, making no attempt to lower her voice now. The guy reached for her again, but she had already grabbed her purse and was walking as fast as she could toward the front door, her high heels sounding as loud as tap shoes.

Her date, red-faced, oblivious to the scene he had made and was still making, tossed a fistful of cash on the table and followed her.

'Enough,' Andrew Crain said as we all watched him go. *'Enough.'*

He took his napkin from his lap and spiked it like he was Gronk, the old Patriot, spiking a football after catching another touchdown pass from Tom Brady. Then Andrew Crain was pushing his chair back. It was like watching a kettle that had now come to full boil.

Crain reached for the Red Sox cap and pulled it down over his eyes, as if that was going to do anything to hide his identity at this point.

'Andrew, no,' his wife said in a small voice.

'Let them go,' she said.

She was the one reaching for his arm. But it was too late for that.

'Spenser,' Susan said.

'Andrew,' I said quietly, 'you're the last guy in this restaurant who wants to be anywhere near this. Let me go deal with that guy.'

Andrew Crain wheeled around.

'I'll take care of this,' he snapped, as if speaking to all of us at once.

'Enough,' he said again.

A man used to being in charge, and having people do what he told them to do.

He followed the couple out of Davio's.

No one spoke at our table as we watched him go. The main dining room had gotten much quieter. I had seen some cell phones go up as Crain made his way across the room. I wanted to check mine, just to have something to do with my hands.

When I couldn't wait any longer, I got up from our table and headed for the door myself.

'See if he needs help,' I heard Laura Crain say.

But when I got out onto Arlington Street her husband was gone.

The only one standing there was the jerk Andrew Crain had followed out of the restaurant. He was staring up Arlington in the direction of the park.

I spun him around.

'Hey,' he said. 'Take your hands off me.'

'Where is he?' I said.

'Was that who I think it was?'

He started to back away from me. I reached down and grabbed his left hand. If I put any more pressure on it than I already was, I would start to feel bones crack. In the moment it was not an unappealing thought.

'Where is he?' I said.

'It was crazy,' he said. 'I'm trying to figure out which way my date went, yelling her name. I don't even hear him come up behind me. Then I feel this tap on my shoulder and when I turn around I see that he's already got his fist back, like he's ready to throw a punch. So I start to back away. But then he stops himself at the last second.' The guy shrugged. 'Like he'd left himself hanging.'

The guy looked down at his hand. 'You're going to break my fucking hand,' he said.

'Not until I want to,' I said. 'Tell me what happened next.'

'What happened next is that rich guy ran like he owed me money.'

47

11

Laura Crain called the next morning to tell me that her husband hadn't returned to their home in Brookline, and hadn't spent the night at their brownstone on Chestnut Street on Beacon Hill, as she would have gotten an alert on her phone if someone had disabled the alarm system there before entering.

'Don't you have the app where you can track his location with his phone?' I said.

She said that normally she would have been able to do that, except that he'd asked her to keep it in her purse during dinner so he wouldn't be tempted to check it every five minutes during dinner like a high school sophomore.

'He keeps saying he's trying to quit acting as if it might explode like a pipe bomb if he misses a text or a call,' she said.

'Has his partner heard from him?' I said.

'I called Ethan first thing. He said that the last time they'd spoken had been at the office late yesterday afternoon. He told me he'd actually been surprised, Andrew had acted more like himself than he had in weeks.'

'What about his assistant?'

'I called Claire right before I called Ethan,' she said. 'The last time she'd seen him was at the office when he'd left for dinner.'

'Why doesn't someone as rich as your husband have a bodyguard?' I said.

'He has several at his disposal. He just doesn't like to use them as often as he once did.'

'Any particular reason?'

'Andrew said that having someone around all the time was another way of making him feel like a prisoner.'

'Of what?'

'Being Andrew Crain.'

I was at my desk. *The Globe* was unopened in front of me. I was working on my second cup of coffee, having had one at the apartment before I'd walked over. I took comfort in the fact that only I was counting.

'Has he done anything similar to this since his behavior began to spin out?'

'There have been occasions when he stormed out, either here or when we were at the brownstone,' she said. 'But he's always come back eventually, usually after taking an epically long walk. Andrew has always thought that long walks can cure everything except beach erosion.'

I drank some coffee, then leaned back and put my sneakers up on the desk, noticing that they were starting to look older than the Paul Revere House. Maybe a visit to Marathon Sports was in order this morning, right past Dunkin', as luck would have it.

'You have his phone,' I said. 'Has anybody tried to reach out to *him* this morning?'

'No.' There was a long pause at her end. 'How long before you start to think about filing a missing-person report?'

'We're nowhere near that, Laura,' I said. 'Once you call the cops and tell them that Andrew Crain is missing, he'll be trending on social media in about five minutes, and then the whole thing blows up.'

'You have to find him,' she said.

'I will,' I said.

I tried to sound far more confident than I felt at the moment. I asked if they had any other homes. She said there was a cabin in the Berkshires, and their place on Martha's Vineyard, but all of them were linked by the same computer security system, and he hadn't been to either one of those, she'd checked to make sure.

I asked if he might have just checked into a hotel, but she said they shared credit cards, and none had been used since he'd paid for dinner at Davio's in advance of sitting down.

Her voice rose suddenly, as if she'd hit the volume button on her phone.

'I have no idea what's going on in his brain right now,' she said. 'I don't even know where to tell you to begin to look for him.'

'How about I begin by talking to his other brain?' I said, and asked for Claire Megill's number.

12

I had my picture taken at the Lith reception desk in the lobby after Claire Megill had left my name down there. They gave me a badge to wear up to the fiftieth floor.

The assistant to Andrew Crain's assistant, a young guy whom I would have thought looked like the kid who'd played Theo on the old *Cosby Show*, if you were even allowed to still reference anything Cosby in polite society without getting canceled.

His name plate read MR BAKER.

'Do I look fat in this picture?' I said to him, showing him my badge. 'They wouldn't let me retake my driver's license picture, either, and now I'm stuck with it.'

He gave me the kind of bored look that I was sure guys his age had to practice until they had it down.

'That's probably the saddest story I'm going to hear all day.' He checked his list. Looked back up at me. 'Mr Spenser?'

'There is but one,' I said. 'Like May in the year.'

'It's September.'

'I was making a larger and poetic point.'

'She's waiting for you inside,' Baker said.

I started to walk away.

'Be nice to her,' he said, barely loud enough for me to hear.

I turned.

'Odd thing to say.'

'Not everybody around here is,' he said. Then he added, 'Kind.'

Claire Megill's office was next door to Andrew Crain's and with the same view, which I thought might extend all the way to the White Mountains. For some reason, I had expected someone older, a headmistress type. But even though her short black hair was flecked subtly with gray, she was not that. Susan had made a continuing and concerted effort to get me to stop objectifying women, at least not in the first thirty seconds of being in their presence, by their physical beauty, or lack thereof. But I continued to fall short of her expectations for me in that regard. Claire Megill was quite attractive, managing to show off a terrific figure in a slim navy skirt suit.

We shook hands.

'Ms Megill.'

'Claire,' she said.

'Your assistant is funny,' I said.

'And a bit of a genius,' she said. 'Mostly with numbers. Which Andrew and I aren't.'

I smiled, but in moderation, not wanting her to overheat, we'd just met. 'You and Andrew seem to be doing just fine.'

'Do you have a first name, Mr Spenser?'

'I do,' I said. 'But I try not to make a big thing out of it.'

I looked around the room, wondering how much bigger and better-appointed her boss's could possibly be next door. It featured an antique desk, the top of which was covered with spreadsheets of some kind, and three TVs bracketing into the wall to my left showing stock-markety things. To my right was a small sitting area with a couch and two chairs and coffee table, giving the office the feeling of being a small suite. Claire Megill gestured for me to take the couch. She took one of the chairs across from it. I sat. She sat. She crossed her legs.

And I heard a melody.

'Laura said I could trust you,' she said.

'Even with classified documents,' I said. 'Including the kind you're not supposed to keep.'

She smiled. Maybe she did think I was funny.

She said, 'Laura told me what you do for a living, but added that you were a friend of a friend who happens to be a Harvard-trained psychologist.'

I shrugged. 'I'm frankly as surprised by that as anyone,' I said. 'But I think it was one of those ancient Greeks who said that fortune favors the foolish.'

I heard her phone buzzing from where she'd left it on her desk. If Claire Megill heard, she didn't acknowledge that she had.

I nodded when the buzzing stopped. 'Aren't you worried that it might have been the boss calling from an undisclosed location?'

'Not on that phone,' she said. She reached into the side pocket of her jacket and pulled out another one. 'He calls on the red phone,' she said. 'Literally, as you can see.'

'I'll ask you what I asked Laura a few minutes ago,' I said. 'Has he done anything like this before?'

'Anything like disappearing into the night after nearly getting into a fight on the street with a stranger?' Just a hint of sarcasm, but I managed to roll with it. 'No, he hasn't done anything quite like that.'

She recrossed her legs. If she did it a few more times, I'd be used to it. 'But has he gone off and not wanted any of us to reach him? He has.'

'In what circumstances?'

'Laura told me I could be open with you, Mr Spenser. But I'm not sure how open.'

She stood now, stiffly, wincing slightly, arching her back the way cats do.

'Sorry,' she said. 'My back doesn't allow me to sit for long periods anymore. From a lifetime of doing too much sitting. The most essential hour of my day is my noon yoga at the Equinox over on Dartmouth. It's like I have a lunch date every day with my back.'

'A friend of mine once said that a bad back is like having a second job,' I said.

'Sounds like a wise man.'

'Woman, actually.'

'I'm not surprised.'

'So has your boss gone off like this before?'

'We call them walkabouts,' she said. 'But they never last long.'

'Overnight?'

She hesitated slightly. 'Yes,' she said finally.

'Has he ever shown up at your place?'

'Yes,' she said. 'But not last night.'

There was a lengthy silence between us then. It did not appear to make her uncomfortable. Nor me. Claire Megill didn't know me well enough to know that I could wait for her to resume speaking until we had both calcified.

'Can I share something with you off the record?' she said.

'I'm not here working on a profile for *The Globe*.'

'What I'm asking is if you're going to share everything I tell you with Laura, even if it's not germane to this particular event.'

'Only after I decide if it's germane or not,' I said.

She took in a lot of air and let it out.

'Andrew and Laura have been spending quite a lot of time apart lately,' she said. 'More than usual, even given their busy lives. And more than she's let on, I gather.'

'Has it been business that's been keeping them separate from each other?' I said. 'Or something else?'

She seemed to be studying me now, like an item in a store she was considering purchasing.

'I'm not much of an expert on marriage, Mr Spenser. I had a bad one. Or maybe the worst one. But Andrew and Laura had a good one, for a very long time.'

'But not so much now?'

'You're a detective and will likely find this out eventually,' she said. 'But there have been some very preliminary conversations about separation, put it that way.'

Oh, ho, I thought.

'Whose idea?' I said.

'Hers, I believe,' Claire Megill said.

13

We both let that settle. I had worked enough divorce cases to know that Massachusetts wasn't a 50/50 state when it came to assets. According to the law, those assets would eventually be divided 'fairly,' but not necessarily equally, by the court. If it came to that in the case of the Crains, whether the split was equal or not, Laura Crain would likely walk away with the kind of heart-stopping money that her friend Melinda Gates had.

The phone on Claire Megill's desk buzzed behind her. She ignored it once again. Probably some B-lister. Probably the number I'd been given.

'I'm curious,' I said. 'Why are you telling me this?'

'What do they say in court?' she said. 'I believe it speaks to his state of mind.'

'But the Crains aren't formally separated, right?'

'When you have as many residences as they do, and you're just operating off the short list, you can be as separate as you want to be,' Claire Megill said. 'Their night out together with you was quite rare these days.'

'You're obviously of the opinion that his marriage is a contributing factor here,' I said. 'But what do you feel is the primary factor for his disappearance.'

'He's come to hate his life, and it's tearing him up inside,' she said, without hesitation. 'Just my opinion. It's as if he's tired of being Andrew Crain, billionaire businessman and philanthropist.' She made air quotes around the two descriptions of her boss. 'A good man who still wants to change the world seems to be constantly carrying the weight of it on his shoulders, if that makes any sense. It's not just one thing. It's everything, in my opinion. His marriage. The merger. Getting older. All of it.'

I was about to ask about the merger when her door opened. No knock. A man stepped into her office.

'Claire, we need to talk.'

She didn't move from where she was leaning against the desk. But she somehow seemed to back up in that moment, or shrink from her visitor, as if whoever the man was, he had done more than simply interrupt us.

'As you can see, Clay, I'm with someone,' she said, her voice tight.

'It can wait,' he said. 'I can't.'

'This is Clay Whitson, Mr Spenser,' she said. 'Our top attorney.' She tried to smile, but didn't do very much with it. 'Just ask him.'

'Is that supposed to be some kind of joke, Claire?' he said.

'Evidently not,' I said now.

He turned to me, as if suddenly remembering I was there. He was about my size. Curly black hair not flecked with gray. Smallish dark eyes. Five-o'clock shadow even in midmorning. Despite his size and barrel chest he was wearing one of those tight suits with tight pants that made him look to me like a bull in tights.

'Who the hell are you?' he said.

'I'm with the band,' I said.

'Mr Spenser is a friend of Laura's,' Claire said quickly.

'What are you doing here?' he said to me.

'We were having a conversation, one that has just ended rather abruptly.'

'A conversation about what?' Whitson said.

I wasn't sure why I felt a sudden urge to annoy him. But I did. I slowly got to my feet now, just to give him a better sense that he wasn't the biggest guy in the room.

'I'll be in touch,' I said to Claire Megill, and walked between them toward the door, coming as close as I possibly could to brushing up against Clay Whitson.

'I asked you a question,' Whitson said.

'Two,' I said.

'What?'

'First you asked me what I was doing here, and then you asked what my conversation with Ms Megill was about. That's two questions.'

'What are you, some kind of tough guy?' Whitson said.

He seemed a bit flushed. But perhaps he went through life that way.

'I am actually a very tough guy,' I said. 'But now I'm leaving, just so Ms Megill doesn't start to get the impression that *I'm* the asshole here.'

And I left.

Not even noon yet, and I'd already made a new friend.

14

Laura Crain couldn't come into the city to meet me at their brownstone, but sent someone she actually described as their houseman instead. Carlos was his name. He said he would wait and lock the place back up and reset the alarm when I was finished looking around inside.

I didn't think I'd find any kind of clue as to Andrew Crain's whereabouts. But I needed to start looking somewhere, and this was closest.

'Just keep telling yourself that he hasn't yet been missing for twenty-four hours,' I told Laura Crain on the phone.

'Keep reminding me of that,' she said.

I had decided I would ask her about possible trouble in her marriage in person.

The inside of the place on Chestnut was both tasteful and spectacular at the same time, with enough paintings hanging on the walls, just on the first floor, to make it look like an annex to the Museum of Fine Arts. I poked around down there for a few minutes, then made my way to the second floor, where Laura Crain said her husband's 'ego room' was located. Up there I found some of the framed certificates for humanitarian awards he'd received from countries all over the globe, and photographs of him posing with everyone from Nelson Mandela to Barack Obama to George Clooney, even one with Mookie Betts. He and Mookie were in front of the Green Monster at Fenway and looked happy. So was I when Mookie was still at Fenway.

There was also a picture on the fireplace mantel of him with Queen Elizabeth, which made me smile, not at the sight of the late monarch, but at something Hawk had said when she passed.

'Still watching *The Crown*,' Hawk had said. 'Thanks for the damn spoiler alert.'

I went through Crain's desk and found nothing interesting. There was an oversized Mac on the desk, but I did not have the password and had not asked for one. I continued to make my way from room to room. The whole house was spotless, but then Laura Crain had told me the housekeeper had been in the day before. On the third floor was a small theater, with recliner seats and a large screen and even a popcorn machine.

The master bedroom was on the second floor. I stopped back in there, went through his closet and hers, which was about five times the size of his. I went through the drawers of the two bedside tables, hoping I wouldn't find things that would make me feel like a voyeur. Fortunately I did not, just a small bottle of cannabis oil, probably a sleep aid. Her side of the bed.

There was no sign that Andrew Crain had been here recently. Or that she had. Or that anybody except the housekeeper had. I went back down to the ego room again, then down to the first floor to admire the art, both paintings and sculptures. Despite the personal touches, there was no sense that this was someone's home. Instead it felt like a lavishly furnished and designed spec house for the rich and famous, as if the Crains might be ready to turn it around and sell it to some other rich guy.

As I stepped outside, I was thinking about the lawyer again, and how quickly he *had* annoyed me to the extent that he had.

I had mentioned him to Laura Crain.

'Have you ever seen *A Few Good Men*?' she asked.

I told her that by now I was pretty certain I nearly had the movie memorised.

'Clay is the company's version of Colonel Jessep,' she said. 'He was Ethan's hire. My husband's partner has convinced himself and keeps trying to convince Andrew that they need Clay on that wall.'

She hesitated and then said, 'I just think he's mean.'

I told her what I'd said to Whitson on my way out of Claire Megill's office.

'I'm sorry I missed that,' she said.

'Not a fan?'

'My husband occasionally fantasises about shooting him out of a cannon. But Ethan won't allow it, not this close to the big merger.'

Carlos was waiting in his car out in front of the house. He got out when I was back on the street. He went inside. I was picking up a sandwich at DeLuca's once I got to Charles Street when I picked up the tail.

15

I didn't want to stop and stare, which would let him know I'd spotted him. But I had gotten a good enough look to see that I was being casually followed by a slightly larger version of Hawk. Like the next size up.

If I wasn't working as diligently as I was at non-objectification, my first reaction would have been that he looked as if he should have been playing power forward for the Celtics.

He was bald and wore a soft-looking gray hoodie and jeans and white high-top sneakers. Even from a distance I could see the midday sun gleaming off the top of his head, and giving the illusion – literally – of a headlight.

He was hanging back about a block, sometimes switching sides of the street as a way of not making himself obvious. But he was clearly following me, finally making the turn on Charles that I'd just made. When I crossed over and acted as if I were taking a picture of the Charles Street Meeting House with my phone, he stopped, too.

I headed for the park then. When I slowed before getting to the corner of Charles and Beacon, I allowed myself a brief look over my shoulder and saw that he had stopped in front of DeLuca's, as if studying their assortment of cheeses with great interest, nose practically pressed to the glass.

I crossed Beacon and walked into the park and made my way diagonally toward the statue of George Washington. I meandered my way toward Boylston and Berkeley, where my office had been since the British were coming. If he knew where my office was, which he might if he knew who I was, the route made sense.

I crossed Arlington against the light, jogging to dodge traffic as a way of putting some distance between the two of us, heading toward The Newbury. He was still about a hundred yards behind me, talking on his phone or at least wanting it to look as if he were.

I did not feel threatened. But I did not believe in coincidence. I had been to the office of Andrew Crain's executive assistant that morning, had met with her and then gone out of my way to insult their lawyer. Maybe after I had left she had told the lawyer that I was looking into Andrew Crain's disappearance. And I had just come from the Crain residence on Chestnut Street.

Now I was being followed.

Before I got to The Newbury I took a hard right, ducking into the Public Alley and sprinting for the first cover I could see, a blue dumpster. I crouched behind it, having decided in that moment not to let the game come to me, and still angry at myself for letting Andrew Crain get away from me at Davio's the way he had.

I looked down the alley from where I waited and saw that there were no other people between here and Berkeley.

I heard him before I saw him. But when I did see him walking tentatively past the dumpster, I was up and out of my crouch and bum-rushing him across the alley and toward another dumpster across the way, getting hold of his right arm as I did and twisting it behind him, in the general direction of his shoulder.

Then I shoved him harder into the dumpster and said, 'Got an existential question, I guess you could call it.'

If I was hurting him, he wasn't showing it. Or making any move to get his arm loose, perhaps afraid I might snap it like a twig.

'What's the question?'

British accent. He sounded a bit like Hawk doing Jeeves.

'Why are we here?' I said.

He still made no attempt to separate himself from my grasp. 'I was following you. But you obviously know that, don't you, mate?'

'I don't like being followed,' I said.

I twisted his arm more, bringing it up. He turned his head just slightly. And I could see him smiling.

'Now please let me go,' he said, 'before I'm the one who has to hurt you.'

'How do I know you won't try to do that if I do let you go?'

He was still smiling.

'Because we're both gentlemen,' he said, 'and know that fighting rarely solves anything.'

I told him to speak for himself.

16

In the spirit of hands-across-the-globe internationalism, we were in my office a few minutes later, neither one of us having tried to prove who was the better fighter.

He somehow appeared even bigger sitting down than he did standing up, making the client chair in which he sat look as if I'd borrowed it from a kindergarten class.

He said his name was Reggie Smythe. He spelled the last name out for me and said it rhymed with 'blithe.' I told them there had been a Reggie Smith, which rhymed with Smith, who'd played with the Red Sox on their Impossible Dream team in 1967.

He greeted the news with far less interest than if I'd just told him his fly was open.

'I'm a football man myself,' he said.

'Yours or ours?'

'There is only ours,' he said.

'Don't tell Belichick that,' I said.

I asked if he wanted coffee. He said he'd prefer something stronger. I told him it was a little early for that.

'Maybe in your country,' he said. 'Not ours.'

I got the bottle of Jameson out of the bottom drawer of my desk and one of the glasses I kept in there with it and poured him some and he drank.

'Why are you following me?' I said.

'As head of security at Lith,' he said, 'my responsibilities are both plentiful and diverse.'

'Happy for you.'

'And being quite good at my job, I thought there might be a chance that you could save me some trouble and perhaps even lead me to Mr Crain.'

'How did you know that I'd be at his brownstone?'

He smiled again. His teeth were almost as white as his sneakers. 'None of your bloody business,' he said.

'So you don't know where he is, either,' I said.

He shook his head. 'It's not yet reached the point where it's a problem at the company,' he said. 'But we'd very much like it to not become one, especially not at the present time.'

'Because of the merger, you mean.'

'Imagine, if you will, if Tim Cook the Apple man suddenly disappeared right as he was about to buy another company, something he does almost on a monthly basis, were you aware of that?'

'I wasn't,' I said. 'But I do know the date when Benny Goodman and his orchestra recorded "Sing Sing Sing." Want to know what year?'

'Do I have a choice?'

'Nineteen thirty-seven,' I said. 'Sixth of July. In Hollywood.'

'Brilliant,' he said.

He drank. He seemed quite comfortable sitting across the desk from me. He probably didn't know that I had my .38 in the slightly open top drawer next to my right hand.

'This isn't the first time Crain has disappeared,' I said.

'Has he disappeared,' Smythe said, 'or have we simply not found him yet?'

'A distinction,' I said, 'not a difference.'

There was still a lot of whiskey in the glass. I could practically taste it, no matter what the hour, knowing what the first sip would feel like, the way it would feel making its way through me like warm, running water. But even the thought of drinking hard liquor this early in the day made me start to feel sleepy. And would do nothing at all to get me to where I wanted to go with Reggie Smythe.

'Did you follow me from the Hancock and I just didn't make you sooner? If so, it could only be Claire Megill or the lawyer who put you on me before I'd left the building.'

He ignored the question, finished his drink in a healthy swallow, and stood.

'Since you're of no use to me,' Smythe said, 'it would be best if you leave the search for Mr Crain's whereabouts to us.'

'I have a client who might feel differently about that,' I said.

'I don't care,' he said.

'You must know who my client is.'

'Same answer.'

'And if I choose not to back off?'

'Then the next time we meet you won't see me coming,' he said.

He finally nodded in the direction of my top right-hand drawer. 'Gun?' he said.

I nodded.

'So we're clear,' I said, 'I'll be out of it when my client tells me I'm out of it.'

'You've now been told,' he said. 'What you do from here is entirely up to you.'

'You think it's harder to sound tough with a British accent?' I said.

I stood now, looking up at him, but not enough to make me feel less like a tough guy myself.

'Are we done here?'

'For now,' he said.

'Brilliant,' I said, affecting an accent of my own.

He walked out and left my door open. I could hear him whistling 'God Save the King' until he was all the way down the hallway and gone. If I had intimidated him, he'd kept a stiff upper lip about it, I had to give the Limey bastard that.

17

L ater in the afternoon I met Hawk in what had long ago become our own private boxing gym at the Harbor Health Club. The only reason the gym was still part of Henry Cimoli's club was because Hawk and I were both ex-boxers and so was Henry, who had once been the most accomplished of the three of us.

The gym had gotten smaller recently after Henry had knocked down a wall to build another yoga studio.

'You really need more damn yoga here, you old dog?' Hawk said.

'That's downward dog to you,' Henry said.

Before I had left the office I had bagged the glass that Reggie Smythe had used, planning to drop it off with Lee Farrell at police headquarters tomorrow, just in case the gentleman bruiser might have something on his résumé other than the ability to talk pretty.

Hawk was showing off on the speed bag when I arrived, having already finished the rest of his workout. I was about to start my own progressions on the contour bag Henry had purchased for us, one that was shaped slightly more like a human body and which gave you more realistic targets for your punches than the normal heavy bag next to it.

'Who had faster hands when you were a kid,' I asked Hawk when he finished. 'You or Ali?'

'Me.'

'Then explain to me how come he's the one who became the greatest.'

'He didn't have to augment his income as a thug,' Hawk said.

He was wearing white Adidas boxing shoes and long black satin shorts and another of his endless supply of 'Black Mamba'

T-shirts, this one with Kobe Bryant's likeness on it. In comparison, I was the one who looked like the thug, in a Red Sox T-shirt cut to the shoulders and baggy gray sweatpants and sneakers to match.

'Good news for you,' Hawk said, watching me move from side to side in front of the bag, 'is that your workout clothes won't never go out of fashion, on account of never having been in no fashion in the first place.'

'You planning to review my workout along with my functional attire?' I said.

'Don't require much planning. You been letting your elbow fly out from underneath your shoulder lately when you throw your hook.'

'You're just pointing that out now?'

'Been workin' up to it, I know how sensitive you are 'bout what's left of your form.'

I quickly sped up my progressions, Hawk having made it clear that he was ready for a beer as soon as he showered. But it didn't take long for me to feel as if I had found a perfect rhythm, what Hawk liked to call synchronice-ness, with my movement and with my punches and my breathing. Jab, cross. Slide step to my left and do it again. Then to my right. Same combination. Then jab, cross, hook. The contour bag helped you get a sense of where punches would be landing on an actual opponent. The other benefit of the new bag, because of the material with which it was made and a softer core, is that your hands bounced off it more easily, almost like a spring effect.

'Cross is still too damn long,' Hawk said. 'Like you sending an email it's on its way.'

I grunted in response.

'What's that you say, my good man?' he said.

'I hate it when you're right.'

'Shit, you ought to be used to that by now.'

I concentrated even harder on both form and footwork now. Jab, jab, cross. Putting a little more snap into every punch, knowing I could do it because my core was as strong as it was. Jab, cross, jab, cross, hook. The hook was a beauty.

'Good,' Hawk said.

'You like me,' I said. 'You really like me.'

'Still gonna make you buy the drinks for keeping me waiting.'

I told him I had my reasons for getting here late, but would wait to tell him when we got to the bar, which today was the Rowes Wharf Bar at the Boston Harbor Hotel, one of our favorites.

Rowes was starting to fill up by the time we got there about forty-five minutes later with the after-work crowd, mostly young. But despite that demographic, it was everything a good bar should be. Not exactly The Street Bar at the Old Ritz, but not all that far away, either, the atmosphere and feel of the place and the looks of it. Mahogany walls, wine-red carpet, old-school light fixtures hanging from a coffered ceiling that looked as if they came out of another time, which seemed to be the point.

We were both drinking Lord Hobo Boomsauce out of cans, an IPA that had become one of my favorites and was now one of Hawk's when he was in a rare mood for beer.

'So why you think somebody at the home office would send some hard case after you?' Hawk said.

'You don't think he was telling me the truth about hoping I might lead him to Crain?'

'Fuck no,' Hawk said.

He was smiling now, but not at me. And perhaps getting ready to write songs of love, also not for me. I followed his eyes and saw a striking young woman sitting at the far end of the bar, shyly looking at Hawk over her phone. She had flawless skin the color of coffee, short-cropped black hair that served only to accentuate features that seemed pretty flawless to me as well, from a distance and in this light. Even only seeing the top half of her, the body was clearly by God.

'I thought you were in a committed relationship with the Bank of America lady,' I said.

'Changed banks,' Hawk said, 'like people do.'

He turned back to me. 'So Idris Elba threatened your ass?'

'Right before he left my office,' I said. 'But I managed to remain steadfast.'

'Maybe they just all more worried about the big boss being cuckoo for Cocoa Puffs than they letting on,' Hawk said. 'But what I can't figure is why they seeing you as the threat when the threat seems to be the guy nobody can find, leastways not yet.'

'This seems to be a major concern to all concerned,' I said. 'It sounds like they're trying to mitigate any possible risk until they close the deal, and before the SEC signs off.'

'Look at you,' Hawk said, 'going all *Squawk Box* on me.'

'You watch *Squawk Box*?'

'Don't everybody?'

By now the young woman had been joined by a date. But when the bartender placed new beers in front of us, he also slid a piece of paper to Hawk.

'Uh-huh,' Hawk said.

'You starting to think that maybe it ain't all one big happy family over there on the fiftieth floor?' Hawk said.

'Did I mention that Crain's assistant said there might be problems in the Crains' marriage?' I said to Hawk. 'Just to add a little special sauce to the whole thing?'

Hawk drank down about half of his new beer and smacked his lips after he did. 'You a big-picture guy,' he said to me now. 'What happens when you step back and just look at what you got so far?'

'A bad feeling, that's what I've got,' I said.

'Wouldn't be the first time,' Hawk said. 'Look at it that way.'

18

Laura Crain said that instead of meeting for coffee the next morning I should join her for her morning walk near her home in Brookline.

'I've talked myself into believing that today's the day I hear from him,' she said. 'Or that he's just going to come walking through the door as if he's just taken a longer walk than usual.'

'Put me down for either one,' I said.

At a little after eight o'clock I met her at the Edith Baker School in Brookline, next to the Blakely Hoar Sanctuary, between Leatherbee Woods and Hancock Woods. Laura said that she varied her morning walks, but the sanctuary was close to her house, and the hiking place she considered most beautiful, even if the trail was shorter than others in the area to which she had easy access. I told her I'd actually walked it myself a few times with Susan Silverman when she was having Walden Pond urges and didn't want to drive to Concord.

'There's nothing wrong with being at one with nature closer to Linnaean Street,' she'd explained at the time, and I told her I could respect that, but wasn't entirely certain how Henry David would have reacted to selfish thinking like that.

Even though there were those longer trails in Brookline, Laura Crain explained, none of them filled her with the sense of peace that Blakely Hoar did. And said she was looking for some peace this morning, the more the better.

She had received no phone calls from her husband last evening, or this morning, had seen nothing on social media that even hinted that anyone had heard from Andrew Crain for the past few days, which meant that everybody at Lith was keeping the company's circle tight.

And she still wasn't ready to contact the police.

'He's been acting out lately, no one is more aware of that fact than I,' she said. 'Perhaps what's going on right now is just extreme acting out. There's so much going on at the company. But I think it's something more than that, I just don't know what.'

'But it's still his company, in terms of control,' I said.

'Are you sure about the control part?' she said.

'You aren't?'

She started to say something, then shook her head and said, 'It's something we can talk about another time. Perhaps sooner rather than later.'

We were just beginning our walk, passing the tennis courts at the Baker School and making our way toward a path that had made me feel, on my previous visits here with Susan, like a trip back in time, the trail occasionally guarded by low stone walls that I knew had been here for hundreds of years.

'I have to ask you something,' I said. 'Actually, there is more than one thing about which I want to ask you this morning. But I need to know if you think your husband is capable of harming himself.'

She had taken a slight lead as the path briefly narrowed, and had to look back over her shoulder now to answer me.

'I'm not seeing depression from him, Mr Spenser, if that's what you're asking. I'm just not, and believe me I've looked. What I see is high anxiety. And occasionally manic behavior, without question. But not classic or clinical depression. I understand that Susan is only going off what I've told her, but she agrees with me.'

'Something triggered that reaction at the restaurant.'

'I agree. But you have to agree with something: When my husband did get outside with that awful man, and with whatever rage he was feeling in the moment, he did pull himself back.'

'Before running as if being chased,' I said. 'I almost would rather he'd stayed and started a fight that I could have broken up.'

As we went deeper on the trail, she pointed out pools and

69

ponds and various wildlife, getting as excited as a bird watcher when she spotted a goldfinch. I didn't feel as if she were trying to change the subject as much as trying to distract herself, if only momentarily, from the reality of why we were here.

'That's a bat house on that tree,' she said at one point.

'Thanks for the heads-up,' I said. 'And I mean that sincerely. I like bats as much as I like snakes.'

I told her then about having been followed by Reggie Smythe, and my conversation with him at my office.

'Andrew has no use for Reggie, just so you know,' she said. 'It's probably the biggest reason he doesn't like using him as a bodyguard. He was Ethan's hire all the way and Andrew just went along, the way he often does when Ethan gets stuck on something, and the way he goes along with Clay Whitson. Ethan had gotten stuck at the time on extra security, for the company and for himself. Ethan sees the world as an increasingly dangerous place, and has become increasingly paranoid, especially the last year or so.'

'I don't think anyone thinks it's getting safer,' I said.

She nodded. 'Ethan even takes Reggie with him now when he travels. Andrew asked Ethan one time if it wouldn't be cheaper to have a night-light. He said Ethan didn't find that amusing.'

I hoped she didn't see me take one last look back at the bat house. You couldn't trust the gnarly bastards, whether it was daytime or not. Flying snakes, that's how I looked at them.

'Who do you think sent Reggie to follow you?' she said.

'Since I'm assuming it wasn't you, only Ethan and Claire Megill know I'm looking into Andrew's disappearance. And perhaps the charming lawyer.'

'I've already mentioned that Andrew has no use for Clay.'

'Then why is he still around?'

'Because Ethan also managed to convince Andrew that Clay is indispensable, having done so much of the heavy lifting on the merger. A merger over which both Ethan and Clay have become increasingly paranoid, as if the whole thing is going to blow up in their faces any second. I can't prove it, but I think they're keeping things from Andrew about it.'

'He could find them out, I assume.'

'He has always trusted Ethan, occasionally to a fault.'

'Sounds like a fun shop these days.'

'Tell me about it.'

'Does your husband want the merger to happen?'

She sighed. 'He understands why it *should* happen,' she said. 'I guess that's the way to put it. It's a way for them to eventually pass Tesla and Musk and dominate the electric-car business into the future, which Clay assures everybody they will.'

We were walking under what felt like a cathedral ceiling of white hemlocks and maples and oaks. The experience was as peaceful as she said it would be.

'But Andrew's position has shifted lately. He increasingly talks about enough being enough. Others disagree, as you can imagine.'

'But he has sixty per cent of the company.'

'He does. And the right to buy out Ethan if it ever comes to that. But I don't believe he ever would, even with cause. He and Ethan have always been like brothers. Loving each other like brothers, fighting like brothers, making up afterward. And even though Andrew has the biggest stake, Ethan has always had a way of getting my husband to where he, Ethan, wants him to go. I've always thought his greatest ability as a salesman has been selling things to my husband. And managing him. More like an agent than a partner.'

'You didn't mention any of this when you came to my office.'

'My husband hadn't run off and hidden at that point,' she said and sighed. 'I've told you a lot about my husband and his current circumstances, Mr Spenser. But not everything.'

'Now his head of security has come around telling me to back off.'

'How did you respond to that, by the way?'

I told her what I had told Hawk about remaining steadfast.

'I'll bet,' Laura Crain said.

We had made the turn at the end of the trail and were headed back by now. She was dressed in leggings that had some sort of floral design and a black nylon vest over a long white T-shirt. Her hat said NATURE CONSERVANCY.

'If *you* had to pick one person you think might have sent Smythe to watch me, who would it be?'

'Clay Whitson. One hundred per cent. Clay's really the same kind of enforcer that Reggie imagines himself to be, he just has a law degree.'

'But why would he be this threatened by me?'

'Clay believes in keeping the circle tight, and doesn't trust anybody he doesn't know,' she said. 'He is obsessed with any hint of bad publicity that could somehow slow the merger. Andrew said to me not long ago that Clay would be willing to kill to see this thing through. I don't think he was exaggerating, frankly.'

She stopped and looked at me. 'He called me last night, furious that I'd brought someone from the outside into this without telling him.'

'What did you say?'

'I told him to kiss my ass.'

In that moment, it was Laura Crain I wanted to kiss.

We were still standing at the point where we'd begun our hike.

'You have to find Andrew,' she said. 'Tell me you'll find him.'

'I'm very good at this kind of work,' I said.

Then I told her there was one more question I needed to ask.

'Are you and your husband contemplating divorce?' I said. 'Because if you are, that's something else that would have been helpful for me to know.'

'*Who told you that?*'

There was no point in not telling her who had. She would easily be able to figure it out for herself. And she was my client.

'Claire Megill,' I said.

'If wishing could only make it true for the long-suffering Claire,' she said.

72

Then she added, 'That bitch.'

Then she turned around and headed back up the trail without saying goodbye.

I continued to have a very bad feeling about all of this. About what I knew already and the new information that kept coming in, on what felt like an hourly basis.

I recalled that Thoreau had written once that an early-morning walk could be a blessing for the whole day.

If he were around right now, I would have told him he could kiss *my* ass.

19

I had invited Susan and Pearl to a family dinner at my apartment, with the promise to Susan of a flight of heavenly transport afterward.

'So the usual?' Susan said.

I told her that was my ambition, yes.

'Then I'll have what he's having, bartender,' she said.

I was making us turkey burgers and fries seasoned with salt and pepper and black truffle oil. Not everything in the modern world had made things better. But it was my opinion that truffle oil had vastly improved French fries if you knew what you were doing in the kitchen. And I did.

'I could have cooked tonight,' Susan said when she and Pearl arrived. 'Especially now that you've given me multiple tutorials on how to make turkey burgers.'

I poured us each a glass of Riesling and put the bottle in the ice bucket on the kitchen counter.

'Why don't we hold off on having you cook us turkey burgers for a special occasion,' I said.

'Such as?'

'Jesus coming back?' I suggested.

'That kind of talk isn't going to help you get me out of these clothes, mister.'

'I've got a solid game plan, don't worry.'

'With turkey burgers?' she said.

'The food of love.'

'You think Cheetos are the food of love,' Susan said.

She sat at the counter and watched me cook. While I did, I told her about my nature walk with Laura Crain, and the way she had reacted at the very end when I'd asked about divorce.

'Has she ever mentioned that they're considering divorcing each other?' I said.

'She has not. We have talked about a lot of things. Not that.'

I caught her up on the rest of it, Ethan Lowe and Clay Whitson pushing harder than anyone for the merger, almost as if the lawyer had become a third partner in the firm. I told her what Laura had said about her husband being opposed to the merger. And about Reggie Smythe ending up in my office. Susan did not interrupt, letting me tell it my way, my own rhythm and pace, with as much or as little detail as I saw fit. When I told her about the goldfinches, her eyes lit up and she did interrupt long enough to say, 'I love finches.' I told her that's why I'd brought them up.

Otherwise her focus, as always, was almost fiercely present, part of what I knew, if only anecdotally, about her immense skill as a therapist, even if all she was doing in my kitchen was listening to me as I went through the preparations for our dinner.

When I finished, she was smiling.

'It sounds as if the security man was less than intimidated by my cutie,' she said.

'He will be when he gets to know me better,' I said.

'Which I'm assuming he will,' she said.

'Hey, he started it,' I said.

Susan was in no rush to eat and neither was I. I had already chopped the mushrooms and onions before she arrived, sautéed them until they were soft, and had them cool. Now I was ready to mix them in with the ground turkey and bread crumbs, one egg, salt, pepper, and just a splash of Worcestershire sauce before carefully making the patties. I always made extra patties. They were for me, not Susan. It was more of an understood-type thing.

The fries were already in the oven. When the skillet was ready I put the patties into it. Generally I cooked them for four minutes a side. But I wasn't a slave to the clock, I just waited until I thought I had the firmness just right.

'You're sure I can't help?' Susan said.

'Actually, I do have an important job for you.' I grinned. 'You can toast the English muffins.'

'Now you're just being mean,' she said.

She set the table while she toasted the muffins. I removed the truffle fries from the oven. She poured us more Riesling. After that it was just like all the dinners we'd ever had, at her place or mine, because it didn't matter where we were sitting, just that we were sitting across from each other, and I was again breathing the same air as she was.

'So what do you think?' I said.

'It's wonderful.'

'About the Crains, I mean.'

'I assume you're looking for a symptomatic psychological diagnosis?'

'No such thing as a free lunch,' I said. 'Even when it's dinner.'

Another smile from her, which reminded me of a line from the poet who happened to be my namesake, if not a distant relation. The other Spenser, as Susan liked to call him.

Her eyes look lovely and upon them smile.

'Clinically speaking,' she said, 'I think job one is finding the sonofabitch. But you don't need me to tell you that.'

We ate and cleaned up and drank a little more and then the transport part was as promised, and like the first time, all over again.

*

We were both asleep later, Pearl snoring away from her spot on my couch, when my cell phone chirped.

Belson

'Stop me if you've heard this one before, but we got a body,' Frank Belson said.

I waited.

They were never social calls from Belson, and never at this time of night.

'Mrs Andrew Crain,' Belson said. 'Quirk says you know her.'

20

Susan offered to go with me to Brookline, but I knew she didn't want to be anywhere near a crime scene, especially one involving a friend.

I told her I'd talk to her when I got back, whenever that was. She said there was no way she was going back to sleep, and said she was going to take Pearl back to Cambridge now, she had an early appointment today she couldn't move.

'This is like waking up to a nightmare,' she said when I was dressed and on my way out the door, and I told her I had nothing to add to that.

By official definition, the unattended death scene really began all the way back at Independence Ave, the construction site for a new community center. That's where the television trucks were set up. The media already knew who the victim was because the media always seemed to know, at the highest speed of high-speed Internet.

I knew Belson and the Crime Scene Response Unit would be somewhere up the path I had walked with Laura Crain, wherever the body had been found. They'd be tagteaming with a State Police unit, which probably meant Brian Lundquist, the homicide captain who'd replaced my old friend Healy, who'd finally retired from scenes like this and nights like this.

Belson had left my name with two of the uniforms at the edge of the perimeter, between the construction site and the Baker School. I saw a variety of police vehicles, some with flashing lights, between the television trucks and the uniforms. A couple Ford Explorer hybrids. Two sedans marked BROOKLINE. As I headed up the trail, I saw the first couple investigators in their white Tyvek jumpsuits, carrying evidence bags. Because this was Norfolk County, there were two guys in windbreakers about fifty yards up from the white jumpsuits who had to be assistant district attorneys. Hail, hail, the gang was all here.

Now I was, too.

There was more activity when I got to the place off the trail by a few yards, which Belson had described as a body-sized spot between the root system of the trees and one of the rock walls Laura Crain had pointed out to me the other day. The path was muddy, I could feel it more than see it, the forest floor having almost risen up with water because of a heavy rain the night before. This is where a man taking a late-night walk with his dog had discovered the body of Laura Crain.

I was confident as I approached Belson and Lundquist that there would be no jurisdictional turf war going on between the Boston Police and State Police. Belson and Lundquist had worked together before the way Belson and Martin Quirk had worked with Healy once, and somehow managed to do that without one of them threatening to steal the other's lunch money.

There was a photographer taking still pictures near where the body must have been found, yellow tape now extending from one tree to another across the trail. There was another guy, BPD on the back of his blue jacket, carrying a digital recorder. It takes a village. They had left the crime scene sprinter van at the mouth of the trail, which wasn't wide enough for it to come any farther. All in all, there were nearly enough of Belson's guys and Lundquist's guys for a pickup basketball game. I counted at least eight but may have missed the ones who had fanned out into the woods.

Laura Crain's body must already have been bagged, because behind me I could see the sprinter van slowly starting to back away from the trail.

I nearly bumped into one of Belson's guys, a sergeant named Chris Connolly, walking around with a notebook and a pen, keeping a log.

'You made good time,' Belson said.

'Highly motivated,' I said. I nodded at Brian Lundquist. 'Hey,' I said.

'Hey,' he said.

Before I could ask, Belson took the unlit cigar out of his mouth and said, 'Strangled, from the looks of it.'

'How long was she here before the dog walker found her?'

'To be determined,' Frank Belson said.

'She liked to come here in the morning,' I told them. 'We walked right past this spot the other day.'

'She mention ever coming here at night?' Lundquist said.

I shook my head. 'Hard to believe she'd come out here alone, though.'

'What about with somebody?' Belson said.

I shrugged. 'Something else to be determined.'

Belson said, 'You got any theories about who might have done something like this to the wife of the fifth-richest guy in the US of A?'

'Sixth,' I said.

'Fuck off,' Belson said. 'She mention anything about being concerned for her safety?'

'Maybe she didn't think she needed to be worried because she had me,' I said.

'How'd that work out for her?' Belson said.

Then I told him that I'd known Laura Crain for only a few

days, that she'd come to me for something other than bodyguard work.

'Why had she?' Lundquist said. 'Come to you.'

There was no point in confidentiality at this point, she was gone.

I told them of her concerns about her husband.

'Stop me if you've heard *this* one before,' Belson said, 'but with an event like this, the first person we very much like to have a sit-down with is the spouse. But he's not at their house here, and he's not at their place up on Chestnut, we already checked. You have any idea where he might be?'

I described the scene outside Davio's for them.

'I might have been the last person to see him,' I said.

'And maybe her,' Belson said. 'What are the odds?'

21

At a little before four in the morning Belson and I were drinking coffee at an IHOP on Soldiers Field Road, north of Brookline and south of the Mass Pike. Even in the middle of the night, I found myself wanting to order everything on one side of the menu. I hadn't been inside an IHOP for a while, and found it pleasing that the menu still consisted of pictures, as if the world had forgotten what a short stack with eggs on the side looked like.

'You know you want to,' Belson said when he saw me slide the menu away.

'I eat now,' I said, 'and it throws off my whole schedule of good intake the rest of the day.'

'So you're worried about fitting the donuts in later, is what you're telling me.'

'No wonder you finally made lieutenant,' I said. 'By the way? Where was Nurse Ratched tonight?'

'If you are referring to my immediate superior, Captain Glass, it turns out that just this week she once again tested positive for COVID,' he said. 'Though I'm frankly surprised that COVID didn't test positive for her.'

I took him through what I knew, even if it wasn't *everything* I knew so far. I wasn't entirely sure why I held back what Claire Megill had told me about problems in the Crains' marriage. But I did.

Belson had placed his cigar on his saucer. I nodded at it now and said, 'You use those things like chew toys.'

'Pacifiers,' he said. 'And *you* suck on it.'

There were a few other booths occupied. Late-shifters getting off work. Early-shifters on their way in, most likely. There were a couple college boys, at least they looked like college boys to me, trying to get a jump on what I was pretty sure were inevitable hangovers, caught somewhere between the end of the party and the point later when they would have to decide whether or not they were waking up or coming to.

'The husband could be dead, too, we just don't know it yet,' Belson said.

'The thought has occurred.'

'Guy's wife is dead,' Belson said. 'Somebody at his company is going to have a hard time getting out in front of this if he's missing when she is dead.'

Belson shrugged. 'If we assume he is still among the living, where the fuck is he?'

He looked tired. But that seemed to be his natural state. He was as great a cop as Quirk had been when he was the one who was the star of the Homicide Division. He would just never have Quirk's management skills. Or had ever expressed any interest in acquiring them, or any other people skills for that matter. Sitting across the booth from him, it was as if I could see the accumulated weight of a thousand nights like this one.

'What aren't you telling me?' he said.

'I gave you all I got,' I said. I grinned and held up my hand. 'Scout's honor.'

I was holding up two fingers. Belson shook his head as if I'd just flipped him off.

'That's the Cub Scout salute, you dumb shit.'

I poured us both more coffee out of the pot they'd left. 'With the husband,' I said, 'I keep going back to the scene at the restaurant, and how the way the dumb shit was acting with his date pushed Crain's buttons. If he didn't get the head start he did, I would have gone after him.'

'You said that people in his office were worried how bad publicity might affect this merger,' Belson said. 'Well, they're about to have a shitload of bad publicity now.'

'Or maybe she did take a walk in the night by herself and it turned out to have nothing to do with who she was or who he is.'

'So, scout,' Belson said, 'do you honestly think it was just bad luck? After she hires you and her husband does a runner and the husband's company has about a gazillion more dollars on the table?'

'I need to find him, is what I think, Frank,' I said. 'After that I need to find out if he's got any thoughts about who might have done this to her.'

'Staying out of my way in the process.'

'I thought that was an understood-type thing.'

'Yeah, since when?' Belson said.

He picked up the cigar and dipped the end of it in his coffee and put it back in his mouth.

'The husband isn't my client. She was.'

'You said yourself she didn't ask you to watch her. So it's not as if this happened on your watch.'

'You know me better than that, Frank,' I said.

'Yeah,' he said. 'Unfortunately, I do.'

22

When I had parked my car behind the building it was still not yet five in the morning. I had no way of knowing whether or not Susan somehow had managed to get some sleep, so I didn't call.

I didn't want to talk right now. Or try to sleep, at least not at the moment. I needed to walk. So I made my way across the Public Garden and then across the Common and up to Tremont, back down Boylston to Arlington, and around again. It was dawn by now, the soft gray light changing by the moment, the morning becoming brighter, as if a retractable roof over the park was slowly being opened. I thought back to the drunk college boys at the IHOP, and felt suddenly as if I were the one walking something off.

Could Andrew Crain have done this to his wife? She had spoken of him pulling himself back from the edge with a perfectly obnoxious stranger when we'd all dined out together. What if it had been his wife who had set him off and this time he wasn't able to bring himself back from the edge?

Hawk had once described what I did for a living as opening closed doors, then finding out what was on the other side of them. But what did I know, really, about what had gone on behind closed doors with Andrew Crain and his wife?

Belson was right, I knew, the first thing any good cop needed to do was eliminate the spouse as a subject.

But first you had to find the spouse in question.

Instead of turning right on Arlington, I walked down Boylston to the Dunkin' and got a large coffee with cream and sugar. It was still only seven-thirty when I got back to the apartment, Susan and Pearl already long gone.

I remembered then that I had left my phone in my car, walked around back and got it, saw a text from Susan telling me that she and the baby had left early and that she would call me when she had some free time so I could catch her up, and how horrible it all was, and how sorry she was.

I saw she had made the bed. Of course she had. She was Susan. I lay down with my clothes still on, stopping only long enough to take off the muddy Red Wing boots I'd worn to Blakely Hoar.

Somehow I managed to fall asleep then, having no idea how long I'd been asleep when Frank Belson awakened me for the second time that morning.

'Turn on the TV,' he said.

23

The press conference, about to air live, was being held at a conference room at the Lith, Inc. offices on the forty-ninth floor of the Hancock. I observed that they were correctly calling it 200 Clarendon for their viewing audience, which now included me.

It meant the stars of the show were one floor below where Andrew Crain's office was, and Ethan Lowe's, and Claire Megill's. Ethan Lowe was standing behind a lectern with what I knew was the Lith logo on the front, sparks coming out of a battery.

Andrew Crain was standing next to him.

'Shazam,' I said in my living room.

Lowe thanked everyone for coming on such short notice, and then informed the media in the room that they wouldn't be taking any questions about what he described as 'a tragic death in our family.'

Then Lowe introduced Andrew Crain, as if he needed introducing, and stepped away from the microphone. You could see the small piece of paper in Crain's hand fluttering like a single leaf on a tree in the winter.

'There are no words' is the way he began.

He stared down at the paper, almost as if he were afraid to look out at the audience in front of him.

'I have lost the love of my life,' Crain continued, 'who has become one more victim of random violence in America. I will step aside now and allow the authorities to do their work finding out who committed a crime like this against such a good and gentle creature of not just our country, but the world, because my Laura was a true and valued citizen of the world. Ethan and I will spare no expense in aiding that effort. Thank you all very much for coming here today. I will have no further public comments on this tragedy, or my loss.'

Then he walked away from the lectern and out of the conference room, the cameras tracking his movements until he finally disappeared down the glass-walled hallway. There were questions shouted at him as he made his way toward the door. Andrew Crain did not acknowledge them, or look back, or slow down.

I called Belson back.

'You plan to talk to him?' I said.

'Trying,' Belson said. 'I believe Quirk is handling the official request for an interview.'

'You think he'll do it?'

'Most people think they're required to talk to the cops,' he said. 'You and me, we both know they aren't. But I have a feeling that a high-profiler like Crain isn't going to want it out there that he refused.'

I had no way of knowing whether or not Andrew Crain had left the building once he was out of the conference room. But even though he said he didn't want to talk to anybody right now, it didn't change the fact that I wanted to talk to him. His wife had hired me to find things out about him and, up to now, what I had found out could have fit inside a shot glass.

Martin Quirk might have to go through channels. I did not. Andrew Crain wasn't my client. His wife had been, and still was, and would be until I decided she wasn't.

I was going to head over to the Hancock and wait for Andrew Crain in the hope that he was still inside and, being a trained investigator, find out how he exited the building when he did exit the building.

But when I came walking out the front door of my own building, Reggie Smythe was standing on the sidewalk, in front of a black Lincoln Navigator parked illegally on Marlborough.

'Let's take a ride,' he said.

'I'm not sure I know you well enough to get into a car with you,' I said.

'Just get in the fucking car,' he said.

I did.

24

The ride to Brookline took about twenty minutes. The Crains' estate was, appropriately enough, in what was known as the estate section of the town, on Cottage Street. I knew that the man who owned the Red Sox also lived somewhere in this part of Brookline. Maybe before I headed back downtown I could stop in and give him my thoughts on improving the Sox next season, and how much of his money I thought it might take to do that.

I worried sometimes that he didn't fully grasp how important his team was to me.

Smythe stopped at an elaborate wrought-iron gate and punched in a code before we made our way up a driveway that seemed as long as the Commonwealth Ave Promenade. The Navigator finally came to a stop in the circular drive near the front door of a massive colonial, mostly brick, that reminded me of an exterior for *Downton Abbey*.

There was another car, also a Navigator, already parked there, and a sleek-looking silver Mercedes. Smythe hadn't said much during the ride. Nor had I, seated next to him in the front seat.

At one point I did ask how his boss was doing, and Smythe, without taking his eyes off the road or changing his expression, said, 'You're the detective. Why don't you see if you can figure it out now that we're here.'

'I'm starting to sense that the two of us have gotten off on the wrong foot, Reg.'

'See, there,' he said, 'you're detecting at a high level already. Brilliant.'

Because of the other cars, I expected to find company with Andrew Crain once I was inside, perhaps Ethan Lowe, perhaps Claire Megill. But the only person occupying the living room was Crain himself, seated at the end of a long wraparound sofa. He had changed out of the blazer he'd been wearing at the press conference. Now he wore a red v-neck sweater with a plaid shirt showing underneath it and jeans and boat shoes.

He did not stand to greet me, just motioned for me to sit across from him in an antique chair that looked as if it might collapse underneath me like some kind of prop once it absorbed my full weight.

I carefully lowered myself down.

'I'm very sorry for your loss,' I said, because I couldn't think of anything better to say at the moment, and also because it happened to be true. His loss, my loss, everybody's.

At first I was afraid that he hadn't heard me, or hadn't processed what I'd just told him. He seemed to stare past me, blinking rapidly, his eyes fixed on some point on a wall covered by more expensive art.

'I understand you were one of the last people to see Laura alive,' he said.

The only people who knew about my walk with Laura Crain were Susan and Hawk. But obviously Crain's wife had told someone about it, unless Belson had told Quirk and Quirk had told Crain.

'I'm curious as to how you know that,' I said.

He stared past me again without answering. It was as if there were some kind of technical delay at work here, the kind you got on the Zoom calls I'd been forced to use with clients during COVID, on the rare occasions when I'd actually had clients during COVID.

'She... Laura kept an old Filofax organiser,' Crain said. 'It was on the kitchen table. Your name was in it for the other morning.'

'May I see it?' I said.

'No,' he said, 'you may not.'

I let it go.

'We took a walk along the same trail where they found her body,' I said.

He nodded now, like a bobblehead doll, as if this were the most fascinating piece of information he would receive all day.

'How... How did she seem? Was she anxious?'

'She was worried about you.'

Then he was nodding again, as enthusiastically as before, eyes wide.

But said nothing in response.

'Where have you been, Mr Crain?'

Another slight pause. 'Away.'

'Away where?'

Now his eyes focused on me. 'Does it matter?'

'It would have mattered to your wife,' I said. 'And thus matters to me.'

He pointed to his right now, in the direction of the front door. 'We have a place out in western Mass.'

'How did you get there?' I said. 'And how did you get inside without Laura having gotten an alert on the alarm system?'

'It was, ah, deactivated.'

'Without her knowing?'

'Is this a grand jury, Mr Spenser?' he snapped at me then, as if I was the one who had tripped an alarm inside him.

'It's not,' I said, keeping my own voice even. 'I'm sorry if it sounded that way.'

Susan often told me that there was no proper way, or even educated way, to quantify grief, or analyze it with any great certainty. But in this moment, in the big room in the big house, he seemed more upset about my line of questioning than he was about his wife's death.

'I'm simply honoring her wishes in wanting to know your whereabouts, just after the fact,' I continued.

'This isn't the way the story was supposed to end,' he said, his own voice quiet again. 'Can you appreciate that, Mr Spenser?'

'Of course.'

'We were… supposed to be together forever.' He smiled. 'I always knew that, that we were meant for each other, long before she did.'

He took a couple deep breaths.

'I did everything for her,' he said.

He was like a drunk at the end of the bar at closing time, talking and not listening. Nobody in the place, 'cept you and me.

'There was more she needed to know from me,' he said. 'Things I'll never get to tell her now.'

He had tucked himself into a corner of the couch, as if using the arm as a ballast.

'We were meant to be together,' he said, and started nodding again, in self-affirmation.

There was no point, at least not today, in me raising the subject of divorce, or asking him about behavior that had brought his wife to me in the first place.

'I need to pay you,' he said. Nodded again. 'Yes, I do.'

'For what?'

'I was under the impression that Laura was worried enough about me that she hired you.'

It was something he could have learned only from his partner or from his assistant or cops trying to set up a formal interview and maybe giving him information as an enticement. Because why would Laura Crain have told him she hired me? Because she wanted to share that she thought he had snakes crawling around inside his head lately?

'You don't owe me anything,' I said. 'I did nothing for your wife. I certainly didn't help keep her alive.'

'I need to pay you something for your services,' Andrew Crain said, as if everything in his life were transactional, even now.

'I never expect any kind of compensation for a job I don't finish, or sometimes don't even start,' I said. 'Your wife died while she was a client of mine. It's why this is no longer business with me, just personal.'

I stood. 'I'll be in touch.'

Somehow in this moment, he seemed intensely focused on me, as if I'd just now come into focus.

'No, you won't.'

Now I was staring at him.

'I'm not sure I understand.'

'I don't want to see or hear from you ever again, Mr Spenser,' he said. 'I do not want you to contact me or anyone with whom I associate. Your business with my wife, whether you consider it personal or not, is now concluded and her death is in the hands of the police.'

He was blinking again, and nodding.

'Now please leave my house,' he said, and got up from the sofa and walked out of the room.

'Okay, be that way,' I said when he was gone, my voice sounding quite loud in the empty room, as if I'd just shouted something at Monet.

25

'Well,' Susan said, 'it's not as if you haven't been fired before. So you can take some consolation in that.'

'But I've never been fired by somebody who'd never hired me,' I said.

'Maybe it's a sign you're still evolving,' she said. 'God, you're good.'

'Why I make the big bucks.'

'Good thing, now that I'm unemployed again.'

'Just when job numbers in the country have been improving.'

We were in her living room. She had just finished with her last client of the day, a few minutes before five. I poured her a chardonnay. I had already begun my own cocktail hour with a Boomsauce while waiting for her. She was still in her work clothes. Today that meant a sleek black dress with a scoop collar. Or what I thought should be described as a scoop collar. She had kicked off her low heels and curled up in her favorite chair, organising her legs underneath her, somehow managing to show off just enough of them as she did, and making me want to scoop her up.

We talked some about how she was still trying to process, even though we had done that already at a point earlier in the afternoon when she'd been between clients. She told me again that there was no point in me blaming myself, there was nothing I could have done to change the outcome.

'Are you trying to shrink me?' I said now.

'I'm a full-service girl.'

It got a smile out of me. 'You don't have to tell me that,' I said, and then proceeded to describe my odd meeting with Andrew Crain, in great detail.

She seemed to be relieved that we were talking about him for the moment and not his wife.

'This may just be a continuation of some kind of breakdown,' she said, 'exacerbated by grief and shock. Him telling you this isn't the way their story was supposed to end was both sad and predictable at the same time.'

I drank some of my beer. 'Before we continue, Doctor, I have a question. How come you always manage to look so elegant and swellegant and I look as if I just carried in some furniture and you were nice enough to offer me a beer?'

She winked. 'Maybe you've touched on one of my fantasies about hunky deliverymen.'

'Got another question,' I said. 'Do your male patients find you as distracting as I do?'

She winked again. 'Why limit it to male patients?' Susan said.

It was something the two of us had done plenty of times before, in moments like this, using small talk and humor to deflect from the subject at hand, the murder of her friend, in this case. I noticed that she had finished most of her wine, which, for Susan, was the equivalent of drinking out of the bottle. But she told me it had been an emotional last hour for her with a patient outside the clinical definition of gender binary, not elaborating beyond that, just that the person was adrift in no-man's-land. Or no-woman's-land.

She held out her glass now for me to refill it, somehow managing to look elegant doing that.

'What are you going to do?' she said when I sat back down on her couch. 'I know you well enough to know that you're not going to walk away from this.'

'Not even at gunpoint.'

'So?'

I grinned at her. 'Actually I'm the one with the him/her problem.'

'I see what you did there,' she said.

'I was originally hired to find out what Andrew Crain's problem was. His wife seemed quite sincere about wanting to know, as she had made that clear to you as well. But now I have to find out why what happened to her happened.'

'And whether it might possibly have something to do with the issues she wanted you to investigate.'

'And who done it,' I said, 'as we crime-stoppers like to say.'

'Any theories?'

'Not a one.'

'No wonder you got fired,' she said.

We were dining tonight at Alden & Harlow on Brattle, just a few minutes away by car. Sometimes, when feeling ambitious, we walked the mile or so to the restaurant. Not tonight. I asked Susan if she were planning to change. She looked at me as if I'd just asked if she were planning to get a neck tattoo.

'But I won't be long,' she said.

I knew from experience that even though the lie was benign, it was still a lie.

'I need to know more about the life and times of Laura Crain,' I said.

'Any thoughts on where you plan to start?' Susan said as she headed for the bathroom.

'I was thinking Harvard.'

'You'll never get in,' Susan said.

26

In my reading about Andrew Crain I had discovered that his best friend as an undergrad at Harvard had been a graduate assistant in the English Department named Paul Dockery, whose name popped up in several articles about Crain's younger years, Crain often pointing out what an unlikely friendship it had been, since Dockery barely knew one end of a double-A battery from another. But according to what I'd read they had hit it off, to the point where when Crain came back to Boston after the wanderlust years, Dockery allowed him to live rent-free in the second bedroom of his house in Watertown.

Dockery had also been friends with Laura Crain, even providing some tutoring for her during her senior year.

'What I didn't have to pay in rent I was able to put toward the small lab Ethan and I had fashioned for ourselves,' Crain once told *Forbes*. 'And more than anybody, with the possible exception of Ethan, it was Paul who convinced me to chase my dreams.'

Susan helped me find a phone number for Dockery in the Harvard directory, as he was now a fully tenured professor in the English Department. I called the office number and left a message on his office phone, explaining who I was, and that I had questions about Andrew and Laura Crain that he might be able to answer. He called back about an hour later, telling me he was finishing up a brief writers' conference in Bretton Woods, New Hampshire, but would be happy to meet with me when he was back tomorrow.

I didn't say I was a cop. Didn't say I wasn't one, either. But he was a Harvard man. I was confident he'd figure it out.

I called Claire Megill the next morning, but was sent straight to her voicemail. I texted her that we needed to talk, and as soon as possible, without specifying about what. She didn't respond to either my message or my text. She probably would have if I'd been special enough to have the inside number for the Batcave.

I did not have her home address. I knew I could find it if I had to, either with trickeration or with the assistance of the Boston Police Department. But for now I decided to take the more direct route to her, remembering her telling me about her yoga class at the Equinox club, a short walk from the Hancock, every day at noon.

When in doubt, follow someone.

Or annoy someone.

On good days, I had frequently managed to do both.

I decided to walk to the club, over next to Dartmouth Street and Back Bay Station. I stopped at the Starbucks on Dartmouth and bought a large coffee and a blueberry scone and found a bench on Dartmouth about twenty yards from the entrance to Equinox. I sat on it and watched the incoming traffic of people on their way to exercise or on their way home, or to the office. I saw more women than men. Most wore their exercise pants, all of the pants form-fitting to the extreme, on their way into the gym. Few seemed to need the work, at least to my trained eyes. I tried to remember the dark place men were in before women wore exercise pants so routinely on the street, whether they were on their way to exercise or not.

I made short work of the scone. I was more judicious with my coffee, not wanting to leave my post and head back to Starbucks to use the restroom, for fear of missing Claire Megill when she arrived. It was still only eleven-forty-five. I imagined her to be a creature of habit and organization, particularly since she worked for a man she must have occasionally tied a rock to, for fear he might float away.

I sat on the bench while I waited for her and observed the life of the city, this part of the city, anyway, in the middle of the day. I had grown up in the west. But I loved city life, its rhythms and energy and soundtrack. When I was in New York City, I found myself walking even more than I did in Boston. But now I was walking Boston again, every chance I got. Perhaps I was the creature of habit and organization.

I sat and watched people navigate their way up and down the sidewalk and into the train station, some cutting off others like cars swerving in front of others as they changed lanes. I wanted to ask some of these people where the fire was, but then wondered if anybody even said that anymore.

I finished my coffee. There was a Dunkin' close to where I sat. But I stayed where I was and waited for Claire Megill, still not certain she would show up. There were other ways for me to contact her. For now, this one made the most sense. And afforded the path of least resistance, a method of detecting I had always employed whenever possible.

Or was it the road less traveled by?

I saw her then, heading in my direction. Now she was one of the fast walkers on Dartmouth Street. Bag slung over her shoulder. Wearing sunglasses and what was obviously a work dress, just with sneakers as an accessory.

I tossed my cup into the wire bin next to the bench and was about to head her off before she entered Equinox when I saw Clay Whitson appear, almost out of nowhere, to block her way.

When she tried to get around him, he grabbed her arm and jerked her toward him.

Jerk, I thought, being the operative word.

I felt as if I were back at Davio's with Andrew Crain, close enough to hear her say, 'Don't touch me!'

Then I was one of the fast walkers on Dartmouth.

27

It was as if they were both trying not to make a scene even as they were in the process of making one on the busy street.

Whitson held on to her arm and pulled her in the direction of a brick pillar between the Dunkin' and the entrance to the station, away from the pedestrian traffic.

'Just tell me who you told,' I heard Whitson say.

His back was to me. Claire Megill was focused entirely on him, as she tried to get her arm loose. I covered the last few yards and clamped my hand on Whitson's shoulder and spun him around. Once we were facing each other and I had his full attention, I used both hands to shove him hard into the pillar.

'See, there, Clay,' I said. 'I was right at the office that day. One of us *is* an asshole.'

He tried to come off the wall. But I was too close to him and he was too slow getting his own hands up. I shoved him back, even harder this time. Then I had him by the lapels of the skinny suit he was wearing today, one I was wrinkling the hell out of at the moment.

'Please let go of him,' Claire Megill said from behind me.

'Not just yet,' I said.

'You need to mind your own goddamn business,' Whitson said.

He tried to raise up both of his arms now and break my grip. But he was still too close. I jerked his jacket up a little higher. If I kept going, pretty soon it was going to be a bonnet.

'Clay,' I said, 'I am going to release you now. But if you annoy me further, I am going to take one of your elbows and see if it's possible to shove it down your throat.'

His face was the color of an apple, and his jacket being as tight as it was around his throat was making breathing difficult. His eyes looked slightly unfocused.

He finally nodded, having decided that escalating our interaction further was not in his best interest.

'Mr Spenser,' Claire Megill said. 'This is between Clay and me.' She was standing to my right.

'Well,' I said. 'Not at the moment.'

I stepped to the side so I could see both of them. To her I said, 'What's this all about?'

Before she could answer, Whitson said, 'Like the lady said. It's between us.'

'You should have considered that before taking the matter into the public square.'

'Please go now,' Claire Megill said. 'Please... You will only make things more difficult than they already are.'

I kept my eyes on Whitson.

'More difficult for whom?' I said.

'For me,' she said. 'Now, please. *Both* of you, leave me alone.'

'Is there some sort of problem between you and Ms Megill?' I said to him as she walked away from us and into the Equinox club.

'The one with the problem now is you,' Whitson said, 'if you don't stay away from her, and me, and our company.'

'Or?' I said, dragging the word out.

'Or maybe next time it will be somebody coming up from behind you,' Whitson said.

People kept telling me that.

Whitson moved past me then, and confidently made his way across Dartmouth, avoiding the two-way traffic as he did, as if he were back to being a tough guy and he'd just jammed me up and not the other way around.

When I had lost sight of him, seeing no reason to follow him, I called Hawk and informed him that I'd just been threatened on a street corner by a corporate lawyer.

'He threaten to scratch your eyes out?' Hawk said.

'In fairness,' I said, 'I did threaten him first.'

'Man needs a hobby,' Hawk said.

28

Paul Dockery's office was in the Barker Center. I had passed the building on multiple occasions while attending events on campus with Susan, who had gotten a terminal case of Harvard while getting her degree there.

I had always liked walking around the school. I knew that some of *Good Will Hunting* had been filmed there and likewise knew that Matt Damon, who wrote the movie along with Ben Affleck, had been an English major there. I was more impressed with the fact that Damon was a Red Sox fan, and wondered if he was still as upset about Mookie being traded or had finally managed to let it go.

But there had never been a time when I was on the campus or near it when I hadn't expected to be asked for some sort of ID. Or at least asked to explain my thoughts on *Discourse on the Method*.

Dockery had left my name at the front desk in the lobby.

'I'm here to see Mr Chips,' I said to the young man checking his list.

The kid looked up at me with complete indifference.

'Are you referring to the original, or the remake with Peter O'Toole?' he asked.

'Sorry,' I said. 'Forgot where I was for a moment.'

'We hardly ever do,' the kid said, and told me that Dockery's office was on the third floor.

Paul Dockery did not look anything like Peter O'Toole. He just looked like an older version of the grad student he'd been when he had first met Andrew Crain. He was tall, slightly stooped, with shaggy, silver-blonde hair, wore a denim shirt with a frayed collar, jeans. His reading glasses were on top of his head. The desert boots he was wearing looked as old as the Yard.

'You're a policeman, I gather,' Dockery said.

'Former.'

'But on the phone you said you were investigating Laura's death.'

'I am,' I said, and explained my professional relationship with her, as brief as it had been.

He ran a hand through his hair, nearly knocking his glasses off before he remembered they were up there.

'I've tried to reach out,' he said. 'To Andrew, I mean. But he's harder to reach lately, for obvious reasons.'

'But you two have stayed in touch?'

'We did until the past few months,' Dockery said. 'Then he stopped returning my calls.'

He checked the Apple watch on his wrist. 'Listen, I've got a student coming in about fifteen minutes,' he said. 'Maybe you could explain exactly what you need from me.'

'I'm just trying to understand them both better,' I said. 'I feel as if I came to them about halfway through the book, without having read the first half.'

'You could be one of my students talking like that,' he said.

I grinned. 'Where I could dream my time away?'

He nodded approvingly. 'Wordsworth,' he said. 'Not bad.'

'Got it off a fortune cookie.'

'Somehow I doubt that.'

He leaned back down, put the boots up on his desk, clasped his hands behind his head. 'They were always such an odd couple,' he said. 'Andrew and Laura. When they finally became a couple, that is.'

'Just from my research,' I said, 'it sounds like unrequited love that finally got requited.'

'Andrew was a geek,' Dockery said. 'Like *The Big Bang Theory* geeky. Like the Sheldon character.'

I nodded as if I understood the reference. I was vaguely aware there had been a TV series with that title, but had no idea who Sheldon was.

'Hell, Andrew and I were an odd couple, when I think back on it. I'd only taken a couple science courses here because I had to. He had no interest in any book that didn't involve diagrammatic illustrations. But we met one night at Cambridge Queen's Head. It's a pub nearby.'

I told him I'd been there.

'And for some reason we hit it off. Maybe because we were different. His senior year. Somehow we got to talking about girls. And I got an earful about the fair maiden who belonged to another.'

'Laura was in another relationship at that time?'

He nodded. 'A heavy one, according to Andrew. With someone Andrew characterised as a bad guy unworthy of her. I just thought it was because the other guy was with her and he wasn't.'

'Do you remember the guy's name?'

He leaned forward now and tapped his forehead with a closed fist. 'Rob. I'm pretty sure it was Rob. If I ever got his last name, I don't remember it. I think Laura broke it off with him at one point, but then right before graduation, Andrew told me that the guy was still coming around.'

'What finally happened?'

'Sometime after graduation, as best I can recall, they broke up for good. Laura and the Rob dude. But Andrew and Laura didn't get together then, because he picked that moment in time to go off and find himself. Like he wasn't worthy of her yet. He told me once he wanted to come back from his travels a better man.'

'But they finally got together when he came back to Boston, right?'

'And love was born of the heavenly line.' He winked. 'More Wordsworth,' he said.

I thought about Andrew Crain saying that this wasn't the way what he obviously considered a great love story was supposed to end.

Paul Dockery checked the Apple watch again. I felt like one of Susan's patients coming to the end of a session.

'You've known Andrew Crain a long time,' I said. 'And the two of you are obviously friends. I still have to ask if you think he's capable of having killed his wife?'

'Not in five million years,' Dockery said. 'You need to understand something, Mr Spenser. Andrew had his dreams. He's told the world how often I was in his ear telling him to chase them. But the only one dream that ever really mattered to him was having her.'

'Who can you remember from those days who might know something about the old boyfriend?' I said.

'You think he might have come back after all this time?'

'If he did, I need to know about it.'

'It would mean the guy might have been more obsessive about

Laura than Andy was.' He shrugged. 'Maybe you don't need an English professor to help you out. Maybe you need a shrink.'

'I'm sleeping with a Harvard-educated psychologist,' I said.

I asked him if he might possibly come up with a list of Laura Crain's classmates, and roommates. He said he'd do a little digging and come up with some names.

'I wish I could be more helpful off the top of my head,' he said. 'But I was smoking a lot of weed in those days.'

'I would have expected nothing less of an English major.'

I gave him my card, one that had all of my phone numbers on it, and my email address.

'I get the impression,' Dockery said, 'that you can be pretty obsessive yourself on occasion.'

'To the point of compulsion,' I said.

'Where do you go from here?' he said.

'Not entirely sure,' I said. 'It's too early for the Yale game.'

29

Susan had another committee meeting tonight.

She'd actually told me which committee it was, and whom it benefited, but I had forgotten. I did know that it was somewhere in Cambridge and that her attending it meant I was on my own for dinner.

Before she left the house I called and asked if she wanted me to come collect Pearl and bring her to my place, or at least take her out and allow her to pull me up and down Linnaean Street for a while.

'The baby is fine,' she said. 'I just took her on a long walk myself.'

I told her I loved her then, and wished her good luck saving the whales.

'It's for the bike and pedestrian paths along Memorial Drive,' she said.

'Hey,' I said. 'I was close.'

Frank Belson called and told me, because he said he knew I cared, that Blakely Hoar was still being treated as an active crime scene. As hard as his ME had looked, he could find no physical evidence on Laura Crain's attacker, and any footprints that might have been useful upon what he called further review had been washed away by the heavy rain the night before.

'Am I allowed to go back and walk the trail without fear of being arrested?' I said.

'The BPD has gotten together as a group and decided it's too late to find any new evidence there, after the rain.'

There was a pause at his end.

'I assume you got nothing useful for me.'

'Less,' I said. 'But you know that if I do come up with anything...'

He hung up on me.

On my way to the sanctuary I stopped in Watertown at Not Your Average Joe's for the BBQ meatloaf. I ate at the bar and drank Samuel Adams draught with my meatloaf and mashed potatoes and watched the start of the Red Sox game. The empty seats at Fenway told you everything about the way their season was ending.

'Well,' I said to the bartender, 'wait till next year.'

'Make me,' he said.

It was dark by the time I drove over to Brookline. I wanted to walk the trail in the night, experience the same sights and sounds and hopefully even the solitude that Laura Crain had experienced in the last moments of her life.

Tomorrow I would try to learn more about her old boyfriend, as little as I had to go on so far. At some point I knew I would have to come up with a creative way to ask Andrew Crain about him, since Dockery had made it clear Crain considered Rob with no last name to be a member of the bad boyfriend club.

'You got yourself fighting one of your two-front wars,' Hawk had said on our morning run along the river. 'You still haven't found out what she wanted you to find out about him. And now you gots to find out what happened to her.'

'But I have the strength of ten,' I said.

He'd snorted. 'One more thing you exaggerate the size of.'

'Snob,' I said.

When I arrived at the sanctuary I parked my new Jeep Cherokee at the construction site. I was going to bring a flashlight with me on my walk, but there was more than enough light from the moon tonight. I did take my new Smith & Wesson .38, the 586 model I'd gifted to myself on my last birthday, out of the glove compartment and stuck it into the side pocket of my leather jacket.

Then I started up the trail I'd walked with Laura Crain that morning. The brook that stretched all the way back to the tennis courts at the Baker School was swollen from the previous night's rainfall, the sound of the water loud in the night.

Had she come out here alone? Or had the person who had killed her been someone she knew, someone she had come here to meet?

The yellow tape was still stretched across the trail. I ducked underneath it and walked over to the place where they'd found her next to the rock wall.

'It always gives me the feeling that I've taken a walk back in time,' she'd said on our morning walk.

Now the moon lit the crime scene like a spotlight, and there were the night sounds all around me. I leaned down and picked up a tree branch the size of a baseball bat that must have fallen there in the storm. I started back up the trail finally, pretending the branch was a walking stick, on my way back to my Jeep.

I heard my phone then, that marimba ringtone that sounds like everybody else's and always has everybody reaching for their own phones when it goes off in a public place.

But now it was just me, and my phone.

I looked at the luminous screen.

Unknown caller

'This is Spenser,' I said.

'I'm supposed to tell you this is your one and only warning,' a voice said.

The Boston accent made it come out 'wah-ning.'

Before I could say anything I got hit with the first blow from behind.

30

It was some kind of club, a free shot behind my shoulder blades, one that staggered me and knocked me forward but didn't put me down even though it hurt like hell.

My phone came flying out of my hand.

The guy who'd hit me tried to wrap his arms around me as a second muttonhead came out of the woods to my right. There was enough light from the moon for me to see he was wearing a ski mask, and was my size, at least. And heavier.

The second guy had what looked like a tire iron in his right hand, and started to swing it at me. But I broke the grip of his partner in time to slip-step to my right and force the one with the tire iron to miss, even though I could feel the breeze from the swing close to my face.

I cleared just enough space then to turn and swing the branch in my hand at the legs of the guy behind me, hearing the crack as I connected with what I hoped was one of his knees. He went down like he was the tree falling.

If they had come here to kill me, I'd be dead already, I told myself.

They were just here to give me a beating after what hadn't been frankly much of a warning.

I could hear the guy I'd knee-capped groaning and could see him rolling around in the mud out of the corner of my eye. There was no time for me to clear the .38 from my jacket as the second guy was back on me, the tire iron connecting with my left shoulder.

But he still didn't put me down this time as I managed to set my feet like I was Mookie still swinging for the fences at Fenway. I didn't go low, and instead swung for the middle of him like a shooter aiming at center mass, and heard a crack from him now.

'*I think he broke my fucking arm.*'

I swung at him again, but missed, and then the second guy was back up and on me, hitting me on the side of my head with his fist, connecting enough that I felt as if sirens were going off.

I went down, but with purpose.

'Kick the shit out of him, Eddie,' I heard.

But as Eddie's work boot came forward I rolled toward him and grabbed it and flipped him to the ground, and then I was back up. The second guy had one arm hanging at his side, but kept coming. The branch was somewhere around me but would do me no good now, so I stepped toward him and threw a hook to his stomach and heard the air come out of him with a *whoosh* and then threw a straight right to the middle of his face.

He went down, but the guy already on the ground hit me with something across the ankle and this time I went down for real. Somehow I managed to roll away into the grass and mud and get my hand on the .38 now and fire a warning shot into the air.

They ran then, two shadows running into the woods, one of them limping badly, the broken arm of the other one flopping at his side.

I let them go and then the night was silent again, except for the screech of what sounded like a single owl.

I found my phone and started limping myself toward my Jeep

and tried to take consolation in the fact that I'd just given a lot better than I'd gotten before I called Hawk and told him what had happened.

'Shit,' he said. 'Maybe you do have the strength of ten.'

'Told you,' I said.

31

Hawk said, 'Whoever sent them boppers only sent two? You ought to be insulted.'

'They seemed to be under the mistaken impression that bad intentions made them bad men.'

'How come you didn't shoot them, you had the chance?'

'It didn't seem like an appropriate response after I determined they weren't there to kill me.'

'Weren't there to kill you this time, you mean.'

Hawk had a key to my apartment and was already there when I got back from Brookline. After I cleaned up and assessed the damage, he asked me where it hurt. I told him everywhere. He asked if I could be a little more specific and I told him that the hit parade started in my upper back and went all the way down to my right ankle, which miraculously hadn't been broken when Eddie or the other guy, I'd lost track at that point, was the one swinging for the fences. Hawk went and got two ice packs from the freezer and told me to place one of them behind my shoulders and then had me stretch out my right leg and placed one of them behind my knee.

I told him I'd taken a blow to my ankle, too.

'What's your point?'

'Thank you, nurse.'

'Now I'm a damn caregiver,' Hawk said. 'Probably be like this when you're old.'

'Why can't Susan be the caregiver?'

'She be long gone by then.'

Then he said, 'Beer or whiskey?'

I told him where to find the bottle of Bushmills. He came back with a glass for himself and handed me one. He'd asked for champagne and I told him sorry, I was fresh out.

'I don't know how I put up with somebody as common as you,' he said.

'If I'd known I was going to entertain tonight,' I said, 'I would have run to the wine store and picked up a bottle of Dom.'

'Think you meant to say Veuve Clicquot,' Hawk said, 'not to make too fine a point of shit.'

He was dressed in a soft-looking hoodie I knew had to be expensive, jeans, boxing shoes. There was no way for me to know if I had woken him, if he'd been alone when I called or with somebody. He had moved again, this time to Mission Hill, without giving me an exact address. As always, as close as we were – and we were as close as brothers – there were parts of him that I could not reach, parts he held back because he always had. He'd come back from Paris a month ago, having gone there to determine whether a young woman there was his daughter. She was not. When I'd asked upon his return if he wanted to talk about it, Hawk had said he did not, and we did not. And I did not ask whether he was sad about that or happy or relieved because that was another part of himself he held back.

'Looks like you've done gone and poked another bear.'

'Which bear is the question.'

'Didn't that lawyer tell you that maybe somebody'd come up behind you one of these days?'

'So he did.'

I drank some whiskey. The warm feeling as it made its way through me went nicely with the ice packs, I thought.

'So you think maybe he sent a couple proud boys after me because I made him look like something less than a manly man in front of Claire Megill?'

'Uh-huh.'

'I sensed some tension between them,' I said. 'Whitson and Claire Megill, I mean. I thought it might be sexual.'

'Best kind,' Hawk said.

I moved my ankle slightly and the ice pack fell off. Hawk got up and walked over to me and put it back where he'd had it before.

'I give and I give and I give,' he said.

We sat and drank. The whiskey wasn't making all of the places where I'd been hit hurt any less. But they weren't hurting any more. I knew I'd been lucky tonight, even if the guys who had come for me had been amateurs in the end, punching above their weight.

'Last warning,' the guy had said on the phone, before he hit me.

My friend Wayne Cosgrove told me once that all stories came from somewhere, and that once they did, the first question you always had to ask was who benefited from them.

So who benefited by sending Eddie and his pal to give me a beatdown tonight?

'Say you're right and it is the lawyer. Why would he or anybody else at Lith be worried about me getting in the way of a merger?'

Hawk smiled. 'You too banged up, I could go ask him.'

'Let's hold off for the time being.'

He drank. I drank. I had no idea what time it was by now. I couldn't even make an educated guess about how many late nights there had been with Hawk and me talking like this. Or not talking, when we'd worked our way around to that.

Finally Hawk said, 'You give a rat's ass about a merger gonna make rich people even richer?'

I slowly shook my head no, feeling myself wince as I did.

'Knew before I asked,' Hawk said. 'Why we got to focus on who did that to the man's wife.'

'We?'

'Hell, yeah,' Hawk said. 'Look what happens, I let you go off on your own. And if something happens after this and whatever

108

you got yourself into is bigger than we think and you get yourself killed, you know Susan's gonna blame me.'

'You told me one time you weren't afraid of anything or anybody,' I said.

''Cept for her,' Hawk said.

'Same,' I said.

32

Paul Dockery called in the morning with enough information on Laura Crain, maiden name Mason, that it was as if he were one of his own students and had just pulled an all-nighter.

I had told him I was mostly interested in her senior year, which is when she had begun dating the old boyfriend.

'I called the Alumni Office,' Dockery told me over the phone. 'Got a buddy there. He already knew a fair amount about her time here because he'd done some research when Andrew Crain's name went up in lights. Her mother died when she was young. Her father was a high school teacher in Perrysburg, Ohio, and *he* died when she was a sophomore here. No other living relatives he knew about.'

Laura had lived in Claverly Hall, on Mount Auburn, in a three-bedroom her senior year. One roommate was named Missy Jones. The other was Angela Calabria. Both, Dockery said, were now married, according to school records. Missy Jones, a lawyer herself now, had married a Seattle lawyer and moved there. But Angie Calabria, now divorced, was an elementary school teacher in Carlisle, Mass.

Dockery had a number for her. I told him I appreciated the legwork he'd done. He said, 'Nobody should die like that, whether they've got all the money in the world or not.'

'I've done a lot of reading since she died on her own charity work,' I said. 'Her husband wasn't the only one who wanted to save the world.'

I called Hawk after I got off with Dockery and asked if he wanted to take a ride to Carlisle with me.

'Carlisle where the great Jim Thorpe grew up?' he said

'That was Carlisle, Pennsylvania.'

'So it finally happened,' Hawk said.

'What finally happened?'

'You know something I don't know other than baseball or some song got written when FDR was president.'

He asked if we were going to have breakfast first. I told him we'd be fools not to, and that's how we came to stop at Jimmy's in Burlington. I had Irish eggs Benedict and Hawk had eggs with Greek sausage and pancakes on the side. While we ate as if both of us were on our way to the chair, I called Angie Calabria and caught her between classes. I told her who I was and how I'd gotten her number and what I wanted to talk to her about. She asked if I could be there by twelve-thirty, which was when she took her lunch break.

Hawk had picked me up in his new Jaguar. How he seemed to have one expensive ride after another was just something else about him that I accepted as part of the natural and mysterious order of things.

It meant one more thing he knew and I didn't, and if he wanted me to know, he'd tell me and until then not to fucking worry about it.

'I like her already,' Hawk said. 'Harvard girl like herself gone off to teach kids.'

'We might even run into a clue while we're with her.'

'You always have been an optimistic bastard.'

'It's the Irish in me.'

'Hell it is.'

An hour later Angie Calabria sat with us on the front steps of the Carlisle Public School complex on School Street underneath a warm midday sun. She looked younger than I knew she had to be, pretty and blonde with violet eyes. She had been waiting for us when Hawk pulled up and parked the Jag as if the school zone signs didn't exist.

'Is that your car?' Angie asked Hawk. 'I *love* cars.'

"Course you do,' Hawk said.

She wore a cotton pullover and jeans and sneakers and made it easy for me to see her as the college girl who had been Laura Mason Crain's roommate.

'Did the two of you stay in touch?' I said.

She smiled. 'You mean after she became *Laura Crain*?' She practically shouted out the name. 'Yeah, we did. She liked to remember where she came from, even if it was Harvard.'

'When was the last time you heard from her?'

'I guess it was a couple weeks ago. She called me, which was unusual, most of the time it was the other way around. She said that Andrew's behavior was starting to freak her out and she had no idea what was causing it, because he refused to talk to her about it. I told her she needed to see somebody about it. A shrink. Somebody. I don't know if it was our conversation, but apparently that somebody turned out to be you, Mr Spenser.'

She looked intently at me, almost fiercely, the effect intensified by her eyes. I knew how rare the color was. Back when dinosaurs roamed the earth, Elizabeth Taylor had eyes like hers.

'She came to you for help and now she's dead,' Angie Calabria said, in response to absolutely nothing.

'Is that an accusation?'

'More an observation,' she said. 'I meant no offense by it.'

'None taken,' I said. 'Nobody feels worse about what happened than I do.'

'*Were* you able to help her?'

'Still efforting that,' I said. 'Just after the fact.'

I asked her then about Laura Crain's old boyfriend.

Her eyes widened, almost in fright.

'Oh, God,' she said, as if I'd thrown a fright into her. 'Is that why you're here? Did he come back into her life?'

'Wouldn't she have said something to you if he had come back into her life?'

Angie Calabria shook her head. 'She didn't like to talk about him then, maybe she didn't want to talk about him now.'

'Did you ever meet him?'

She shook her head again. 'It was like she had a whole separate life with him. He never came around school. She always went to him, sometimes for a week at a time even while she kept going to her classes. I think he had a place in Watertown. Or maybe it was Allston. She wouldn't say where.'

She looked at me again. 'But when he called, she went running, almost like she was afraid not to.'

'She was afraid of her own boyfriend?'

She nodded.

'Toward the end of senior year I asked why she didn't just break up with him once and for all, because she'd done it once before,' Angie Calabria said. 'We'd gotten into a bottle of white wine pretty good that night and it had gotten late. We were both pretty drunk. But she didn't sound drunk when she told me that if she ever did try to break it off again, she was afraid of what he might do.'

She heard a bell ring from inside the building closest to us.

'That was the night she told me he hit her sometimes,' Angie Calabria said.

33

Susan and I were watching Pearl the Wonder Dog chase pretty much everything moving in the Public Garden.

'I just don't understand people who don't love dogs,' she said.

'How much did you love her last week when she turned those new Christian Arroyo shoes of yours into chew toys?'

'Christian Louboutin,' she said. 'And the Arroyo person is a baseball player, right?'

'Look at you. Next you'll be reading box scores.'

'And if you're being fair, you'll recall that I didn't raise my voice about what the baby did to my shoes until she was out of the room.'

'At which point a nice Jewish girl from Swampscott swore like a rapper.'

'Fuckin' ay,' Susan said.

As we sat on a bench and watched Pearl dash hither and yon, I caught her up on my meeting with Angie Calabria.

'She said he was abusive,' I said.

'Physically?'

'Yes.'

'What did he do for a living?'

'According to Angie he was a bartender. But Laura would never tell either of her roommates *where* he bartended. It was as if Laura were ashamed of him, of the relationship, his hold on her, all of it.'

'Ashamed of herself,' Susan said. 'A classic element to the dynamic.'

Pearl came back to me with a stick in her mouth, dropping it at my feet. I threw it as far as I could in the direction of Charles Street and was sorry as soon as I did, because it felt like my sore shoulder had just exploded all over again.

'And the roommate did not have this man's last name.'

'She did not.'

'And she really never laid eyes on him?'

I shook my head.

'And she never knew of the abuse until that night?' Susan said.

'Angie told me that Laura just suddenly pulled up her sweater and showed her some bruises. Angie said she was going to call the police. Laura begged her not to, she said that the argument had been her fault.'

'Isn't it always,' Susan said drily.

113

Pearl came back with the stick and plopped down, finally exhausted. From experience, we both knew it wouldn't be for long.

'How and when did the relationship finally end?' Susan said.

'Angie said it lasted at least into the summer after graduation,' I said. 'Angie went off to backpack through Europe with some other girlfriends, and when she came back, Laura told her it was finally over.'

'Did she finally screw up the courage to walk away?'

'I asked Angie. She said Laura didn't want to talk about it, that it had ended horribly but that at least had ended. That his hold on her, literally, had finally ended.'

'Did the guy leave town?'

'I got the impression from Angie that he had, but that Laura didn't know where at the time. And didn't seem particularly interested in finding out.'

Susan knelt in the grass now and gently scratched Pearl behind the ears. But I could see her processing the information I was giving her, focusing all of her intelligence and curiosity and education – all of her immense self – on the young woman that Laura Crain had been when she was still Laura Mason.

She looked up at me. 'And she never heard from him again?'

'Angie said that if Laura had, she was certain Laura would have mentioned it. But she never did.'

Susan hooked up Pearl's leash to her harness and the three of us began to make our way past George Washington, toward Marlborough Street.

'*Could* he have come back?' Susan said as we were crossing Arlington.

'It would be useful for me to know,' I said. 'But I don't even have a full name for him.'

'Which would also be useful for you to know.'

'You don't miss a trick, do you?' I said, grinning at her.

She had handed the leash to me, and took my free hand then, and gave it a squeeze.

114

'What can I tell you,' Susan said. 'I have a master detective as a love slave.'

I asked her if she was willing to prove that, even in the middle of the afternoon, and Susan said, as luck would have it, she was.

34

I thought I could perhaps enlist Claire Megill in my effort to get Andrew Crain to see me, so I could ask him what he might know about his wife's old boyfriend. But Claire still wasn't returning messages or texts and it was starting to affect my self-esteem.

So I took a walk over to the Hancock in the late afternoon as people were beginning to leave work on the outside chance that even with security, Reggie Smythe or somebody else, Crain might come walking out the main entrance. By six o'clock, he had not, and I gave up.

On my way back to my own office I called Vinnie Morris and told him I needed help trying to locate a bartender who had worked around town twenty years ago, or thereabouts.

'Where'd he work?'

'I don't know.'

'What's his name?'

'Rob.'

'Rob what?' Vinnie said.

'All I got.'

'Are you drunk?' Vinnie said, and I told him I wished, and he said he'd ask around and that I should say hello to Susan for him, he'd get back to me as soon as he could, he was in the middle of something, which he so often was, and about which I rarely asked.

When I got back to my office Hawk was back on my couch

and got up only long enough to get two beers out of my small refrigerator.

'Ask you something?' he said when I'd settled in behind my desk.

He pronounced it 'axe,' but we both knew that was just part of the act. As always, it was difficult, even for me, to separate the mask from the man. But the quest to do that remained endlessly entertaining to me, and endlessly fascinating.

'Please don't make it a hard question,' I said.

'Always try not to,' Hawk said, 'since I know that can make your head hurt something awful.'

He sat up on the couch so he was facing me. 'Where does a Boy Scout like you come down on the end justifying the means?' he said.

'So it's a philosophical question you ask,' I said.

'Uh-huh.'

I had my feet up on my desk. The refrigerator kept beer very cold. If it didn't, what was the point of even having it?

'You're asking me how far I'm willing to go to set things right in this crazy world?' I said.

'Like you did that time in San Francisco,' Hawk said.

It was a long time ago and we were fugitives, out there to rescue Susan from a rich control freak named Russell Costigan, with whom she'd had an affair but then had been held against her will. Hawk and I were on the run because I had broken him out of jail in a town called Mill Valley, one owned by Costigan's father, and we had finally holed up in the apartment of two prostitutes.

I had eventually killed their pimp because if I hadn't I was certain he would have killed the two women himself.

Hawk and I rarely spoke of it. Susan and I did more frequently. But now here we were, and back there.

'You're asking me if the outcome would be the same now?'

'Uh-huh.'

'I honestly don't know.'

Hawk smiled. 'Sho' you do.'

116

I said, 'What I do know all this time later is that I couldn't let two innocent people die because of something the two of us had done, something that had nothing to do with them. They only took us to that apartment because they thought we were a couple tricks.'

'I offered to do the pimp so you didn't have to,' Hawk said.

I let that go, like a batter letting a pitch go by.

'And then,' I said, 'acting as an agent of the federal government, I took out a different kind of pimp named Jerry Costigan.' I swiveled my chair so I was more fully facing him. 'Why exactly are we revisiting this today?'

'I'm just curious, on account of we mostly having the same code, you and me,' Hawk said. 'But we both know I'm willing to do things you can't, or won't, except there was that time with the boy Costigan and his old man you did things I never thought you'd do on account of we had to save Susan.'

'Call of duty,' I said.

'Ain't that a video game?' Hawk said.

'Not with us.'

'Laura Crain ain't Susan.'

'She was still my responsibility.'

I got up and went into the refrigerator and came out with two more beers. Susan was threatening to cook for all three of us tonight at my apartment, and Hawk and I, without coming right out and saying it, were just fortifying ourselves, almost certainly with stronger stuff later.

'What if you can't find out who the bartender was or where he went?'

'Then we go to Plan B.'

'You ain't got no Plan B,' Hawk said.

I told him I was hoping he wouldn't notice.

35

I sat at my desk the next afternoon and drank coffee, which usually made me feel better about everything, and wrote out a timeline of everything that happened since Laura Crain had shown up at my office.

Quirk had told me once, a long time ago, while we were working a different case together, how he'd never understood why the line about throwing shit against the wall and hoping some of it stuck had somehow managed to become a cliché.

'Guess what?' Martin Quirk had said. 'You do it right, some of it will stick eventually.'

'But how do you know if you are doing it right?' I'd asked him.

Quirk had shrugged and said, 'Beats the shit out of me.'

I put my pen down and made myself another cup of coffee, telling myself I could walk off the caffeine later. I finally got around to reading *The Globe*. I wondered if the man who owned the paper and owned the team even bothered with reading the sports section these days. I wondered if he missed Mookie as much as I did.

I wondered if somebody sent two headbangers after me because they didn't want me nosing around Laura Crain's death, or they didn't want me nosing around her husband's company, and its impending merger with a car company whose name escaped me at the moment?

'We know what we are but know not what we may be,' I said aloud.

I knew who'd said that in *Hamlet*. Ophelia. I knew a lot of things. Just not a single one that was helping me solve the murder of a client who'd gone for a walk in the woods in the night.

I looked back down on Berkeley for a few more minutes, then called the number Paul Dockery had given me for Missy Jones, Laura's other roommate at Harvard, which had the Seattle area code 206.

'This better not be another spam call today,' she said when she answered. 'Or I will find you and beat you.'

'You can decide about that later,' I told her, then told her who I was and how I'd gotten her number and why I was calling her.

There was a brief pause at her end. I could hear people yelling at each other on a television in the background. I assumed it was either cable news or one of those *Housewives* shows. From my limited knowledge of both, it could have gone either way.

The sounds disappeared suddenly.

'Why did Laura need a private detective?' Missy Jones asked me.

I told her, as succinctly as I could, Laura's concerns about Andrew Crain's increasingly troubling behavior.

There was another pause, not lasting as long as the one before. 'Did he hit her, too?'

'You mean the way the old boyfriend did.'

'So you know about Rob.'

'I do.'

'I'm no therapist,' Missy Jones said. 'But I know about destructive patterns in people's lives. It was a logical question for me to ask.'

'I had no indication that he had been abusive in their marriage.'

'Do you consider yourself a therapist, Mr Spenser?'

I knew we needed to get past this.

'A therapist to whom Laura did speak is the one who sent her to me.'

'A grasp of who and whom,' Missy Jones said. 'You don't sound much like a private eye to me.'

'Me talk pretty sometimes.'

'Okay,' she said. 'How can I be of assistance to *youse*?'

First indication of a sense of humor. A start.

'I'm trying to find out as much as I can about this Rob.'

'Did she tell you about him?'

'Angie is the one who got me up to speed on the bartender boyfriend none of you ever saw.'

'I saw him,' she said. 'It was the night I threatened to kill the sonofabitch.'

36

Missy Jones asked if I were pressed for time. I told her that presently I had nothing but time.

'There are some things you need to know about me,' she said. 'First off, I'm a lawyer. My father was also a lawyer. Maybe you've heard of him. His name was Kenneth Jones.'

'Oh, ho,' I said again.

'You have heard of him.'

'Kenneth Jones, the Mob lawyer.'

'Dad was resistant to that description. But yes, that's him.'

'He was Gino Fish's lawyer when Gino was still with us.'

'Yes,' she said, 'he was.'

In my professional career, there had been an All-Star team of Mob bosses in Boston. Tony Marcus. Eddie Lee in Chinatown. Joe Broz. Jackie DeMarco. Desmond Burke. A handful of others. But the late Gino Fish, in the day, had been as powerful as any of them. I had never actually met his personal lawyer, as many times as Gino's interests and my own had intersected. But Kenneth Jones had been well known in that world, which also meant my world.

'So Big Ken's daughter got into Harvard,' I said. 'I have to say that was very open-minded of them. Or at least ecumenical.'

'I earned it, asshole.'

I laughed. 'I take it back,' I said. 'Tell me about your meeting with Rob.'

It was, she said, the summer after they all graduated, her and Laura and Angie and Andrew Crain. Missy was living with her boyfriend in Brighton. Laura had a place of her own off Brattle, not far from Harvard, busy with freelance copywriting. Missy and Laura hadn't spoken for a month or so, until Laura called one night from Mount Auburn Hospital and asked Missy to come pick her up.

After the doctors had seen the extent of her injuries, she'd told them that she'd tripped over her dog and fallen down a flight of stairs.

'She didn't have a dog,' Missy said. 'Unless you counted Rob. She'd finally decided to break it off with him, and this time he'd beaten her within an inch of her life. And told her that if she ever mentioned leaving him again, he'd kill her.'

Missy Jones insisted Laura spend the night at her apartment and drove them both to Allston. Laura finally told Missy where Rob worked, a bar called Marino's. When Laura was asleep, Missy had called her father. Her father called Gino Fish. The next night one of Gino's enforcers, a guy named Mitch, picked up Missy and they drove to Marino's, on Comm Ave in Allston.

'Had Laura told you Rob's last name at this point?'

'I didn't even bother to ask,' Missy said, 'as I was confident that my relationship with him – and his with Laura – wasn't going to progress past that night.'

Rob had closed up that night. Mitch and Missy were waiting for him when he came out the back door and into the alley behind Marino's, where he'd parked his car.

'For what it's worth, he looked a lot like Brad Pitt,' she said. 'Just not for long.'

Mitch pistol-whipped him until Rob's face was what Missy described as a beautiful mess. Then Mitch rolled him over and sat on his stomach and stuck the barrel of his gun in Rob's mouth. Missy knelt down and told him that if he ever went near Laura again, if he even attempted to *contact* her again, the only thing that would change the next time Mitch came looking for him was that he would pull the trigger, something Mitch said he'd done plenty of times before.

'Maybe you get the idea,' Missy said. 'I had arrived at the "time's up" point long before the MeToo'ers did.'

All Missy ever told Laura was that her father had taken care of her problems with Rob. Laura had asked if that meant killing him. Missy said it hadn't been necessary, and Laura, as best she could recall, had said, 'Pity.'

A few nights later Missy called Marino's and asked for Rob. The bartender who picked up said Rob had stopped coming to work, wasn't answering his phone, seemed to have disappeared. Missy called a few days later and was told that Rob hadn't come back.

'Laura never heard from him again?' I said.

'If she did, she never mentioned it to me,' Missy said.

I told her she had been a good friend. She said she didn't need me to tell her that.

'You're a tough cookie,' I said.

'My father's daughter,' she said. 'What can I tell you? And if you do find out who did this to Laura before the cops do, I think I still have Mitch's number in Florida.'

I told her I would keep that in mind.

'And because I *am* my father's daughter?' Missy Jones said. 'You can choke on that cookie comment.'

I told her I took that back, too.

37

I went over to the Harbor Health Club in the late afternoon, determined to grind my way through the lingering soreness from the beating I'd caught at Blakely Hoar.

Henry Cimoli watched me from a chair against the wall

as I went from the light bag to the contour bag, even skipping rope, something I rarely did, to test my knees. Then over to the old heavy bag. Henry was generous enough to offer a running commentary on my form and my hand speed and my footwork, as if this were some sort of livestream event.

'Jesus H Santa Claus,' Henry said. 'No wonder you got your ass handed to you.'

'Not to make excuses or point fingers, Henry, but there were two of them, and they jumped me from behind, and one of them had a goddamn Louisville Slugger.'

'Whiner,' he said.

I took a break. Henry handed me a towel. He remained an ageless wonder, dressed in black boxing leggings and a white harbor T-shirt and still looking lean enough and fit enough to go twelve rounds for the featherweight title, something he had thought was within his reach when he was a kid on the way up. Full head of white hair. Bright blue eyes, full of fun and constant eternal mischief. You would have needed Special Forces to find an ounce of fat on him even now. He had been a second father to me for as long as each of us could remember, and to Hawk.

'Shouldn't you be leering at women doing Pilates?' I said.

'We only do Pilates in the mornings, smart guy,' Henry said. 'Barre method and yoga in the afternoon.' He grinned. 'And it's not leering. Scouting, is what it is.'

'You're a dirty old man, is what you are.'

'And proud of it.'

I showered and changed there and drove back to my apartment and parked behind my building and then walked back to the office. I knew that Marino's had closed its doors for good during COVID, because I'd looked it up online after speaking with Missy Jones.

So I called another private eye in town I knew, Sunny Randall, a long-standing client of Susan's whom I'd met when Hawk helped her out on a case a couple years ago. Her father, Phil, now retired, had been a legendary detective with the BPD, and longtime friend to Martin Quirk. Her ex-husband, Richie Burke, was the son of Desmond Burke, still the head of the Irish Mob in Boston, and someone powerful enough to have had Gino Fish and all the other All-Stars cross streets to avoid him.

That wasn't as interesting to me, at least not today, as the knowledge that Richie Burke had owned a saloon on Portland Street. And the saloon business, even in a big city like Boston, could feel like as small a world as the one Richie's father inhabited.

'Spenser and Sunny,' Sunny Randall said when she answered her phone. 'It would be a dream team. I can already see it on the door.'

'Do you want to break it to Hawk that I was dumping him for you?' I said.

'It's because I'm a girl, isn't it?'

'You've managed to overcome it,' I said, and told her why I was calling and why I needed Richie's number, which she gave to me.

'Weren't you and Richie supposed to be the dream team?'

'Don't be hurtful,' she said.

I called Richie Burke and asked him about Marino's and asked if Joe Marino, who'd owned it, was still around. Richie said he'd get back to me. I asked him how things were going with his ex.

He laughed and told me to shut the fuck up and that he'd call me when he knew something.

I was about to call Susan about dinner when there was a single knock on the door and Reggie Smythe came in, followed by Ethan Lowe.

'I think we're in a position to help each other out,' Lowe said.

'You first,' I said.

38

I pointed at Reggie Smythe.

'He can wait outside,' I said.

'And why is that?' Lowe said.

'I don't know you well enough to know whether or not I can trust you. But I know Reg here well enough to know I don't trust him.'

Lowe looked at Smythe and nodded toward the door. Smythe hesitated but left, closing the door a little harder than necessary, I felt.

When it was just the two of us Lowe said, 'I'm thinking I might want to hire you.'

'Should I thank you now?'

He closed his eyes, then sighed, somewhat theatrically. He hadn't even made me an offer yet, and already I'd disappointed him.

'I'd like to talk to you about doing the same sort of thing you did for Laura, but with me as your client.'

'Laura is still my client.'

'Laura is also dead.'

I shrugged, also theatrically. 'I've decided not to hold that against her.'

'But as a practical matter, by working for me you'd still be working for her.'

I asked if he'd like some coffee. Lowe asked if I had anything stronger on hand. I told him it was too early for whiskey, but there was beer. He said that would be fine. I went to the refrigerator and came back with two cans of Boomsauce.

'You've got good taste in beer,' he said.

'Yeah,' I said, 'but let's face it, as long as it's cold, bad beer is better than none.'

We both took healthy swallows from our bottles.

'Andrew has withdrawn even further following Laura's death,' he said. 'But even though I've always handled the business side of things, he remains the majority shareholder, and the face of Lith around the world. This merger can't go through without his blessing.'

'Is he still prepared to withhold it?'

'He hasn't come out and said that,' Lowe said. 'But no matter how clear I make it to him that this deal only makes our brand stronger, and Lith bigger than it's ever been, he's become more hesitant about it.'

'What's the worst that happens to Lith if the merger doesn't happen?' I said. 'Smaller Christmas party?'

'It's not as if we're going to suddenly go belly-up,' he said. 'But there are other people out there looking to make synthetic materials even cheaper and more affordable than ours, while working just as well. The line keeps moving, Mr Spenser.'

He drank more beer. I wouldn't have made him for a beer drinker.

'Are you a sports fan?' he asked.

'Sadly yes.'

'Let me offer you an analogy, then,' he said. 'The Patriots had one kind of brand when they were winning all those championships. Now they're just another team that *used* to win all the championships. Do you understand the distinction?'

'I do,' I said. 'But don't expect me to be the one who tells *their* owner that.'

He took off his glasses, cleaned them with a cloth he pulled out of his pocket, looked through the lenses, put them back on.

'So many people, including consumers, will benefit from this merger,' he said. 'And in the end, so will so many of Andrew's charities. But if his behavior scares off our potential partners at Prise, then it's not just Lith that gets hurt.'

'You practically make this merger sound like a public service,' I said.

'I just want to help Andrew through whatever has gotten him off the rails to this extent,' Lowe said. 'But I can't do it without knowing what it is. It's why Laura came to you and why I've come to you.'

'My priority is finding out who killed her, not what might kill your merger,' I said. I shrugged. 'As another practical matter.'

'It doesn't mean our interests can't align here,' Lowe said. 'And you should know that money is no object.'

I smiled again. 'Is that ever really true?'

'In my case, almost always.'

'Let me ask you something,' I said. 'Is everybody else at your company on board with this merger?'

He had the bottle almost to his lips, but stopped now and put it down on my desk. 'Why do you ask?'

'I'm just curious as to whether someone other than Andrew Crain might be motivated to sabotage the deal from within, whether he's acting like a nutjob or not.'

'Sabotage it by killing his wife?' he said. 'Now who sounds like a nutjob?'

We sat there in silence then. It seemed to make Ethan Lowe somewhat fidgety, as if not filling any gap in conversation made him somehow negligent. Or less in charge.

Finally I said, 'Would you mind if I changed the subject?'

'It's your office.'

'What do you know about the bartender Laura dated her senior year at Harvard, and then beyond?'

He frowned.

'That *is* a change of subject.'

'Humor me.'

'I don't know very much in terms of specific information,' he said. 'Mostly just that Andrew seemed to hate him more than he hated bin Laden at the time.'

'I only bring him up,' I said, 'because when I discussed him with both of Laura's roommates, they both expressed concern that he might somehow have come back into her life, and been the one to put her at risk.'

'I really wouldn't know,' he said. 'I graduated a semester early, which means I left all of that drama behind me. Then before I knew it, Andrew had gone off to find himself. And when he came back to Boston, he and Laura finally fell in love with each other.'

He checked his watch, almost as if he wanted to make me feel as if my office were his now. 'Do you honestly think Laura's old boyfriend might have had something to do with her murder?' he asked.

'Somebody once said that what's past is prologue,' I said.

He grinned. 'I hope it was a Harvard man.'

'Shakespeare,' I said.

He checked his watch again, and said he needed to be going, he had a late meeting back at Lith. 'Name your price,' he said.

'I don't want your money,' I said.

He looked at me as if I'd suddenly started speaking in tongues.

'Laura gave me a generous retainer,' I said. 'All I want is some cooperation from you and your partner and Claire and even your lawyer, if I can manage to restrain myself from bouncing him off the nearest wall when I'm next in a room with him.'

'I can't make any promises on Andrew, at least not right away, we go day to day with him and occasionally moment to moment,' Lowe said. 'But the rest of us will be made available to you.'

He stood. 'I know what you think,' he said. 'But this is only partially about saving the merger. It's about saving my best friend, or I wouldn't be here.'

He was out the door and gone when Reggie Smythe came back through it.

'You rather enjoyed him dismissing me like that, didn't you?' he said.

'Well, I didn't hate it, Reg, put it that way.'

'To be continued, then,' he said.

'Brilliant,' I said.

I tried to make my British accent more subtle than the first time he'd been in my office. But being men of the world, we both knew it was there.

39

Susan and I were spending the night together in Cambridge, but our reservation at Oleana wasn't until eight because of another late client for her.

'Waiting that long to eat dinner might make me faint from hunger or pass out or do something along those lines.'

'You could eat earlier over on your side of the river and I could sleep alone on my side,' she said.

'Meet you at the restaurant or pick you up?' I said.

Richie Burke called and said that Joe Marino had died last year, and hadn't been much of a bookkeeper when he was alive. Richie added that he was still trying to track down an old bartender of his who might have worked at Marino's about the same time Rob had, and would get back to me if he managed to track him down. I told him I appreciated his best efforts in the matter.

'Sunny made me do it,' he said. 'I think she might have a crush on you.'

'I'm too old for her,' I said. 'How's your father, by the way?'

'Starting to slow down finally.'

'Who the hell isn't?'

'Sunny doesn't seem to think you are.'

Susan and I took our time at Oleana. It was ten-thirty by the time we paid the check. When we got to her house I told her I would walk Pearl while she prepared herself for yet another trip to the moon on gossamer wings.

'I think it's adorable that you still quote Cole Porter,' she said.

'Who am I supposed to quote, Taylor Swift?'

She kissed me on the cheek as she handed me Pearl's leash.

'Only bought this dress so you could take it off,' she sang.

'Don't tell me,' I said. 'Taylor?'

'I try to stay current,' Susan said.

Pearl, as always, treated this late-night outing like a jailbreak. I tried to explain to our dog, as patiently as I could, that I needed her to take care of her business. But she pulled me up to Raymond and all the way past the Harvard University Press on Garden.

We had made the turn back on Linnaean and I was trying to see how many lyrics I could still remember from 'You're the Top' when Ethan Lowe called to tell me that they had found the body of Claire Megill's assistant, Darius Baker, outside his building in Charlestown.

'They think he threw himself off his balcony,' Lowe said.

40

Darius Baker had lived on 1st Ave, an older residential building in what had become one of the most gentrified areas in town over the past several years, his building a few blocks from the old Charlestown Bridge.

It was actually called the North Washington Street Bridge now and had finally been declared structurally deficient about twenty years earlier, which is why they were building a new one next to it. But the original, construction of which dated back to the late eighteenth century, was still open to pedestrian traffic that could take you from the Navy Yard all the way over to the North End.

The police presence stretched up and down 1st. Belson was there when I arrived. So were Lowe and Claire Megill and Clay Whitson.

Andrew Crain was a few yards away from his people, standing next to Reggie Smythe, so close to Smythe I thought he might be leaning against him for support. Smythe nodded at me. I nodded at him. The vacant look on Andrew Crain's face was reflected in the flashing police lights, as if Crain were staring past the USS *Constitution* Museum to infinity, and perhaps beyond.

Belson walked over to me.

'Oh, thank God,' he said, 'you're finally here.'

'What happened?'

'Young couple on their way to walk over the bridge and meet some friends for drinks on the other side of the river hear him land behind them on the sidewalk,' Belson said. 'He lived on the top floor of 275. Fifth floor.' He pointed. 'Not a pretty picture.'

'I would imagine not.'

Belson's eyes were fixed on the balcony as he told it. 'She gets hysterical, the boyfriend calls nine-one-one, I get the call because the guy worked for Lith and Mrs Lith was the dead body before this one. Lundquist was rolling up a shooting at a party up in Marblehead, but says he's on his way.'

He looked at me.

'You know this guy?' he said.

'I met him just one time, at the Lith offices,' I said. 'Spoke to him for a minute or so. That was it. He was the assistant to Crain's assistant. She called him a genius.'

'His boss says the kid wasn't suicidal,' Belson said.

'She'd know better than anyone,' I said.

'Your girlfriend's the shrink, not Ms Megill,' Belson said. 'A lot of young people are depressed these days and nobody knows it until it's too damn late.'

'Andrew Crain's wife gets killed,' I said. 'Then the assistant to his assistant gets killed. Maybe the universe is trying to tell us something, Frank.'

'I'll be sure to keep that in mind,' he said.

'You check the cameras at his front door?'

'Aren't any.'

'Talk to the people on his floor?'

'Shit!' Belson said, slapping his forehead. 'Why didn't I think of that?'

'Phone?'

'Not in the apartment, not on him, not near the body.'

'Was the guy seeing someone?'

'Ms Megill says no.'

Belson walked away from me then to talk to Lundquist, who'd just arrived. I went to talk to the upper management of Lith, Inc. about the sudden and violent death of another member of the family.

None of them looked particularly thrilled to see me.

But then, I ran into a lot of that.

41

Andrew Crain was still keeping some distance from the others, as if in a barely operational state of shock. Reggie Smythe was still at his side. I assumed Smythe had collected Crain and brought him here, from either Beacon Hill or Brookline.

Before I could get to Claire Megill, Clay Whitson saw me.

'What's he doing here?' Whitson said to Ethan Lowe, pointing at me.

'I called him,' Lowe said.

'What the hell for?'

Lowe didn't change expression. 'Remind me again which one of us is boss, Clay?'

I ignored both of them and motioned with a quick toss of my head for Claire to walk with me. She did. Her eyes were as empty as Andrew Crain's, seeming robotic even in this small movement.

'He wouldn't kill himself,' she said. 'You have to believe me.'

'I do,' I said. 'But if he didn't, who killed him? And why?'

She lowered her voice.

'He hasn't been to the office since Laura died,' she said. 'He said he was ill with the flu, but finally called tonight and said he'd been working on something that he couldn't work on at the office, and needed to talk to me about it.'

'Working on what?'

'He didn't say. Just that it was important, he'd call back, it might not be safe even talking about it on the phone, it had to be in person.'

'Did you tell the police that?'

She shook her head. 'I'm telling you,' she said.

'Let's keep it that way for now,' I said.

Claire Megill started to cry then. No sound came out of her. Her breathing didn't seem to change, nor her posture. There were just the tears. She made no attempt to wipe them away, as if oblivious that they were even there. But they showed no signs of stopping.

Before I could offer her comfort, Ethan Lowe was standing in front of us, as if he'd suddenly felt left out.

'I don't know whether this young man took his own life or not,' Lowe said. 'But what I do know is that two people connected to our company have died in the past week. So, Mr Spenser, let me ask you a question: *Now* are you willing to come work for me?'

I told him I wanted to sleep on it, even though I didn't, I didn't want to work for Ethan Lowe or Andrew Crain or Lith, Inc., and not just because I was about as good a fit in any corporate structure or chain of command as an iguana would have been roaming the fiftieth floor at the Hancock.

Laura Crain might have been the first dead client I'd ever had. She was still my client. Even now. And I still owed her.

Belson waved at me from where he and Lundquist now stood in front of Darius Baker's building. I started to head over to them but then Claire Megill yelled, 'Mr Spenser, wait!' and broke away from the others to catch up to me, alert all of a sudden, quickly covering the ground between us.

When she had, she threw her arms around me and pulled me into a fierce hug and in a loud voice said, 'You have to find out what happened to this beautiful young man.'

133

Before I could respond she pressed her face into my shoulder. 'Please protect me,' she whispered.

I hadn't known any of these people a week ago and now I was suddenly the most popular boy in class.

42

My knees remained too sore for me to consider our normal run along the Charles, so the next morning Hawk and I were walking the McCurdy Track at Harvard.

'So you know,' Hawk said. 'We could do this forever and not break a damn sweat.'

I said, 'There have been multiple studies done on the health benefits of walking if you're able to maintain a brisk pace.'

'This,' he said, 'ain't that.'

'What, you *don't* consider this to be a brisk pace?' I asked, trying to sound hurt.

'Maybe at the fucking *home*,' Hawk said.

'You just wait. Your heartbeat will be up before you know it.'

'Only if I walk to Braintree when we done here.'

'Bitch, bitch, bitch,' I said.

Hawk snorted. 'Man walking like Father Time and calling me the bitch.'

'Nevertheless,' I said, and we began another lap.

Today Hawk wore a T-shirt that had, 'Woke This', on the front of it.

'Claire Megill says that kid knew something, and it was important, and wanted to tell her before he died.'

'Kid?' Hawk said. 'Shit, you are Father Time.'

'Belson said Baker had just turned thirty.'

'Stand corrected,' Hawk said. 'Nobody ought to be thirty.' He smiled. 'Unless I be dating them.'

'If he didn't jump, somebody wanted it to look like he did,' I said. 'Maybe because of whatever it was he'd found out.'

'No suicide note?' Hawk said.

'Nope.'

'No sign of no scuffle or whatnot up on that balcony.'

'Nope.'

The more we walked, the less my knees hurt. But I wasn't going to tell Hawk that. The right one hadn't buckled today, at least not yet.

'You want to keep going?' Hawk said.

'Why not? I'm suddenly feeling fresh as a daisy.'

'Or some other kind of delicate flower. First they looking at you as some kind of threat,' Hawk said. 'Now they falling all over they-selves wanting you on their side.'

'Or so they say.'

'Uh-huh.'

The morning air was cool and clean, as if autumn had already arrived in Boston, and dropped the temperature more than ten degrees from the day before in the process.

'The kid's boss lady say she wants you to save her,' Hawk said, 'right after the other boss comes and asks you to go to work for him. Probably on account of two people they know being dead.'

'It sounds a lot worse when you put it like that,' I said.

Hawk asked when I planned to next talk to Claire Megill. I told him I was meeting her for a drink after she finished work today.

Hawk nodded.

''Less somebody kill her first,' he said.

43

Martin Quirk showed up at my office an hour or so before I was scheduled to meet Claire Megill at the bar at the Capital

Grille, which had moved several years before from Newbury next to Hynes Auditorium on Boylston.

It had begun to rain by then. Quirk took off his ancient Burberry raincoat and hung it on my coatrack, his movements as precise as they were with everything else, as if he were prepared to treat a single drop of water on my rug as some kind of felony.

He was dressed in another of his tweed jackets, another of his knit ties, another blue button-down shirt. I imagined him dressed like this watching a ballgame or playing with his grandchildren or walking his dog.

'Want a drink?' I said when he was seated.

'Thought you'd never ask.'

I poured Bushmills for both of us, handed him his glass. We both drank immediately. The warmth of the whiskey was both immediate and soothing.

'First of the day,' Quirk said.

'None better.'

'Until the second one.'

He slid a coaster close to him and put his glass down.

'You are once again a walking fucking crime wave,' he said.

'To be fair,' I said, 'only one of them was my client. I barely knew the guy they found in Charlestown.'

'Tell me everything you know, whether you already told Frank or not. And then tell me everything you think.'

'You in a rush?'

'I have a PBA dinner at seven-thirty at the new Ritz, one I would fake *my* death to get out of.'

I told him everything, including the parts about Laura Crain's old boyfriend. After a few minutes Quirk held out his empty glass and I refilled it. We were listening to the Bill Evans Trio. Bill on the piano. Chuck Israels on bass. Larry Bunker on drums. All going down as smoothly as the whiskey. Taylor Swift didn't know what she was missing.

Bill Evans was playing 'Who Can I Turn To?'

'The media is already having a goddamn field day with this,' Quirk said.

He held up his glass and stared at it in the faint light from my desk lamp, now that the early evening outside had grown darker with the rain.

'You think somebody would try to kill this merger by killing two people?' Quirk said.

'Or kill two people to save it.'

'How often do we look at either sex or money?' Quirk said.

'So often,' I said.

'The commissioner is up my ass already,' Quirk said. 'So I need you to keep me in the loop on this thing.'

'When haven't I?' I said.

I thought he might almost have smiled. 'You know,' he said, 'I could just stay here and finish the bottle and skip the dinner. I got a driver.'

'Be my guest,' I said. *'Mi casa...'*

'Kiss my *casa*.'

He finished his whiskey and took the glass over to the sink and rinsed it. He was even tidier than Susan. Almost impossible to fathom.

'How could the wife and the assistant be part of the same problem?' he said as he reached for his coat.

'I don't see a connection. But that doesn't mean there isn't one.'

He put on his coat. I could still spot some droplets of moisture on the shoulders. 'I don't want this to turn into more of a shitshow than it already is.'

Quirk stopped when he got to the door. 'You get anything useful out of Ms Megill tonight, you let me know.'

I told him I would.

'Time to head over there,' he said.

'Poor bastard.'

'Yeah,' Quirk said, and then left my office like he was being perp-walked.

44

Claire Megill and I sat at a corner table at the Capital Grille. She said the bar had just the proper lack of good lighting, as any good bar should. She had a glass of pinot grigio in front of her. I had a glass of Napa Hills pale ale.

'The one time I met Darius,' I said, 'he told me to be nice to you, right before I went into your office. When I asked him why he'd say something like that, he said, "Not everybody is."'

She drank a healthy amount of her wine.

'You'll find out the truth eventually,' she said. 'Or maybe have already. I had a relationship, one I'm not very proud of, since we work together, with Clay Whitson.'

'I'm shocked,' I said. 'Shocked, I tell you.'

'Don't make fun,' she said.

'I take it he wasn't nice to you?'

She stared past me, then brought her eyes back to me. 'No,' she said.

She drank more wine. 'I came in one day, and I hadn't done a good enough job covering a bruise on my chin with my makeup. Darius asked me. I denied it. But I knew that he knew what had happened to his boss.'

'But you didn't tell your boss,' I said.

'I was too ashamed,' she said. 'But I think Darius might have.'

'If Andrew knew, why wouldn't he just fire Whitson's ass?' I said.

'Because Ethan either believes the merger can't go through without Clay,' she said. 'Or is afraid that Clay would find a way to sabotage it if he *was* fired.'

She moved her glass slightly on the table, as if giving herself something to do with her hands.

'Anything more you'd like to tell me?'

'I've told you too much already,' she said. 'But as I said, just knowing you a little, I had a feeling you'd find out for yourself sooner or later.'

'But it's over now between Whitson and you?'

'As far as I'm concerned it is,' she said. 'And could we please change the subject?'

The rain had stopped by the time I got to the bar. She wore a short beige linen jacket with a blue T-shirt underneath and white jeans. She said she'd had enough time to stop at her apartment and change after work, and had walked here from there. I told her I would walk her home later. She said it wasn't necessary. I told her that was the plan.

'To walk me to my door?'

'For you to not need saving.'

She told me now, in an effort to change topics, if only briefly, that she'd always loved taking her son to the Capital Grille when he'd visit from school.

'Nothing better than watching college boys eat steak,' she said.

'They should make it part of their marketing,' I said.

Now she ran a finger around the tip of her wineglass. I noticed that her fingernails were the same color as her T-shirt.

'Maybe it's an irrational reaction to what happened to Darius,' she said. 'But I feel as if I'm in the middle of something and might be next.'

'Middle of what?'

'Some toxic mix of family drama and corporate intrigue,' she said.

'I'm not sure I understand.'

'Andrew is the scientist,' she said. 'Ethan is the entrepreneur. Because Andrew invented a cheaper way to produce lithium, he has the larger share of the company, as you know. Mr Inside to Ethan's Mr Outside. They're both well aware that there is no Lith, Inc. without Andrew's genius. But Ethan believes the company would never have grown to the extent that it has without his business genius. He's always telling Andrew to just keep focusing on the science and let him take care of everything else.'

'I got the impression that Laura didn't trust Lowe as completely as her husband did.'

'I don't know whether it was simply a lack of trust, or that she'd just never liked Ethan very much, and got tired of hiding it.'

'So Lith isn't everybody's happy place.'

'Maybe once. But not for a while. Andrew likes things the way they are,' she said. 'Ethan, though, he's become increasingly obsessed with the merger.'

'His idea?'

'From the beginning,' she said. 'He wants the company to keep growing, becoming more profitable than it already is. But more and more Andrew is convinced they have enough money, and should use even more of it, for fear of sounding highfalutin', to make the world a better place. That's *his* obsession.'

I nodded. I had already gotten the sense from Ethan Lowe why the merger mattered to him the way it did. Now I had heard it from her. I'd finished my beer but was reluctant to order another.

'Where would Laura have fit in with the dynamic you're describing?'

'Laura might have been more opposed to the merger than Andrew is,' Claire said. 'And to be honest, Mr Spenser, I was quietly cheering her on, because her voice mattered to him a lot more than mine does. And mine matters a lot.'

'She called you a bitch,' I said.

She sighed. 'Laura was always threatened by me, even though she had no reason to be. But on this matter, we were in lockstep.'

'Why doesn't Andrew just call a stop to the deal if he doesn't like it?'

'Because he doesn't want to do that to Ethan,' she said. 'Their relationship can get complicated sometimes, even though they love each other like brothers. But even brothers who do love each other fight.'

I'd held out as long as I could, and waved at the bartender now for another beer. Trying to problem-solve made me thirsty. Most everything did, especially at this point in the evening. The bartender put the fresh, chilled glass down in front of me.

'Is your relationship with Clay Whitson really over?' I said when the bartender was gone.

'I just told you it was.'

'You also told me you were ashamed of it. Maybe you're ashamed that it's still going on.'

'It's not,' she said.

'The other day when he was bothering you in front of Equinox, he wanted to know what you'd told someone,' I said. 'What was he talking about?'

She sighed again. 'I'd been questioned by the head of Human Resources about the possibility of an affair with Clay. There had been rumors around the office and they finally made their way to HR. Clay wanted to know what I'd told them.'

'Not told anybody he hit you?'

She shook her head.

'I know he has a terrible temper,' she said. 'And there were times when he did hurt me. But he's not a monster.'

'We're going to have to disagree on that,' I said. 'And any man who ever took a hand to a woman.'

'You get into a relationship like that...' She forced a smile. 'And it's very difficult to get out.'

'So I'm told,' I said, knowing this was a conversation she should be having with Susan Silverman.

The bar had begun to fill up. Mostly guys. I was picking up a lot of guy chatter, mostly about sports. The universal guy language. Susan had suggested, and not frivolously, that they should teach it in college. But as a Romance language.

'If Darius didn't kill himself, as neither of us believes he did, I'd be a fool not to think someone might come for me next.'

'But you don't know what he'd found out before he died.'

141

'Whoever killed him doesn't know that,' she said. 'Just that he worked closely with me.'

'Now you want me to protect you.'

She gave me another long look. 'Can you?'

'I can't do it alone,' I said. 'But there are people who can help me help you.'

'Are they as good at what you do as you are?' Claire Megill asked.

'One of them is,' I said. 'But if you tell him I said that, I'll deny it.'

45

We came out of the restaurant and took a left on Boylston, another left on Dalton, and then another on Belvedere, on our way to Huntington. I asked how she'd come to work for Andrew Crain. She said she was a single mom, raising her son, working for one of Lith's satellite tech companies, another start-up, in Silicon Beach.

'Divorced?' I said. 'Widowed?'

'Divorced,' she said. 'I was young. And stupid. And thought I was madly in love. I got pregnant. He left.' She shook her head. 'The reason I never talk about it is that it always starts to sound like a bad country song. If it hadn't produced my son, it was as if it never happened.'

'Don't they say that if you ran country songs in reverse, they'd all have happy endings?' I said.

'It was my first bad decision with men,' she said. 'And that is another subject I'd like to change, thank you.'

'Done,' I said.

She pulled her jacket tighter around her as we waited for the light to change on Huntington with the Colonnade across the street and the shops at the Prudential Center behind us.

'Want to tell me more about how you came to work for your boss?'

'Happily,' Claire Megill said.

'Was he around your company a lot, is that how you first met him out there?'

'I was working somewhere else when he hired me,' she said. 'But a headhunter called one day and asked if I'd be interested in going to work for Andrew Crain. He was out in Southern California and took me to dinner. We talked for a long time that night. He asked how I liked my current job, which was at Apple. I said I liked it fine, but wasn't being challenged, blah, blah, blah. And told him, quite honestly, that I was barely able to support my little boy and me on what I was making. I must have come across pretty well that night, because two weeks later I was working for Lith's tech company out there. Six months after that, I had moved to Boston and became his assistant, with more responsibility, and for more money than I ever thought I'd make in my life.'

We passed the Colonnade.

'How can I find out if there's a fox in the henhouse at Lith?' I said.

She smiled for the first time, fully. Almost happily. 'Do people still use that expression?'

I smiled back at her. 'Only when the wolf is at the door,' I said.

'Well, I'm certain I can help you with that,' she said. 'I just can't have Andrew and Ethan know that I would essentially be spying on my own company. Or have Clay get wind of it, for that matter. So we'll need to be discreet.'

'One of my many specialties,' I said.

'Do I want to know what the other specialties are?'

'We'd need more time for me to list them all,' I said.

We were a couple blocks from her building when we heard the thunder and then saw the lightning over our heads, followed instantly by a violent rain. Neither of us was carrying an umbrella.

We just ran. I had promised to keep her safe, just not from the elements.

When we arrived at the walk leading to the front door of her building, both out of breath, she looked up at me, hair matted to her head, drenched as much as I was. She laughed. I laughed, both of us looking as if we'd been thrown fully clothed into a swimming pool as I told her to get the hell inside.

'You really can keep me safe?' she shouted over the roar of the rain.

'Yes,' I shouted back. 'We start tonight by you not answering your door once you get inside.'

'I think I can manage that!' she said.

She found her key in her bag and unlocked the door. I watched through the glass doors as she walked across her lobby and then disappeared into the elevator, giving me a quick wave as she did.

Somehow the rain came even harder then.

I had turned back toward the street, thinking I would run back to Huntington and into the Colonnade and wait for the rain to subside when I slipped in a huge puddle that had formed on her front walk, and my gimpy right knee buckled underneath me, and I went down, cursing myself and the weather gods as I landed hard on my side.

In the next moment I heard a sound that I knew immediately was not lightning, a sound I recognised even underneath the storm, the unmistakable crack of some kind of long gun behind me, an instant before the bullet hit what turned out to be the shatterproof glass of Claire Megill's front door.

46

I thought I heard a shout from somewhere in the night as I rolled behind the only cover I could find, one of the two huge terra-cotta pots that bracketed the front door, right before a second shot exploded into the top of it and I was showered with pieces of clay.

The rain came harder.

I couldn't pinpoint the place in the park where the shots were coming from as I pulled the nine-millimeter I had brought with me tonight out of the holster I wore at the hip of my jeans. I looked around what was left of the pot and through the driving rain for pedestrians and saw none and fired once in the general direction of where the shots had come from, not expecting to get off a shot of my own at the shooter, but wanting him to know that I was armed, too.

I made out the shape of a man then, running away from me across the park.

Either giving up or not wanting to be seen, or both.

I rolled back out from behind the shattered pot and began to chase him on the bad knee that had likely just saved my life.

There was more light out here in the open, because of the buildings that surrounded the park. If I saw him stop and turn, ready to dive to the ground. He kept running, through the middle of the park, what looked like small gardens fenced on each side of it.

I was not gaining on him.

He was dressed in what looked like some sort of dark slicker and a baseball cap with a long bill and was faster than I was. But just about everybody was these days. His knees were probably stronger and sturdier than Usain Bolt's.

I slipped in the mud and went down again, managing to keep my gun hand high. I liked this gun. But I liked them all, just some more than others.

It was a big, fast man I was chasing, illuminated briefly by a flash of lightning, almost out of sight, on his way out of the park when I was up and after him once again, not just soaked now, but covered in mud.

Underneath another flash of lightning I could clearly see the long gun in his own right hand.

He slowed, but for only a moment, opening the low gate at the far end of the park rather than trying to scale it, and then he was on the street, running to his right. I didn't know the name of the street, but then it didn't matter because he was gone.

I was out of breath. The rain might have begun to subside, but only slightly, as I holstered my gun and began the walk back to Claire Megill's building, my shoes sinking deeper into the mud as I did.

I would have imagined myself as a drowned rat, except that I wasn't the rat out here tonight, a night when the one who needed protecting turned out to be me.

47

Perhaps residents of the building whose apartments faced the park thought the shots fired had been just part of the soundtrack of the storm. Because of the hour, perhaps no one had entered or exited the building after his shots had hit the door, and the pot. As of yet, there were no sirens heading this way, and there might not be unless somebody actually had seen what was happening out a window and called it in.

I called Claire on the number of the phone she carried with her, the one she said she always answered, told her I was still downstairs and what had just happened. She said she could buzz me in and I could come up. I said that wasn't a good idea in my present state. So she came down to the lobby, having already changed into a sweatshirt and jeans and sneakers, though her hair didn't yet look completely dry.

I showed her where the bullet had entered, what I was guessing might be a military-style bullet from the small hole it had left. Perhaps a .223, I told her. She looked at me as if I were speaking Estonian.

'Dear God' is what she said, putting a hand over her mouth.

It was unclear whether she was reacting to the bullet hole or to my appearance. Probably both.

'They weren't after you,' I said. 'Turns out they were after me.'

She said I should really come upstairs and clean up. I said that wasn't likely to happen any time before Veterans Day. I said that I was going to place a call to the police, but that there was no point in having them in her apartment, the guy had been targeting me tonight, not her.

'I only *thought* I was scared before,' she said.

'I still have friends in the department, hard as that sometimes is for me to believe,' I said. 'I'm going to call them now and explain the situation. I'm going to ask them to send a car, and I will wait here in the lobby until it arrives. The car will be out front all night.'

'You're sure the shooter won't be back?'

'If anybody approaches that door looking anywhere near as suspicious as I do,' I said, 'I will shoot them dead.'

She produced a tiny, nervous laugh. 'I assume you're joking.'

'I'm not,' I said.

No one came through the door after Claire went back upstairs. No one came down the elevator. So no chance for my appearance to frighten the decent people. The rain finally stopped. When it did I went outside and finally placed a call to Belson.

'They shot at you and missed?' he said.

'Sorry to be the one to have to break it to you, Frank.'

147

He said he'd send some of his people, one of whom would stay outside until morning. It didn't take them long to arrive. Once they did, three cars arrived one after another in quick succession, one carrying the detectives. Claire had contacted the super by now, who lived in a small apartment in the back. I showed everybody the hole in the glass, and where the bullet had hit the wall next to the elevator. One of the detectives extracted the bullet, flattened and misshapen.

'A .223,' the taller of the two detectives said. He'd introduced himself as Cohan.

'Nailed it,' I said.

'Huh?' he said.

'I know my bullets,' I said.

'Happy for you,' he said.

The other detective said, 'Lieutenant Belson is waiting for you downtown.'

I looked back at Cohan. 'Bet now you're really happy for me.'

He was young. A hard case. Clearly a by-the-book guy. He looked back at me, face impassive. 'Next time we should make a night of it,' he said.

They didn't ask if I had a car, or needed a ride downtown. I walked back to where I'd managed to find a parking place on Boylston, what felt like a very long time ago. On my way to see Belson, I called Susan and told her about my big night out with Claire Megill.

'You were shot at,' she said.

'He turned out to be something less than an expert marksman,' I said.

I could hear Pearl working over a squeaky toy in the background. I was pretty sure I knew which toy. It was new. But none of them ever had much of a life expectancy.

'So you dodged another bullet,' she said.

'A gift,' I said.

'Not funny.'

'Hey,' I said, 'think how I feel.'

There was just a brief pause and then she said, 'I love you.'

It was the same every time she said it, no matter what the circumstances, over the phone or in person, the words making me feel as if I were better than I had been before I heard them, better and more complete and reconnected to the best part of myself.

An hour later I had finished telling it to Belson, and he had typed up his report.

'We take attempted murder seriously around here,' he said, 'even for hot tickets like you.'

We went downstairs then and got into our cars and drove over to Biddy Early's on Pearl Street, which had always advertised itself as the 'best damn dive bar in Boston' despite what I knew, just from my own personal experience with dive bars, was extensive competition.

I looked at my watch. I had left the bar at the Capital Grille with Claire Megill well over four hours ago. Much had happened since. Belson ordered Jack Daniel's. I ordered Johnny Walker and soda. We sat at a high-top directly across from the bar. There was a Red Sox 'B' prominently displayed above the rows of bottles. In bars like Biddy Early's, it was like displaying a crucifix. Or a picture of the pope.

'So he wasn't after her,' Belson said.

'But hiding in the glowing doom,' I said.

'It's too late for that shit,' he said.

'Thomas Hardy,' I said. 'I knew you secretly wanted to know.'

'Maybe he went there thinking he could take a shot at her when she came home,' Belson said, 'and changed his mind and decided to clip you instead. Get you out of the way and come for her another time.'

'But why try to take me out?'

Belson sipped his drink and very nearly smiled. 'Other than for reasons too countless to list?'

'Other than those.'

'The wife goes out for a walk in that glowing doom of yours,' he said, 'and she dies. If you're right about the guy in Charlestown, which my gut tells me you are despite any useful evidence to the contrary, somebody tried to see if he could fly. Now somebody goes after you, in front of the building where the guy from Charlestown's boss lives.'

'Three different ways of getting it done,' I said. 'Or trying to get it done, in my case.'

'Not exactly what you'd call a coordinated effort.'

'Almost,' I said, 'as if somebody is making up this shit as they go along.'

There were a few diehards at the bar, despite the hour. Or perhaps because of the hour. There was an older guy sitting alone at a table against the wall, studying a glass of whiskey as if it were some kind of math problem he was trying to solve. Late-night ESPN was playing soundlessly on the television. There was no music. Who knew? Maybe it was the best dive bar in Boston after all.

'Somebody must be afraid you know something you shouldn't,' Belson said.

'I wish.'

'I know the feeling,' he said. 'I got no leads on Mrs Crain. Got no physical evidence on the Baker kid.'

'But look on the bright side,' I said. 'Now you've got a bullet from the guy who just tried to assassinate me.'

'*Assassinate?*' Belson said. Hunched over his glass, hands around it, but eyebrows up.

'It just sounds more substantial than "attempted hit,"' I said.

I knew it was time to go home. The adrenaline had drained out of me long ago. Despite my best efforts in the men's room on Belson's floor at the BPD, I was still filthy enough that he'd found a print edition of *The Globe* for me to sit on in his office. I'd at least had a clean sweatshirt in the backseat that I'd put on when I got downtown, and a dry pair of ancient Adidas sneakers with the three stripes, my favorites, built to last, somewhat like me. Or so I liked to tell myself.

I still liked places like this, this time of night. Even after a night like this one.

Belson got up and walked over to the bartender and handed some cash to him. When he came back I said, 'You *paid*? Did I die after all? Is this heaven?'

'You look like shit,' Belson said. 'Least I could do.'

I looked down at what was left of my drink. I had nursed it well enough that the ice hadn't melted yet. Always a good sign, no matter the hour.

'What the hell is going on with these fucking people?' Belson said as we walked back out to Pearl Street.

I still had no answer for that, so I thanked him for the drink and got into my car and drove home.

When I arrived at my own front door, nobody took a shot at me. I considered that progress as I went upstairs and took a quick, hot shower and threw down a quick shot of whiskey and fell into bed. My knee was throbbing, but I found the feeling comforting, picturing myself going to the ground in front of Claire Megill's front door until I finally fell asleep.

48

Hawk and Vinnie Morris and I were in my apartment the next morning. It was the first time Vinnie had been there since I had moved back to Marlborough Street.

'Sorry I didn't bring a fucking housewarming present,' he said.

'Stop before I tear up,' I said.

'Gets you right here, don't it?' Hawk said. 'Or maybe there.'

Vinnie wore a gray summer suit with faint pinstripes, a black shirt underneath, black suede oxfords. If there was a best-dressed list for guys who had once been a shooter for Joe Broz and still dabbled in the field when a lucrative opportunity presented itself, Vinnie would have been on it every single year.

There was more silver to his short, dark hair. He was tan enough that I was not surprised when he told me that the job from which he had just returned had been on Gasparilla Island, on the west coast of Florida.

Because it was Vinnie, there was not much of a report beyond that.

'Lot of rich people on that little island,' he said.

'So I've heard.'

'They don't like to get braced by somebody trying to make them less rich,' he said.

'They don't watch out,' Hawk said from where he was stretched out on my couch, 'shit like that can throw the radiative equilibrium totally out of whack.'

Vinnie stared at him. 'Radioactive what?'

Hawk smiled.

'Whatever,' Vinnie said. 'I got it straightened out and flew back last night, right before you didn't get hit and the storm did.'

'Wasn't much of a shootout, all things considered,' I said.

'You sure the guy didn't miss on purpose and not because you got lucky and made him miss?' Vinnie said.

'Somebody had already given me a warning at the sanctuary,' I said.

'Maybe they think you're slow on the uptake.'

'Well,' I said, 'I can see why someone might think that.'

Vinnie was sipping one of the small bottles of regular Coca-Cola. I knew he liked the little bottles, and I had gone out and picked up a six-pack before he and Hawk had arrived.

'You been beat up now and shot at,' Vinnie said. 'What's next? They try to drown you in your bathtub?'

I had asked him if he'd be willing to keep an eye on Claire Megill for a few days. He said he would, and that he assumed I could afford him. I told him that after what Laura Crain had paid me up front, I was bucks up at the moment.

152

'So this isn't one of those jobs where you get paid in donuts or some shit like that?' Vinnie said.

'Happily, no.'

'She gonna know I'm watching her?' Vinnie asked.

'I will call her after you leave and tell her that you and I will meet her outside the Hancock after work as a way of introducing you.'

'She good-looking?' Vinnie said.

'Does it matter?' I said.

'Maybe you are slow on the uptake after all,' Vinnie said.

'Man makes a good point,' Hawk said, and made a shooting motion at Vinnie with his thumb and forefinger.

I saw Vinnie looking around the living room. 'I feel like I got some of that déjà vu going here,' he said.

'Because of the way I've managed to artfully reimagine my old apartment?'

'Nah,' Vinnie said. 'Because here we go again with me watching somebody and Hawk watching you and neither one of you knowing what the fuck is going on here.'

'See there,' I said, grinning at Hawk. 'There is still equilibrium to the universe after all.'

49

So you're my new nanny,' Claire said to Vinnie when we met her at the corner of Clarendon and Stuart.

'Sure,' Vinnie said.

It came out *shoo-ah*.

'I meant that in a nice way,' Claire said.

'It sounded kind of a-feminist to me,' Vinnie said.

I grinned at Vinnie. 'This might be a chance for you to be even more metrosexual than you already are,' I said.

'Bite me,' he said, then nodded at Claire and said, 'Pardon my French.'

'Seriously?' she said to him. 'Thank you for doing this.'

'Sure,' Vinnie said again.

'I feel as if you'll be walking me home from high school,' Claire said to Vinnie.

She turned to me. 'Do I even want to know what your next move might be?'

'Only if you want me to tell you,' I said.

Belson had told me that he'd cleared it with Quirk to keep a car in front of Claire's building for the next couple nights at least. After that, I would leave the overnight shift to Vinnie. I knew he had people. Who had people. By now I trusted Vinnie Morris the way he trusted me. Susan called it a code that only members of our club understood, and maybe even not all the members.

'Do you really think of it as a club?' I'd asked her.

'Or a secret society,' Susan had said. 'Except you guys deal in real skulls and bones.'

'Yale reference from a Harvard girl?' I said.

'I was making a larger point,' Susan said.

I eventually needed to talk to Andrew Crain again, about many things. But Claire said she could not help me with that, that she was more loyal to him than anybody except her own son. If he did not want to meet with me, at least not voluntarily, that was entirely his choice, and she would do nothing to try to change his mind. She told me that she hoped I could respect her choices. I told her that I could. Everybody had codes, whether you were in a club or not.

Andrew Crain, whom Claire said was currently holed up in the town house on Chestnut Street, might know more about his wife's life in college than even he thought he knew. And likely more about the ex-boyfriend than I knew, just because almost everybody did at this point. I was aware that there were other possible links between Laura's death and Darius Baker's. But Crain remained the strongest link between them, as weak as he himself seemed to be these days, a weakness that had brought me into his world in the first place.

For now, though, I wanted to talk to Clay Whitson. I had spoken with Ethan Lowe on the telephone before Vinnie and I had walked over to the Hancock, clearing it with him. Lowe had given me Whitson's cell phone number, which would probably do me no good, and his address at the Seaport, which I suspected probably would.

'Don't tell him you got it from me,' Lowe said.

'You're his boss,' I said.

'And I do my best to keep him on my side,' Lowe said. 'It makes my life a lot easier. The old theory about having him inside the tent pissing out.'

'Is there any other side for him other than yours?'

'His,' Lowe said.

Whitson lived in a high-rise building behind the Boston Harbor Hotel, the view of the water unobstructed by the hotel. Lowe further told me that as part of Whitson's deal with Lith, the company provided Uber rides to and from the office. Whitson's secretary had told Ethan Lowe that he was working late tonight, but that she had booked an UberX for him at seven o'clock to take him back to the Seaport.

I was waiting for him out front when he got out of the black SUV. He was wearing another suit with skinny lapels and what I once would have called pegged pants. Somebody really needed to tell him that he didn't have the body for it, built as he was like a garbage can. He was checking his phone and didn't notice me standing there until he had put the phone away. Reluctantly put it away. He probably didn't go five minutes without checking it. If that.

He stopped when he did see me.

'You don't get to come to my home,' he said.

'And yet, Clay,' I said, 'here we both are.'

'Ethan told me that I had to talk to you, but I assumed you'd make an appointment and come to my office,' he said.

'Then I made the executive decision to come here,' I said. 'I've frankly always thought I had the makings of a first-rate top manager. Not to mention the people skills.'

'You really are a smug sonofabitch.'

I smiled. 'Well, a sonofabitch maybe.'

'What do you want to talk about?'

'Your boss.'

'Which one.'

'Andrew Crain.'

He surprised me by barking out a laugh.

'Boss?' he said. 'More like the guy who's trying to destroy his own company.'

Whitson shook his head, almost sadly.

'You've got this all wrong, Spenser,' he said. 'I'm not the bad guy here. He is.'

50

We walked around to the dock behind the hotel.

'I could have invited you up to my apartment,' Whitson said. 'But I don't want you inside my apartment.'

'No need to sugarcoat it,' I said.

There was a glass-walled gazebo in front of us, a tour boat to our left beginning to board passengers, probably for its last run of the night, smaller boats bobbing in the water. There was a good hard breeze coming from the east. The view from here was timeless, especially at this time of night when the color of the sky seemed to match the color of the water.

I zipped my leather jacket and put the collar up.

'Andrew has never paid much attention to the day-to-day operation of the company, the nuts and bolts of it,' Whitson said, leaning over the railing in front of us. 'He just thinks of himself as some sort of modern-day Edison. He invented a better mousetrap and found a way to make the energy from batteries cheaper and more affordable and more friendly to the ecosystem. And away he went.'

'When did you start working with him?' I said.

'About five years in,' he said. 'I've been with him and Ethan ever since.'

'So why does a company that was rich beyond avarice even before you came along need this merger so badly?'

'You want the long answer or the short one?'

'Either,' I said. 'Just promise not to use too many big words.'

'Jesus, you really are a horse's ass,' Whitson said.

'Well, yeah.'

'Okay, here's the short answer,' he said. 'First of all, he's given away so much money over the past few years, more than ever before, it's like he's got a charity addiction to match any other kind of addiction you want to talk about, including gambling.'

'It has to be more than that, even if he has been giving money away with both hands,' I said.

'Yeah,' he said. 'It is. We got hit hard by COVID the way everybody else did, especially in terms of production. And when we were slow coming out of it, along comes some Australian scientists to produce an even cheaper form of synthetic lithium than we are, those Down Under bastards.' He shrugged. 'So now they're the ones who maybe have built a better mousetrap.'

'So is the sixth-richest guy in America still the sixth-richest guy in America?'

'He is, but not for long, the way he's going and the way we're going,' Whitson said. 'Bottom line? We *do* need this merger. Ethan knows it. I know it. But our looney-tunes founder doesn't want to hear about it.'

Whitson turned to face me. 'Andrew is constantly talking about the greater good. But now he's about to blow a deal that isn't just good for his company, but might save it.'

'Can't Ethan bring him around?'

'He believes he can, he's always been able to keep him in line before,' Whitson said. 'The problem is that the car people are getting impatient. And if they take their offer off the table, they will sure as shit go running straight to the new kids on the block in Melbourne.'

'How did Laura figure into all of this?'

'As far as I can tell, Laura kept telling Andrew that bigger didn't always mean better,' Whitson said. 'That Lith didn't need this, he didn't need this, *they* didn't need this.'

'So she could have been seen as an obstructionist where the merger was concerned.'

'Indeed.'

'Worth killing because of that?'

'Oh, hell, no,' he said. 'We may be a dysfunctional family behind the scenes. But we're still family. I've always thought that Ethan loved Laura as much as Andrew did. Maybe more. He's never said anything like that. But I've always had this feeling that he thought he should have been the one to get the girl.'

The tour boat, looking as if it had been turned into a party boat on this night, began to slowly ease out into the water.

'What about Darius Baker?' I said.

'What about him?'

'Is there any possibility that he could have been seen as a threat to the merger?'

Whitson turned and leaned his back against the railing, as if the view suddenly bored him.

'Sorry, but Darius didn't matter enough,' he said. 'Does that make me sound like a prick?'

I smiled, not able to help myself. 'You're a lawyer. You probably knew the answer to that before you asked the question.'

'I'm trying to help you, and you persist in talking shit at me,' he said. 'So now we're done here.'

'One last thing.'

I put a hand on his arm as he started to push off the railing. He looked down at it, but made no move to pull his arm away. It was just the two of us out here. Maybe he could see something in my eyes. Maybe he was worried that if he said or did anything to escalate the moment, I might throw his ass into the water.

'I'm just curious about something,' I said, tightening my grip just slightly. 'Would Darius have mattered more to you if he knew you were the prick who liked to beat up Claire Megill?'

He jerked his arm back and slid along the railing to create space between us.

'What the hell are you talking about?' he said.

'Just asking a question I might already know the answer to,' I said, and left him standing there, proud of myself for not throwing Clay Whitson's sorry ass into the water.

51

Hawk and I were at Susan's for a late dinner. She had told me in advance that she was more than willing to cook. I had told her that while I could see that the spirit was willing, the flesh was sadly weak.

'Just out of curiosity?' she'd asked. '*Whose* flesh?'

'Mine and Hawk's.'

'In what order?'

'Ordering in,' I said.

Hawk had preceded me to Linnaean Street. By the time I arrived from the Seaport, the food from Dumpling House had arrived. From the looks of the bags and containers spread out on the counter in Susan's kitchen, she and Hawk had ordered just about everything: beef with longhorn peppers, General Gao's chicken, string beans with dried shrimp, white and brown rice, plenty of hot mustard on the side. And an order of pork intestines with pickled mustard greens, which I was certain Hawk had ordered just to torture Susan Silverman.

'Pork intestines?' she said when we were all seated at her dining room table.

Hawk rubbed his stomach and smacked his lips. 'Hmmmm,' he said. 'Good and good for you.'

Susan used chopsticks. Hawk and I did not. I reminded her again that I was able to use chopsticks, but just chose not to.

As we ate I told them about the time I'd just spent with Clay Whitson.

'Doesn't sound like his interests are aligned with the big boss's,' Hawk said.

'No,' I said. 'They certainly do not.'

Susan plucked a single green bean and ate half of it. She looked at me as she did, face serious, all of her focus on me in the moment, making me feel, as always, as if she could look all the way into my soul. I'd mentioned that theory to Hawk once and he'd said, 'Always knew somebody'd find it, they looked hard enough.'

'But does any of this help you find out what brought Laura Crain to you in the first place?' Susan said. 'Or what that might have had to do with her death?'

'Missy here asks a good question,' Hawk said.

He was seated next to her. Susan leaned over and kissed him on the cheek. If I didn't know what a hard case he was, I might have thought he was beaming.

'I've often considered asking questions professionally,' she said.

'So you're suggesting I go back to the beginning,' I said.

'The thought has occurred, yes.'

She finished the string bean that had remained firmly in place between her chopsticks, one I thought she had forgotten and might have just stayed where it was indefinitely.

'You still haven't found out what event, or series of events, brought Andrew to his breaking point.'

I grinned. '*That* thought has occurred to me, yes,' I said.

'So don't you think it might be useful *to* go back to the beginning?' she said.

'Why do I feel as if I'm being shrunk?'

"Bout damn time,' Hawk said.

We both watched as Susan now nibbled on a piece of chicken, though *nibble* might have been a bit of a reach.

'The conclusions to be drawn about Laura's death are limited, just off what I know so far,' I said. 'One theory would be that it was random, and she really was just at the wrong place at the wrong time, though I can't imagine what she was doing on the trail alone in the night. Or she went there because she knew her killer, a person who might have wished her harm because of what's going on with her husband's company, except that she didn't know he wished her harm.'

'Think about something else, since we headed down this path,' Hawk said. 'How much you know about the girl, really, other than her being married to who she was married to, and that she had herself a boyfriend in college she shouldn't've?'

'Not a lot.'

'Is there a chance, and I'm just throwing this out there,' Susan said, 'that Laura could have had a man on the side, or a woman?'

'She didn't seem like the type,' I said.

Susan smiled. 'Trust me. There is no type. I've done the research.'

Hawk spooned more pork intestines onto his plate, making sure Susan saw him do it.

'Now you're really trying to ruin my appetite,' she said.

'What appetite?' Hawk said.

We discussed the conflict between the two partners then, and the obvious drama between Clay Whitson and Claire Megill. And violence. I poured more champagne for Hawk, who was civilised enough tonight to have foregone drinking out of the bottle. I went and got another Boomsauce from the refrigerator.

'Two people are dead, both with strong ties to Lith,' Susan said. 'Here's my last question before I leave the detecting to the two of you: Is there any connection *between* the two dead people?'

Now I stared at her. 'That is an even better question than the other question.'

161

Susan nodded. 'I really should consider doing this for a living.'

Fifteen minutes later, after we had all cleaned up after dinner, Hawk and I were in his Jaguar and on our way to Charlestown.

52

I called Frank Belson on our way to Darius Baker's building. He told me that the tox screen, which he'd fast-tracked, had come back and indicated a high amount of tequila in Baker's system at the time of his death.

'We didn't find tequila in the kid's bar setup,' Belson said. 'But last time I checked, they do serve it in actual bars.'

'Anybody in the area remember serving him that night?' I said.

'We checked,' he said. 'They didn't. Doesn't mean he couldn't have gotten a load on somewhere else.'

'Do we know if he owned a car, Frank?'

'According to his last credit card statement, he was leasing an Audi.'

'Where is it?'

'No clue,' he said.

'My gut tells me he didn't jump, Frank.'

'Prove it.'

The next thing I heard was a dial tone.

Hawk told the super at Baker's building that he was Darius's older brother, just by another mother, and had just arrived back in the country from France after having gotten the news about his baby brother. The super, who'd introduced himself as Ramon, said the apartment was supposed to remain sealed, by order of the police.

It was then that I flashed the fake badge that I'd collected from my glove compartment before we'd left Susan's, and said, 'I'm unsealing it.'

Ramon acted as if I'd pulled a gun on him, said to Hawk, 'Very sorry for your loss,' and took us upstairs and unlocked the door and we were in.

'Can't believe that badge is still working for you,' Hawk said. 'Where'd you get it, inside a box of Cracker Jack?'

'I was more worried that Ramon might start to question the lack of family resemblance between you and Darius,' I said.

'Wait,' Hawk said. 'You saying we all *don't* look alike?' It was a young guy's place. The flat screen on the living room wall looked twice the size of my own. On the coffee table was a video-game controller, though I had no idea for which video game. So I asked Hawk. 'Xbox,' he said. On the wall next to the flat screen was a framed World Series ticket from 2018, Game 2, Red Sox against the Dodgers at Fenway. Those were the days.

Every piece of furniture in the room seemed to have come from Pottery Barn or IKEA or some hybrid of the two. There was a small, well-stocked bar, but without tequila. Combined kitchen and dining area off the living room. You went down a short hallway to the master bedroom, which had a partial view of the water from the balcony where Darius Baker had spent the last moments of his young life.

Hawk stood in the middle of the bedroom. The bed was made. No clothes draped over the one armchair in there, or the chair at his desk.

'Belson's people go over this place good?'

'What do you think?'

'Yeah,' he said, nodding. 'Frank never been one out there flying on the wings of chance.'

He looked around. 'We looking for anything in particular?' Hawk said.

'What we're always looking for,' I said. 'Something that will make us feel smart when we find it.'

'Could be here awhile,' he said.

Belson said some of his guys had checked out the limited presence Baker'd had on social media. Claire Megill had already told me that Darius did not have a Twitter account, or TikTok, and rarely posted things on Instagram.

'Crazy as it sounds, he was too busy actually living his life to record it,' she said.

Until he wasn't.

There were no clues to be found in the drawers of his desk. Some bills that he hadn't paid electronically. One from J Crew. Another that was from Pottery Barn. A couple unused legal pads, and some gel pens. A small, wallet-sized Red Sox game schedule. No photographs on the desk, or anywhere in the apartment. Maybe he hadn't lived here very long, it would be easy enough to check with Claire, his immediate superior. And probably didn't matter, one way or another. Claire had told me he was a product of the New York City foster-care system but had still managed to earn a scholarship to NYU, majored in economics, after that came an internship at Lith the year before he graduated. Then a full-time job with them. Living the dream.

Hawk found nothing other than clothes in the bureau. There was a floor-to-ceiling bookcase in the living room. I went through the books one by one, hoping that a clue might fall out of one of them. One did not. Most of the books were self-help books, a lot of self-help books on how to become a success in business, a leader of men and women.

I need one of those, I thought.

I went to the closet next. A lot of hanging clothes in there, suits and sports jackets and shirts and jeans. Even his T-shirts were on hangers. A lot of shoes and sneakers on the floor, all neatly arranged. There was an array of baseball caps on hooks, most from New York teams, the heathen.

I began to go through the jackets one by one, meticulously checking the pockets.

The note was in the third blazer from the end, a J Crew, inside pocket, almost hidden by the flap.

Belson's people had just missed it because everybody missed things. There had been plenty of times when I could have

164

taught a master class in missing things, no matter how hard I looked.

It was actually a personalised note card.

LAURA CRAIN was at the top.
The message was in neat, cursive script.

D:
  Didn't want to send anything electronically.
  We have to be more careful than ever.
  What you've found could change everything.
  Love you for caring this much.
    Talk soon.
    L.

I whistled softly as I stepped out of the closet.
'Oh, ho,' I said.

53

Claire Megill agreed to meet me the next morning across from the entrance to Trinity Church.

It was one of my favorite landmarks in the city, because of the look of the place, and its history. The original Trinity Church had been built on Summer Street but had burned down in the real Great Boston Fire, the one in 1872. The Public Library was in the distance behind the bench where I waited for her, at the spot on Boylston where the Marathon ended every year. Even though there were taller structures all around the church, it still seemed to dominate Copley Square, with what looked like arms reaching up from both sides to a central tower. I had read somewhere that the Back Bay had originally been a mudflat, and that the church rested now on thousands of wooden piles. But it consistently made the list of the most significant buildings in the entire country. I wasn't sure what that meant, but the old girl had always been significant enough for me.

I had picked up coffee for me and tea for Claire at the Starbucks that was essentially underneath my office on Berkeley. Vinnie walked Claire to the bench on which I was sitting, at the end of a long expanse of well-maintained lawn. I assured Vinnie that I could get Claire safely to her office from here.

'You carrying?' he said.

'If you show me yours, I'll show you mine,' I said.

'Okay, then,' Vinnie said, and told Claire to call him later, he'd be waiting for her downstairs when she was finished at work.

We both watched him go.

'He's really kind of cute,' she said.

'It would be best to keep that between the two of us,' I said.

'You don't want him to know I think he's cute?'

'I don't want him to quit,' I said.

I got right to it then, asking if she knew of a relationship between Laura Crain and Darius Baker.

Her mouth actually dropped open, in almost an exaggerated movie take.

'A romantic relationship?'

'Any kind of relationship.'

'Between the wife of the principal owner of the company and my assistant?' she said. 'The people at Human Resources would have been wearing party hats when they fired him. Clay Whitson and I would have seemed like a speed bump.'

'But that's what I'm asking you, yes.'

She shook her head a few times, slowly, side to side. 'If there was something between them or anything between them, it's news to me.'

'There was one,' I said. 'A relationship. Darius and Laura Crain.'

She had worn sneakers with her beige pantsuit for her walk to work with Vinnie. Knowing how fashion-conscious Vinnie was with his own attire, I hoped it hadn't offended his sensibilities.

I recited the contents of Laura's note to her, word for word.

'What does that all even mean?' Claire said.

'I was hoping you might be able to tell me,' I said. 'At the very least, it indicates a shared interest in something. And probably explains why he called you the night he died.'

'If there was some kind of shared interest, Darius would have told me.'

'Obviously, he didn't.'

'This can't be.'

'Claire,' I said. 'We're way past that now. Maybe he kept silent because the boss's wife told him to.' I turned slightly on the bench. 'You never saw the two of them together in a social setting?'

'Perhaps at the office Christmas party?' she said. 'But Laura and I were rarely together in social settings, and when we were, let's just say we kept our distance.' She shrugged. 'I had long since given up the notion that the two of us were ever going to be friends, even though there was no need for her to be threatened by me.'

'It doesn't mean she wasn't,' I said.

'And then, what, aligned herself with my assistant on some top-secret mission?' she said.

'Strange bedfellows?'

'Are you suggesting they were sleeping together?'

'Figure of speech,' I said. 'But I'm not saying they weren't.'

She drank some of her tea.

'It's a rather cryptic message,' she said.

'Apparently not to them,' I said.

We sat in silence then in the morning sun. I watched the foot traffic to our left on Boylston Street, thinking about how many briefcases I would have seen in another time, briefcases replaced by backpacks and leather bags now, or not replaced at all, because everything they all needed was waiting for them inside their desktop computers, or in the slim handheld cases that probably contained their iPads. All I generally carried to work was a .38.

'Is there any chance that Laura could have gone to Darius and asked him to find out why Andrew has been behaving the way he has?' I said.

'But why him?' Claire said. 'You're suggesting that she went to the assistant of someone – *me* – she apparently thought was a bitch on wheels?'

'Maybe she knew he was a New York City kid,' I said. 'Maybe she was looking for street smarts.' I raised my shoulders and let them drop. 'I'm fumbling here.'

Claire placed her cup next to her on the bench, reached into her bag, came out with her phone, checked it, put it back inside the bag.

'But street smarts for what?' she said. 'And about what?'

'Something not right about the merger?'

'As closely as I work with Andrew, even I'm not privy to what Andrew and Ethan refer to as "being in the weeds,"' she said. 'He's generally aware of what's going on, of course, he's the major shareholder and will ultimately vote thumbs-up or thumbs-down. But Ethan is the one who's in the barrel on this deal. When Andrew needs to know something, Ethan tells him. When Andrew's got a question, he asks Ethan. When there was some part of the finances I didn't understand, I'd ask Darius.'

'But what if it was Laura who wanted to go into the weeds on this thing?' I said. 'And didn't want to ask Ethan. It's become pretty clear, at least to me, that she was like her husband in the sense that she liked things the way they are at Lith and saw no need for expansion, or major change.'

Claire Megill gave a slight jump as a car horn blared behind us on Dartmouth Street.

'In the end, and despite his misgivings, Andrew will do what's best for the company,' she said. 'He and Laura never had children. Lith is his baby, and his legacy, and his opportunity to change things he thinks need changing. He calls himself the nerd who conquered the world.'

'But seems to be losing himself in the process,' I said. 'By the way? I met with Clay Whitson last night. And he frankly gave me the impression that if Andrew doesn't get on board with the merger, the walls might come tumbling down.'

The mention of Whitson seemed to make her color slightly. Or it could have been a trick of the morning light, I wasn't entirely sure.

'Clay said that?'

'He did.'

'The man has no filter.'

'There's a lot of things he doesn't have,' I said. 'But is he right?'

She hesitated, and leaned her head back, and stared up at the tower of the church.

'I swear, he's more dug in on this merger than even Ethan is,' she said. 'And occasionally acts like he's as much a partner in the firm as either Andrew or Ethan. As if wishing could make it so.'

She pulled up the sleeve of her jacket and checked the Apple watch on her wrist. 'I need to get to the office.'

'Did Darius ask questions recently about the merger or anything that you found odd?' I said.

'No,' she said. 'But he would have known better than to raise my antennae, if he was poking around where he shouldn't have been.'

I took our cups and tossed them into a nearby bin, and told her I would walk her to the Hancock. She said it was called 200 Clarendon now. I told her I knew that, but it was too late for me to change.

'I have the feeling you run into a lot of that,' she said, smiling at me.

'Hourly sometimes,' I said.

She said it really wasn't necessary for me to bodyguard her in broad daylight. I told her Vinnie would ask if I'd walked her all

169

the way to the door, and I promised that once she was inside, I was confident nobody would take a shot at me.

When we'd made our way over there, she stopped on the sidewalk.

'What I don't understand is why Darius didn't mention his relationship with Laura,' she said. 'Whether it was personal or professional.'

I was about to answer her when I saw the black Lincoln Navigator pulled up. Reggie Smythe, my old pal, got out from behind the wheel and came around and opened the sidewalk-side door and Andrew Crain stepped out.

As he did, Claire Megill turned without saying goodbye and moved as quickly as she could toward the front door without breaking into a sprint.

54

Reggie Smythe, most certainly paid handsomely to see the whole field, picked me out of the morning rush between Clarendon and the entrance to the Hancock before Crain did.

Andrew Crain was just slightly visible behind Smythe, head down, wearing what by now I knew was his uniform: Sweater, lemon-colored today, blue shirt underneath, slightly baggy jeans, loafers that had seen better days.

It was a wide sidewalk, and there were other people on either side of them.

I stepped in front of Reggie Smythe.

He smiled, as if hopeful for some kind of confrontation. Any kind of confrontation.

'I'd like a word,' I said.

'I'd like to think not,' he said.

I ignored him, took a quick first step past him even on my bad knee, almost daring Smythe to make the move to stop me.

But I had managed to insinuate myself between him and his boss.

Some bodyguard.

For Smythe to do anything about it, he was going to have to make a scene. In the world of cell phone video and social media, he had to know what a truly bad idea that was.

'Would you prefer I remove him?' Smythe said to Crain.

I said, 'You have a better chance of becoming an astronaut, Reg.'

Andrew Crain's eyes were everywhere at once, as if trying to find a place to come to rest.

His eyes finally focused directly on me, almost as a last resort. 'Please don't embarrass me. Or yourself.'

I could feel Smythe's presence close behind me. If he did try to remove me, whatever happened next would happen. And was probably an inevitability between us.

I just didn't want it to happen until I spoke with Andrew Crain, no matter how briefly.

'I'm not trying to embarrass you,' I said. 'I'm trying to find your wife's killer.'

'That's better left to the police,' he said. 'That's their job.'

'And mine,' I said. 'And yours, if you'll just cooperate with me.'

He looked at Smythe and nodded.

'Good day, Mr Spenser,' Andrew Crain said.

I was out of time.

'Are you aware of your wife being involved in a relationship with Darius Baker?' I said.

In the next moment Crain was doing his eye-blink thing again. Maybe this time it was some sort of message in code for Smythe.

'What did you just say?' Crain asked.

'I'm trying to understand why I found a quite personal note from Laura to Darius in his apartment when I was going through his things,' I said.

171

'Reggie,' Crain snapped.

His boss voice coming out of him, just like that, as if he'd suddenly remembered he actually *was* the boss.

I detected some movement to my right, out of the corner of my eye. When I turned my head to determine exactly where Smythe was, the sixth-richest man in America, apparently unconcerned about going viral, screamed, 'I will not let anybody hurt her ever again!' right before he punched me in the face.

55

'You want me to go over there and beat the bad man up for you?' Hawk said.

We were in my office, in the middle of another morning when we were drinking coffee and eating donuts, Hawk on the couch and me with my feet up on my desk. He had enjoyed the story of what had just happened with Andrew Crain and me immensely.

'Do I have to keep reminding you that it was a sucker punch?' I said.

Hawk snorted. 'From the president of the Science Club,' he said.

'Go ahead. Have your fun.'

'Am trying to look at the bright side, however.'

'There's a bright side to me getting tagged?'

'Least the big bully didn't give you another broken nose,' Hawk said.

'You done?'

'For now.'

At some point we were going to head over to the gym. When we got there, Hawk said, he was going to give me a remedial course in ducking punches.

'I clearly touched a nerve when I asked him about his wife and Darius,' I said.

'Though I got to say, touching a nerve with the boy at this point don't seem to me like you had to thread no needles,' Hawk said.

He nodded at the open box of donuts. 'You plan to eat that last sprinkled?'

'With the pink frosting? It's all yours, you candy ass.'

'Look who's talking.'

He finished the last donut in two bites. It meant we had gone through the whole box in almost record time, even for the two of us.

Hawk said, 'You gonna tell Belson about that note?'

'Eventually.'

I drank more coffee, which I had just reheated in the microwave. I didn't fully understand why Dunkin' coffee, cream and sugar, tasted better than fancier and more expensive brands. It just did. Hawk had suggested once that it might have had something to do with them putting enough sugar in it to bake a cake.

'Maybe Belson already found some connection between the two of them by going into her phone or laptop and is waiting to tell *you* eventually.'

'I actually asked him about that,' I said. 'He said Andrew Crain has refused to release either.'

'Scuse me?'

'I happened to place a call to our friend Lieutenant Belson after I stopped at Dunkin',' I said. 'And got a very fast and very salty assessment of the Fourth Amendment and privacy rights for the dead and what Lieutenant Belson further described as "fucking exigency."'

'You think Crain might've gone into them himself and found out something he didn't want the po-lice to know?' Hawk said.

'Or maybe Andrew Crain doesn't want to know what he doesn't want to know about his late wife.'

'But the man just told you, front of God and the world, that he

173

wanted you to stop hurting her,' Hawk said, 'even now that she gone off to her reward.'

'The last time I know of that she was a victim was when she was trapped in an abusive relationship in college,' I said.

'Then she come to you because she say her husband was some kind of victim,' Hawk said, 'even if it was just from all the toys in his attic.'

'Unless she went to somebody working for her husband's top assistant first,' I said. 'Before the two of them both went and got they-selves killed.'

I saw Hawk grin. '*They-selves?*'

'Just reading the room.'

He took his own last, sad look at the empty donut box and picked it up and dropped it into my wastebasket.

'So the cops don't find Baker's laptop,' he said. 'And Crain say he ain't giving up his wife's. Or even her old Filofax.'

'Correct.'

'But maybe it don't matter, since she say in the note she don't want to send anything to the boy electronically.'

'Also correct.'

By now I knew that Hawk was as good a listener as Susan Silverman was, as observant as Belson or Quirk were at crime scenes, and had a memory like an entire herd of elephants.

'We could break into one of Crain's houses and steal one of his wife's laptops,' Hawk said. 'Just thinking out loud here.'

'And criminally.'

'You forget sometimes,' he said, 'on account of my superior intellect, that I is a career thug.'

He asked if I was ready to head over to Henry Cimoli's. I said I was.

'Wait,' I said.

'We wait, we never gonna make it over there and just want to go get more donuts.'

'No,' I said. 'I just thought of something.'

'Egads, Holmes!' Hawk said. 'Enlightened thinking?'

'There's one computer we could check without breaking and entering,' I said, and then called Claire Megill, and told her what I needed for her to do, if she was willing.

She called back five minutes later.

'I am now seated at Darius's desk,' she said. 'I haven't done that since he died.'

'Haven't the police been through it?' I said.

'Andrew and Ethan wouldn't let them.'

'Do you find that odd?'

'Not for Andrew and Ethan.'

She was keeping her voice very low.

'Are you able to get into his files?' I said.

I could barely hear her when she next spoke.

'No,' she said.

'No, you can't, or no, you won't?'

'No, I can't,' she said, still whispering. 'His hard drive is gone.'

56

I put my phone on my desk between Hawk and me and put it on speaker.

'Somebody removed the hard drive from Darius's desktop,' I said to Claire Megill.

'Yes,' she said.

'Who could have done that?'

'A lot of people here,' she said, 'as long as they knew what they were doing, and made sure not to get caught.'

She had walked back into her office, she said, and shut the door. She said it had been the first time she had been able to sit at Darius's desk since his death.

'Isn't there a way to get into whatever he stored on the cloud there?' I said.

175

'How much do you know about how the cloud actually works?' she asked.

I saw Hawk roll his eyes.

'Could you start me off with an easier question?' I said.

'The company doesn't allow the use of a personal cloud for company business,' she said. 'Ethan thinks information like that is too easy to pirate. So without going all techy on you, any Lith-related business is only backed up here, on a personal cloud for each individual station, all encrypted individually. To access your own stuff, you even have to use your own fingerprint. Like your actual fingerprint.'

'So Darius could have had personal stuff on that hard drive, as well as work stuff.'

'It works the same way for Andrew, and Ethan, and Clay and me and everybody else in upper management.' She paused. 'And their assistants.'

'Are there any cameras inside the office?'

'No,' she said. 'As much of a bear as Ethan is for privacy, Andrew won't allow it. The whole "Big Brother is watching" thing. But again: Anybody on either the forty-ninth or fiftieth floor who knew what they were doing could have removed the hard drive, most likely after-hours. They'd just have had to pick a time when no one else was around.'

'Is it possible to check who might have used their key card or whatever to be around after-hours?' I said.

'An awful lot of people here stay at the office into the night. We're kind of the *home* office for worker bees. Like they're all hoping Andrew or Ethan will walk past their desks and see them still at them.'

'So somebody knew that Darius knew something he wasn't supposed to,' I said. 'Nothing else makes sense.'

'And it got him killed?' she asked.

'Put it this way, Claire,' I said. 'It didn't do very much to keep him alive.'

I told her that I would call her later, and that Vinnie would be there when he said he'd be there, because he always did what he said he was going to do. Another part of the code.

I reached over and ended the call.

'All right, all right, all right,' Hawk said, lapsing into a Texas drawl now.

'Matthew McConaughey?' I said.

'Got more game than even you know,' he said, 'accentwise.'

He grabbed his gym bag. My workout clothes were in my locker. Hawk liked to wear something different every time he worked out, the vain bastard.

'Okay,' I said. 'Was it sex or money that got him killed? Or got both of them killed?'

'You asking me?'

'I saw an opportunity to tap into your superior intellect,' I said.

'How come I always got to be the one to figure this shit out?' he said.

'I think of it as the black man's burden,' I said.

'Just one more thing to add to the damn list,' Hawk said.

57

Hawk went to Harbor Health without me, as much as I need to work out. I told him there were some calls I needed to make.

'To who?'

'Whom.'

He gave me the finger.

'I've put together a list of the committees and boards Laura Crain served on in Boston,' I said. 'It occurred to me that I know more about the friends she had in college than I do about the friends she might have had when she died, at least apart from Susan.'

'And you can't ask her husband 'bout that, on account of he might beat you up again,' Hawk said.

Then I gave him the finger.

'Yeah,' he said. 'I is still number one.'

Belson showed up about fifteen minutes later, coming into the office without knocking. He did not look pleased to see me, but then rarely did.

'I keep forgetting to ask how Captain Glass is doing,' I said. 'She recover okay from COVID?'

'Almost,' he said. 'When she does, turns out she'll be fully recovered working at Sex Crimes.'

'That will probably please Lee Farrell to no end.'

Farrell had been transferred to Sex Crimes.

'Glass pissed off Quirk once too often, mostly by acting as if she invented everything except the wording to Miranda.'

'You should look happier.'

'This *is* happy,' he said, and sat down, and then said, 'So you and Black Adam lied your way into Baker's apartment.'

'Look at you with your pop culture references,' I said.

'Eat me.'

'You want coffee? I just made a fresh pot.'

'No,' he said. 'Hawk said he was the dead guy's brother?'

'From another mother. Or maybe father. I can't actually recall.'

'That super, Ramon? He isn't the sharpest knife in the refrigerator,' Belson said.

'But extremely accommodating in light of Hawk's family tragedy,' I said.

'You two find anything we didn't?'

'No,' I said.

'You lying?'

'Why in the world would you assume that?'

'Why wouldn't I?'

'But I did find out something useful a few minutes ago,' I said. 'Somebody took the hard drive from Darius Baker's desktop at work.'

I fumbled my way through explaining how the computer system at Lith worked, including the part about thumbprints.

'There's ways to get around that. I'd tell you how, but I'd have to kill you, which, by the way, is something I consider from time to time.'

I got up and fixed myself another cup of coffee. I'd lost track of how many I'd had today. But this was it. If I didn't stop now, I was going to run to Susan's when it was time to pick her up for dinner.

'I am told,' I said when I was back behind my desk, 'that our friends at Lith were less than welcoming when you asked for access to Baker's desktop.'

'Expectation of privacy,' he said. 'Even for the deceased.'

'Even with a warrant?'

'The lawyer over there, some guy named Whitson, told me what I could do with my warrant when I tried to brace him.'

'I've run into Whitson a few times,' I said.

'Guy's not exactly a charm offensive.'

'Just offensive, mostly.'

Belson said he'd take that cup of coffee after all. 'You got any donuts stashed in the fridge?'

'Black Adam and me ate them all before you arrived.'

When I handed him his mug Belson said, 'So this Baker got himself into something.'

'Sounds like it.'

'The merger?'

'Maybe,' I said. 'Or maybe he got involved with company secrets that had nothing to do with the merger and got caught and got killed because of it.'

'Buying or selling?'

'Be nice to know.'

'Be nice to have his hard drive,' Belson said. 'Or his personal info.'

'But we don't.'

I considered telling him about Laura's note, but did not. I knew I would at some point. Just not yet. Our relationship had always been transactional, one form or another, case by case, even when we were chasing the same outcome, including justice, as lofty as that sounded. Our roles had remained essentially the same, in all the years we'd known each other, Belson the good cop and me, despite my best intentions, still the bad one.

He put cop eyes on me now, as if able in the moment to read my mind.

'Have you heard anything about Laura Crain having any kind of relationship outside that storybook marriage of hers?' he asked. 'I know she was Susan's friend. But I got to ask.'

I made sure to keep my eyes on him, mindful, as always, about how little he missed. And saw things that other people did not.

'I had this same conversation with Susan,' I said. 'When we did, I told her that Laura didn't seem the type for an extramarital affair. And my better half pointed out to me that there is no type.'

'She's a lot more than just half,' Belson said.

I heard a phone buzz. His, not mine. He ignored it.

'Quirk told me he paid a visit here himself the other day,' he said, 'to tell you the bosses are up his ass on this. Which, as you know, puts him up mine. You see that, right?'

'Well, Frank, I'm not gonna lie, that's an image I'd actually like to unsee.'

'My point being,' he continued, 'that if you screw around on this, like you do, you have a chance to screw Quirk and me at the same time. Understood?'

'Understood.'

'Why'd Crain take a swing at you on Clarendon Street this morning?'

'You heard about that?'

'You'd be amazed the shit I stumble into.'

'I basically asked him what you just asked me about his wife perhaps having an affair.'

He rubbed a growth of beard around his chin that seemed even darker and heavier than normal.

'That all of it?'

'For now,' I said.

He stood.

'I'm going to put this to you another way,' he said. 'You hold back information that could help us roll this thing up quicker, you might finally cross a line with both of us.'

I started to say something back to him, but he pointed a finger as a way of stopping me.

'Don't say something smart, smart guy.'

I didn't.

I poured my coffee down the sink, and rinsed the mug, and put it back on its shelf, and then sat in the empty office and wondered, being such a smart guy, if I even knew where the line was anymore.

58

It took some doing, and experiencing enough rejections on the phone that I started to feel like a telemarketer, but Amanda Levinson, who had served on the board of the Dana-Farber Cancer Institute with Laura Crain, agreed to meet for lunch near her home in Wellesley.

'Are you fond of Middle Eastern food?' she said after she'd returned my call, responding to the lengthy voice message I'd left for her about Laura.

'The answer would have been in the affirmative if you'd asked me about being fond of almost any kind of food,' I said.

'Café Mangal,' she said, and gave me the address on Washington Street.

She was, I guessed, at the high end of her forties, bordering on being too thin but not quite there, at least not yet, hair dyed a subdued auburn with streaks in it, nice smile, face relatively unlined, perhaps even without chemical or surgical assistance. She wore a black turtleneck that covered a long neck and hardly any jewelry. She was not wearing a wedding ring.

She'd ordered some kind of salad with figs. I'd gone big, electing to go with what was listed as a Yengen sandwich featuring Turkish pepperoni. The larger tables were in the middle of a long dining room. We sat at a smaller one, for two, along one of the walls.

'So Laura hired a private investigator,' she said while we waited for our food, having just been served our iced teas.

'She was concerned about Andrew,' I said.

'And for quite some time,' Amanda Levinson said. 'I'd suggested therapy, for him or for both of them. I'm a big believer in therapy, especially since my divorce.'

'The girl of my dreams is a therapist,' I said.

'So you're married?' she said.

'Not exactly.'

'I know the feeling,' she said, and smiled. 'I just had to ask. But I do that more and more these days when I meet an attractive man.'

I let that go by.

'We're very much together,' I said. 'For a very long time. We just don't choose to live together.'

She playfully slapped her forehead. 'Why didn't I think of that?' she said.

I had read enough about her to know that she had been married to a hedge-funder named Steve Levinson, the name of his company one I didn't recognise, just because there was no earthly reason why I would have.

Amanda waved at a blonde woman seated with another blonde woman in the opposite corner of the room. 'Oh, goody,' she said. 'I hope Jenny and Millicent think you're my lunch date.'

She offered a half-hearted wave and a fake smile to someone behind me, whispered, 'Hello, bitch,' then turned back to me and said, 'So what can I do for you, Mr Spenser?'

'I didn't know Laura for very long, or very well,' I said. 'But now her husband not only doesn't want to talk to me about her, he took a swing at me the other day when I attempted to do that in front of his building.'

'Wait,' she said. 'Andrew *Crain* took a swing at you?'

'I'd say he punched like a girl,' I said, 'but I make it a policy never to insult women of any age.'

'He used to be a lot more fun,' she said, 'in his nerdy way. But that was before he got so weird.'

'I know why Laura was concerned about him,' I said. 'But what was she like in the time leading up to her death? Was there anything that you found concerning about her behavior? That made you worry about her?'

'I've been thinking a lot about my friend Laura, as you might imagine,' she said. She frowned now, producing very few wrinkles in her forehead. Maybe there had been some help with the unlined thing. 'You know the expression about a person being an open book? That was never Laura, even though she really was my friend. She had never shared much about her life before Andrew, no matter how hard I pried, and I can be so good at prying I should be the private detective.'

She smiled at me. 'You don't need a partner, do you?'

'The hours are lousy and the pay is worse,' I said.

'Well,' she said, 'if you ever change your mind, keep *me* in mind.'

'Back to Laura,' I said. 'Did you get the sense that she might have been dealing with some kind of crisis that didn't involve her husband?'

'What kind?'

'Perhaps a relationship with someone other than her husband?'

I wasn't sure what kind of reaction I'd expected, shock or surprise. Or even Amanda Levinson being offended on behalf of her dead friend. But my question elicited none of the above.

'Funny you should ask that,' she said. 'I'm much more aware of the signs of that than I used to be, mostly because my ex couldn't manage to keep it in his pants, especially toward the end of our marriage. And perhaps well before that.' She sighed. 'I didn't get the sense that Laura was having an affair, or ever would. But I increasingly got the sense that she thought Andrew might be.'

She shrugged.

'He's a nerd,' Amanda Levinson said. 'But a very, very rich one. You may have noticed with other rich geeks. It makes women ignore certain of their shortcomings.'

The waiter showed up with our food then. Café Mangal had gotten far more crowded in the past five or ten minutes, the noise level in the low-ceilinged room rising accordingly.

'So him, not her?'

She nodded. 'She told me about a month ago, or thereabouts, that he was spending what she considered even a more disproportionate time than usual with his assistant.'

'Claire Megill,' I said.

'The one and only,' she said. 'The sainted Claire.'

'Would that be your description of her, or Laura's?'

'Oh, Laura's,' she said. 'She said that she was convinced Andrew was more invested, I guess that's the word, in Claire's well-being than his own wife's.'

I couldn't hold out any longer and took a bite of my sandwich.

'Did Laura think the two of them really were having an affair?'

'She never came right out and said that. But my general sense, just from some of her comments, was that at the very least she thought Andrew and Claire were the ones with the better marriage, whether they were sleeping together or not.'

'So she did manage to open up to you about that,' I said.

'She finally trusted me enough to do that, at least on this particular subject,' she said.

'But I was under the impression that Claire had been seeing someone at Lith,' I said.

'Maybe that triggered a form of jealousy in Andrew, and contributed to the weirdness. But if you're right about that, why wouldn't Andrew just fire this Lith person?'

'I've asked the same question,' I said. 'Maybe because he would have had to fire Claire, too.'

'A tangled web,' she said. 'You're probably good at unraveling those.'

'Used to be,' I said.

She said, 'Would you mind terribly if I ordered a glass of wine?'

I told her to have at it, not wanting to do anything to slow her roll.

'One other thing I should mention,' she said, after she'd had her first taste of wine. 'Laura vaguely said something once about having a friend looking out for her interests.'

'Did *she* mention who that might have been?'

'No,' she said. 'Wait. She never talked about any of this with you?'

'She wasn't an open book with me, either.'

'I can't imagine why,' she said. She was smiling again. 'You're very easy to talk to.'

'They teach it at detective school,' I said. 'Right after the course on prying.'

We ate in silence for a couple minutes. I was more enthusiastic about it than she was. The sandwich was very good. But I rarely encountered a bad one.

'So you didn't get the idea that the friend Laura spoke about was someone with whom she was involved romantically?'

'She wanted to make her marriage work,' Amanda said. 'As vague as she was about her past, she'd told me more than once about the bad choices she'd made with men before Andrew.'

She finished her wine. 'And then she died.'

I had nothing to add to that. My sandwich was gone, even though she had barely made a dent in her salad. I waved for the check. She said no, this was her treat. I told her to think of this as being on Laura, as she had helped me today more than she knew.

'We aim to please,' she said, in a voice I thought had suddenly become huskier.

I'll bet, I thought.

'If you have any more questions, feel free to call anytime,' she said.

I told her I would do that.

On my way past Jenny and Millicent's table, I winked at them.

59

I went back to my office and saw that I had left my legal pad on top of my desk, with my scribblings about all the players on it, one name on the first page in bigger letters, and circled a couple times:

ROB

Who never left the stage completely, even if I imagined him just standing in the wings sometimes.

The bar at which he had worked was gone. The owner of the bar where he'd worked was dead. According to what Missy Jones had told me, Rob had left town at some point after she and one of Gino's boys had paid him that visit, never to return.

Or so she had hoped.

Missy Jones didn't have a last name. Nobody seemed to have a last name, not her, not Angie Calabria, not Professor Paul Dockery. Maybe Rob wasn't even his real name. Maybe he had changed his name. Maybe he *had* left town.

Or not.

If not, maybe only Laura had known.

Or maybe, and more likely, it was time for me to move on from him once and for all, and focus on two dead bodies, connected to each other by Lith, and by a note I had found in Darius Baker's pocket, linking him to Laura Crain.

According to Susan, though, I'd always had separation issues in matters like this. She actually called it the dog-with-a-bone syndrome, which I was sure she hadn't been taught at Harvard.

My phone was on the desk next to the legal pad. I reached for it and called Ethan Lowe and asked if he might happen to recall the last name of the guy Laura had dated her last year at Harvard.

'You could have stumped me if you'd asked me for his first name,' Lowe said.

'Is there any way you could ask your partner?'

'And tell him what, that I'm asking for a friend?' Lowe said. 'How do you think that would go over considering how things went the last time the two of you were together?'

There was a pause.

'Why does it matter, anyway?'

'Not entirely sure that it does, unless he came back into Laura's life and nobody knew it except her,' I said.

'If I see an opportunity to casually ask him, say, what was that asshole's name, I will,' Lowe said. 'But I can't make any promises.'

'I'm rumbling and stumbling here,' I said.

'Hey,' Lowe said, 'everybody's got to be good at something,' before quickly adding, 'Just kidding.'

He didn't sound as if he were kidding.

I next called Richie Burke and asked if he'd found out anything more about Marino's.

'There was a guy,' he said, 'who went from Marino's to the Five Horses Tavern, over on Columbus. Know it?'

'I know just about all of them,' I said. 'Does he remember the guy I'm trying to locate?'

'He might've if he hadn't gotten shot at another bar in Somerville a few months ago,' Richie said.

'Shot dead?'

'Quite.'

I stayed at the office for the rest of the afternoon and accomplished little. Susan and Pearl were coming to the apartment later before Susan and I went for a late dinner at Piccolo Nido in

187

the North End. It was my favorite Italian restaurant in the whole city and Susan's, too. We used to see Larry Lucchino in there sometimes when he was president of the Red Sox. Susan knew him slightly from her work for the Jimmy Fund. I was certain Larry would have never traded Mookie.

When I got back to the apartment I remembered that I'd meant to call Detective Lee Farrell, now of Sex Crimes, and ask him what he'd do if he were trying to find someone whose last name he didn't know and who had left town without a trace twenty years earlier.

So I called and asked him now.

'Is this some kind of trick question?' he said.

'What would you do if you had that little to go on, from that long ago?'

'Let me think on it.'

'By the way,' I said, 'should I congratulate you on Captain Glass coming to work at your shop?'

'Did you really call to ask for help or just to bust my balls?'

'What, I can't do both?'

'I happen to be in the middle of something,' he said. 'Can this wait until breakfast tomorrow?'

I said it could.

'Before you go, let me ask you something else,' I said. 'Do you think rumbling and stumbling is one of my strong suits?'

'Maybe your strongest,' he said, and then said he'd meet me at the Newbury at eight tomorrow and that he had no intention of buying, he wanted that off the table right now.

I sat on the couch in my living room and pondered whether or not the only structure I had in my life these days was going from restaurant to restaurant, meal to meal. But then concluded that any kind of structure, or semblance of order, was better than none.

Susan called and said she was running late, then told me that she had pushed our reservation to nine o'clock.

'If you can wait and not be tired by waiting,' I said.

'Wait,' she said.

'I see what you did.'

'No,' she said, 'I meant wait, because I happen to know what the next line is, I've heard you use it before.'

'Hit me,' I said.

'Or being lied about, don't deal in lies,' she said.

'Wow,' I said.

'That's what I'm talking about,' she said triumphantly.

'Marry me,' I said.

'No,' she said.

I iced my knee while watching Maria Stephanos read the news on Channel 5, telling myself as always that Maria was speaking directly to me and, further, was ready to leave her family for me if Susan ever dumped me. I had mentioned having these thoughts about Maria to Susan once and she said, 'You just keep thinkin', Butch. That's what you're good at.'

I ate some cheese and crackers after my shower and drank a Boomsauce and began the cruel wait until our reservation, and remembered what it was like when we were in Paris and Susan insisted that we eat at nine every night the way the goddamn French did. Sometimes later than nine.

I had switched from the news to *SportsCenter* on ESPN when Vinnie called.

'She just buzzed in a visitor,' he said.

He was outside Claire Megill's building, about to turn the watch over to one of his young Vinnies for the overnight shift.

'I'm going to assume it's not DoorDash,' I said.

By now Belson had informed me that the Boston Police Department would no longer have a car outside the building, there was no point, I had Vinnie.

'It's a guy from one of the pictures you sent me you said I should call about if the guy ever showed up,' Vinnie said.

'Don't tell me,' I said, 'it's Whitson, the lawyer. The one who looks like a bouncer squeezed into a suit.'

'Nope.'

'Are you going to make me guess?'

'The boss.'

'Crain?'

'The other,' Vinnie said.

60

I told Vinnie to have the other Vinnie call me when Ethan Lowe left the building.

'His name is Ronnie, for fuck's sake, how many times do I have to tell you?' Vinnie said.

'I'm terribly sorry,' I said. 'Have Rocky call me.'

'You ain't that funny.'

'Am so.'

There was no call while Susan and I dined at Piccolo Nido, nor when we were on our way back to Marlborough Street. My phone was with me when I walked Pearl down Commonwealth and back until she performed her nightly duties.

When we were back inside the apartment, Susan said, 'I know you might be expecting a call. But would you mind terribly shutting off your phone while I jump your bones?'

She smiled one of her wicked smiles. 'I have these urges.'

'And the world is a better place for them,' I said.

Afterward, once my breathing had returned to normal, I turned the phone back on and saw there was no call from Ronnie, nor would there be one during the night.

Claire Megill knew that either Vinnie or someone working for Vinnie was watching over her, so it wasn't as if she and Lowe were sneaking around, he'd walked right through the front door for what would have been an innocent visit, except for the fact that he had stayed the night.

She'd had more than one opportunity, especially when I'd asked her about Clay Whitson, to tell me that she was in a relationship with one of the owners of the company, if that was in fact what was going on, even if it turned out not to be the owner with whom Laura Crain had suspected her of having one.

I explained all of this to Susan before she headed off to Cambridge in the morning, having rebuffed my last-ditch effort to elicit more urges out of her.

'Maybe the problems of these two little people don't amount to a hill of beans in this crazy world,' I said.

'I've asked you to please not do Bogie,' she said. 'And for your information, the line is "three little people."'

Once Susan was gone, I checked with Ronnie.

'Still in there?' I said.

'Sure.'

He also pronounced it *shoo-wah*, same as Vinnie.

'I'm on my way,' I said, telling him not to leave until I got there.

Ronnie was in an Audi. I waved at him as I came around from the Colonnade and he pulled away. So I was the one standing in front of Claire's building when Lowe came out the front door, one whose glass, I saw, had already been replaced.

No car waiting for him, no driver.

Just me.

He stopped a few feet outside the door when he saw me standing at the end of the walk.

'Aren't you worried about doing the walk of shame at the office?'

'This isn't what it looks like.'

'Are you sure?' I said. 'Because it sure looks like a sleepover to me.'

'It is, but not the way you think.'

'You and Claire?' I said. 'I gotta say, Ethan, I did *not* see that coming.'

'Repeat,' he said. 'Not what it looks like, not what you think.'

'Enlighten me, then.'

'Walk with me,' he said.

'Okay,' I said, 'but I hope people at the office aren't going to think I'm the one you spent the night with when they see you in the same clothes you wore yesterday.'

'Could you please cut the shit?'

'You first,' I said. 'Shouldn't Reggie be with you, or one of his guys?'

'I came here alone,' he said.

'I thought you were the one always looking over his shoulder,' I said.

'Trying to quit.'

'Even though two people connected to your company are dead.'

'I've decided I can't live my best life thinking I might be next.'

'Claire's afraid she might be next,' I said. 'It's why I've put some people on her.'

'I know,' he said. 'And she has a right to feel that way and you have a right to protect her. I have my people when I need them, as you know.'

We were walking up Huntington by then, on our way toward Copley Plaza.

'Claire and I aren't having an affair.'

'If you say so.'

'I wouldn't put her in that position, and I wouldn't do it to Andrew, knowing how close the two of them are,' he said. 'I just needed to talk to her away from the office, and once we started talking we got into the wine pretty good. And before I knew it, she was offering to let me sleep on her couch and I accepted.'

'Must have been a lot of wine.'

'It was, trust me. I haven't felt this hungover in a long time.'

I figured it was about a fifteen-minute walk to the Hancock. We were already halfway there, but as Lowe was walking at hangover speed, we might not arrive until lunchtime.

'What did you need to talk to her about?' I said.

'We were talking about the merger, what else?' he said. 'I should have had Andrew locked down on this long ago. I still don't. I thought Laura could help me, but she was even more opposed to it than he once was. But now Laura is gone, and I know how much he leans on Claire, maybe now more than ever. So I went there to ask for her help in bringing him around before it's too late, for all of us.'

'You're just trying to enlist her now?'

He had picked up his pace just slightly by the time we got to Stuart.

'I've tried this approach before,' he said. 'But not to the extent that I did last night. This time I offered her a substantial raise, and I do mean substantial, if she could do a better job lobbying Andrew than I have to this point.'

'Is she willing to do that?'

Lowe shook his head. 'She told me that what I was offering was too big to be a gift and too small to be a bribe. So then I offered to give her a small piece of the merger, as even more of a sweetener.'

'You really must have been drunk.'

'The money would be a drop in the bucket in the whole grand scheme of things.'

'Did she accept?'

'She did not. She told me that her loyalty was, and always will be, to Andrew. He'd given her and her son a future, and a life after her husband left them.'

'Hard not to respect that,' I said.

We were at Clarendon now, the Hancock dead ahead.

'I begged her one last time before we called it a night to reconsider, that she wouldn't just be saving the company, but Andrew at the same time. Because if we lose the company, if *he* loses the company so soon after Laura, I'm not sure what's going to happen to him.'

'"Lose the company" sounds a bit over-the-top.'

'There's a lot of plates spinning, Mr Spenser. I'll just leave it at that.'

Lowe turned to face me. His pallor was still gray, his eyes bloodshot. I didn't know how much sleep he'd gotten on Claire's couch. But it clearly hadn't been enough.

'This company is the only child either one of us has ever had,' Lowe said. 'What would you do if you were faced with losing the thing in the world that mattered the most to you?'

'Fight like hell,' I said.

'That's all I'm doing here,' he said. 'I just want my partner to fight with me, one last time.'

Then he said, 'Have a good day,' in front of the Hancock.

It didn't sound as if his heart was really in it. The part about me having a good day. But at least he hadn't taken a swing at me.

So there was that.

61

When I had walked over to my office, I called Lee Farrell and told him that we would have to reschedule breakfast, something had come up.

'We gay men are used to dealing with this sort of heartbreak,' he said.

'Better than straight guys?'

'My experience is that we just do the heartbreak way better.'

My friend Marty Kaiser was already on his way to my office. Marty described himself as being the world's greatest accountant. When I'd called him, I'd asked if he was still the greatest.

'Of all time,' he said.

'Modest much?' I said.

'I have so little reason,' Marty said.

He looked as he had always looked, just with more gray in black hair still worn long. He still carried a pigskin attaché case, still wore white shirts with Windsor collars and silk ties, a blood-red one today that matched his pocket square, everything set off nicely against a black pin-striped suit.

'Dress-down day?' I said.

'I continue to dress for success,' he said. 'You might think about it one of these days.'

I was wearing a black T-shirt, jeans, and some old Merrell hiking shoes that I felt were being kinder to my knee lately than regular sneakers.

'What's wrong with my outfit?' I said.

'Nothing,' he said, 'if you're on your way to bouncer school.'

I made us both coffee. He drank some of his and put his mug down on my desk and crossed his legs, smoothing out the crease on the top leg as he did. Unless he'd changed his buying habits, I knew that the wingtips he was wearing came from Tricker's of Jermyn Street, the shirt from Turnbull & Asser.

'So how can the world's greatest accountant be of assistance?' he said.

I told him about my relationship with Laura Crain and my brief interaction with Darius Baker, and my various adventures and misadventures with Andrew Crain and Ethan Lowe and Reggie Smythe and the two men who had jumped me at the sanctuary and another man who had shot at me.

'How closely do you follow Lith?' I said.

'Fairly closely, as a matter of fact,' he said. 'I think of them as one of our hometown teams, and have always wanted them to succeed for that reason alone.'

'Okay, then,' I said. 'I'm going to ask you some money questions, and feel free to treat me like an idiot.'

'You told me once that as long as I did that with you I would never be disappointed,' Marty said. 'And I never have been.'

'What is the most fundamental difference between a privately owned company and a public one?' I said. 'Start there.'

'Well, the most obvious one is the most fundamental one,' he said. 'A privately held company doesn't trade on the stock exchange, and doesn't have to disclose financial information to the public.'

'So it would be easier for market analysts, say, to value a public company as opposed to a private one.'

'Much,' Marty said.

'But you can obviously track how a private company is doing, correct?'

He nodded. 'There are several ways,' he said. 'Comparable company analysis is one. Capital market transactions is another, and discounted cash flow, provided you could get the data. There's a longer list than that.' He grinned and raised bushy Groucho black eyebrows. 'Am I going too fast?'

'Much,' I said.

Marty said, 'We could continue with this tutorial, and I could continue to show off, or you could ask me what you got me over here to ask me.' He drank more coffee. 'I can't even remember the last time you enlisted my services.'

I could. I had forced a white-collar criminal named Bob Cooper to open the books of a private company called Kinergy, which only people on the inside knew had become a house of cards in an almost Madoffian way. When Marty had gone through the books, he had discovered that the accounting there was more fun than a theme park.

I reminded him of those heady times. 'Some of my best work,' he said. 'Thanks for reminding me.' He whistled. 'And those *pishers* nearly got away with it. And murder, as I recall.'

I asked him if he'd heard about the prospective merger between Lith and the Canadian electric-car company. Marty said it wasn't as if anybody were keeping it a secret, even though he hadn't read much about it lately.

'Ethan Lowe has indicated that they badly need the merger to go through,' I said. 'Why would that possibly be?'

Marty nodded. 'If it is,' he said, 'it's probably because of Aahil.'

He spelled it out for me.

'It nearly turned into a hill to die on for our friends at Lith,' he said.

Marty explained that it had all gone down right before COVID, and much of what he was about to tell me was thirdhand and largely anecdotal. But what he'd heard, from sources he considered to be good ones, was that Lowe had thrown a lot of Lith money behind a proposed golf and gambling resort empire called Aahil.

'Paradise in the desert, that was the theme,' Marty said. 'Qatar, Abu Dhabi, Dubai, Riyadh. If I'm not mistaken, I believe the bulk of the money came from Qatar. They were going crazy for sports at the time because they'd gotten the World Cup. As that man used to say, it was all going to be huuuuuuge. But then along came the pandemic and the world closed down, and all of a sudden the rich guys that Lowe was partnering with decided they didn't want to play in that particular sandbox, literally and figuratively – 2019, 2020, in there. Long story short? Lowe, who I know to be a very savvy guy, got caught holding the bag. Or with his pants down. You pick. But he ended up highly leveraged, with no equity cushion.'

'I know that he and Crain were diversifying at that point,' I said. 'So Lowe must have thought it was a sure thing.'

'But when it turned out to not be a sure thing, Lowe ended up in the worst place you can be, whether you think you're too big to fail or not.'

'Which is where?'

'The place where the debt is due, and to guys who don't deal well with disappointment.'

'Was this widely known at the time?'

'Let us go back to the beginning of our conversation, my friend,' Marty Kaiser said. 'They're not on the market. But again, just going off what I heard from people who would know better than me, Lowe suddenly found himself in a position where the world he and Crain had built for themselves wasn't nearly as battery-powered as it once had been, put it that way. It needed a boost.'

'Meaning he needed cash.'

'Lots.'

'But he's still here and Lith is still here, which means he found a way to get it,' I said.

'And Lith is once again a business that the car people want to do business *with*,' Marty said. 'And because the world's greatest accountant keeps his ear to the ground when money is about to change hands, what I am hearing is that Lowe might be looking to cash out once this deal goes through.'

'But not Crain?'

Marty shook his head. 'Not sure about Crain. Just Lowe. I think what happened in the Middle East made him feel as if his balls were in a lockbox somewhere, and he might be ready to go off and count the money he already has before things go *plotz* the next time, as we say in the faith.'

'So does he want this merger more, or need it?'

'Maybe both,' Marty said.

He stood then, checked himself for wrinkles or lint or both, picked up his ancient attaché case, the kind you don't see much of anymore. But then you don't see a lot of accountants who were larger-than-life characters the way Marty Kaiser was.

'There's one more thing I heard,' he said. 'It's that the electric-car people from Canada aren't just looking to merge with Lith. They're looking to *acquire* it.'

'Be interesting to know if that's true,' I said. 'And how Lowe managed to save their collective asses along the way, starting with his own.'

'Not my department,' Marty said. 'You're the one who's supposed to be the world's greatest detective.'

62

Ethan Lowe didn't return my calls the rest of the day. Maybe we hadn't done as much male bonding as I thought we had. But when we did next speak, whenever that was, I wanted to hear from him, at least in general terms, about what Marty Kaiser had heard.

I called Hawk then and told him this case really was starting to make my head hurt something awful, and he said what did I mean *starting* to make it hurt? So we decided to meet at Parker's Bar at the Omni Parker House and do the only sensible thing and discuss it over a drink. Or perhaps drinks, plural, as the case might be. Which was almost always the case for Hawk and me.

I stopped at the apartment and put on a blue shirt and blazer and loafers. When I got to the bar I saw that Hawk wore a double-breasted charcoal blazer and black jeans and a white shirt.

'You didn't have to clean up for me,' I said.

'Got a dinner date,' he said.

'Do I know her?'

'No.'

'Might I ever?'

'Too early to tell.'

We both ordered martinis. I told him about Marty and what he knew and what I now wanted to know from, and about, Ethan Lowe.

'Maybe you just ought to hold your little friend up and shake him till he tells you what you want to know, and stop fucking around,' Hawk said. 'Because it sure sounds to me as if he knows a lot more than he's told you so far. And you don't know how much he *has* told you is true.'

'I don't think we're there quite yet,' I said. 'The shaking part.'

'You sure?'

Our drinks were delivered, in martini glasses that looked bigger than normal, which nearly made my heart skip a beat. We had both gone with lemon peels this time around. The vodka was as cold as vodka in a martini was supposed to be, tiny beads of ice still visible on the outside of the glasses.

I drank and Hawk drank.

'God*damn*,' Hawk said. 'Something this good could make a man change his religious persuasion.'

'You don't have a religious persuasion.'

'If I did,' he said.

'Where were we?' I said.

Hawk smiled and took another sip of his drink and said, 'Who gives a shit?'

There had been a time when the Parker House had been one of the best hotels in Boston. Then came the Four Seasons and Ritz, the new one on Avery Street, and Mandarin, and the hotels that had sprung up at the Seaport. But the Omni people had come along to fix up the old girl, including the bar. The gilded entrance outside, though, looked the same to me as it always had, just with *Omni* now written above the front doors underneath the green awnings adorning the windows of the second floor.

'Ask you something?' Hawk said.

'Anything,' I said. 'I am in a very happy place right now.'

'Who you trust over there at Lith for real?' he said.

Normally he would have finished his first martini by now. But he appeared to be pacing himself. I would've thought that he might be wanting to present his *best* self to his date, whomever she was, except that Hawk had only one self.

'At this point,' I said, 'I'm not sure I'd trust the receptionist.'

'You can't trust either of the damn owners for shit,' Hawk said. 'You can't trust the lawyer.'

'Not as far as I could throw him.'

'Not even off a balcony.'

'Wow,' I said.

Hawk shrugged. 'Too soon?'

'Little bit.'

'What about Claire Megill?'

'What about her?'

'You trust her to be, ah, forthcoming?'

'Yeah,' I said. 'But maybe only to a point.'

'What point would that be?'

'The one where she'd be afraid of compromising her boss.'

'The boss Crain.'

'Uh-huh.'

'So they could all be lying they asses off to you.' He grinned.

'We going somewhere with this?' I said.

'Seems to me the best you can hope for right now is figure out who's lying to you the least,' he said. 'And decide if somebody over there really might think this merger is worth killing over.'

My martini was less cold than it had been, but still delicious. I drank more of it.

'What time you got?' Hawk said.

I told him.

'Gots to go,' he said.

'I still don't know what happened to Laura Crain's old boyfriend.'

Hawk said, 'I'm working on that, matter of fact.'

'Now you tell me?'

'Not there yet.'

'By the way? I'd still *like* to know who sent those two stooges after me.'

'And who tried to shoot you up, don't forget that.'

'Marty Kaiser called me the world's greatest detective.'

'Easy for him to say,' Hawk said.

I told him I'd pick up the check, and to have a good time.

He smiled again. 'Hope it's as good as the one she's gonna have,' he said. 'If such a thing even be possible.'

I paid the check and sadly finished my martini. I took my time walking home. When I got there I fried some onions. Then I cooked up a burger in the air fryer Susan had given me last Christmas after convincing me that using it wasn't a form of cheating.

The literature with the fryer had promised burgers both tender and juicy and so far had delivered every time.

And did tonight.

I then set up a tray and forced myself to watch the Red Sox game, telling myself that it was all going to be over soon. They were losing to the Orioles in the fifth when I called Missy Jones in Seattle.

'You better be calling to tell me that you or somebody else caught Laura's killer,' she said.

I could once again hear a television in the background, this time with the sound of baseball announcers, excitement in their voices about something in the game they were broadcasting.

'Is that the Mariners I hear?' I said.

'It is,' she said. 'And even though I know you didn't call to talk baseball with me, I might point out that my team is better than your team this season.'

'Hold on,' I said. 'You're from here. How come my team isn't still your team?'

'Not after those clowns traded Mookie,' she said.

'Got a question about Laura,' I said.

'I didn't think you were calling to talk baseball,' she said.

'Is there any chance that Rob might not have left town when you thought he had?' I said.

There was a long pause at her end and then I heard the ballgame noise disappear.

'In a relationship like the one that they had, there's a form of madness that takes over, on both sides. It's why abused women stay in them long after they should have run for the hills, and even end up defending their accusers. So maybe it was a form of madness for her to still keep secrets from me about this guy after I tried to save her from him.'

'So it wasn't verifiable for you that Rob left Boston after Gino's guy gave him that beating,' I said.

'No,' she said. 'It was not.'

'You just made the assumption that he beat it, after catching that kind of beating from your guy and not going back to work.'

'Technically Gino's guy. But yes.'

'So we don't know if he stayed or came back,' I said. 'And might never.'

'Sounds like a Spenser problem to me.'

'Damn it,' I said. 'I was afraid of that. Here's maybe the best question of all. How the hell did Laura end up with a guy like this prick in the first place?'

'There's something about bad boys, what can I tell you,' she said. 'Always has been, always will be. Even for good girls.'

'Are you speaking from experience?'

'Whoever said I was a good girl?' Missy Jones said.

63

September turned into October in Boston. The leaves began to change and the baseball playoffs began without the Red Sox, and without me. And Lee Farrell called one morning to tell me he had some information on Joe Marino's bar.

'It seems Joe was averse to paying his taxes,' Lee said.

'Isn't our government averse to a practice like that?'

'Very much so,' Lee said. 'I'm now thinking that if a heart attack hadn't gotten Joe, the Feds would have.'

'So nobody with a name like Rob on the books?'

'Are you listening to me?' Lee said. 'There weren't any books! I think Marino's was like some cozy little Mob hideaway. I asked a couple vets from Organised Crime Control, and they told me that the joint had a relatively young clientele. College kids who wanted to take a little walk on the wild side. They also told me at OCC that Joe might have had some of the boys behind the bar dealing some drugs. Coke, grass, like that. Nothing major.'

'Thanks for trying,' I said.

'You know what they say. No medals for trying.'

'Well, there should be,' I said.

'Speaking from personal experience?'

'Very much so,' I said.

I no longer needed Vinnie Morris to watch Claire, because she had flown to California on business with Andrew Crain a few days earlier, telling me before they left she wasn't sure when they'd be back. At least they knew where they were going.

That night I had cooked risotto with seafood for Susan and me at her place, having picked up shrimp and mussels and scallops and oysters from the New Deal Fish Market on Cambridge Street. When we were in bed later, she asked if I had made any progress, with either Laura Crain or Darius Baker. I asked her to define *progress*. She asked then if it might be time to piss on the fire and call in the dogs.

'Did I just hear you say that?'

'A client of mine from Texas said it to me the other day.'

'It would be better than pissing on the dogs.'

'Hush,' she said. 'The baby might hear you.'

We had not yet let Pearl back into the bedroom after our recently concluded lovemaking.

'I don't quit,' I said.

She tucked herself more firmly into my side. I could feel the heat coming off her, if not as much as there had been a few minutes ago.

'Not exactly breaking news,' she said.

'There's still so much I don't know,' I said. 'But what I do know is that Laura and Darius knew something.'

'And who knows,' she said, 'maybe when you find out what that was, it will help you finally solve the riddle of Andrew Crain.'

'*When* I find out?'

'My money's still on you, big boy.'

She got up and walked naked to the door. Pearl must have been right behind it, because she was in the bed before Susan was.

'Laura Crain's old roommate says that there's just something about bad boys,' I said. 'Do you concur?'

'Oh, God yes,' Dr Susan Silverman said in a husky voice.

64

The young woman was waiting for me outside my office when I got back from Henry's gym the next morning.

'I probably shouldn't be here,' she said as her opening line.

'I often bring that out in people,' I said.

Even at a time when young women kept looking younger and younger to me, she seemed as if she had stopped in on her way to her nine o'clock class.

Her name was Cindy Patton. She informed me that she worked as one of Clay Whitson's assistants at Lith, describing herself as a 'forty-niner.' Meaning she worked on the forty-ninth floor. She had blonde hair cut short, a shirt cut almost as short, a slate-blue sweater that in a less enlightened time – and a less evolved time for me, certainly – I would have thought accentuated the positive and eliminated the negatives entirely.

I had been at the Harbor Health Club at seven-thirty. I was glad I had showered there and changed out of my workout clothes, even if I still wasn't dressed for success.

'So why *are* you here even though you don't think you should be?' I said.

I had just fixed myself my first cup of coffee of the day. She declined when I offered her one.

'Darius told me about you after you came to the office that

205

time,' she said. 'He'd never met a real live private detective. And knew that Mrs Crain had hired you.'

'How did he seem?'

'He had become very mysterious lately,' she said. 'All he told me then was that he was working on a project. I asked if it was a project for work and he smiled and said, "Kind of."'

'But gave you no indication of what the project might be?'

She shook her head.

'Did you ever hear him talking about Mrs Crain?' I asked.

I was walking a fine line with this young woman, and knew it. I had met her only a few minutes ago. Even though she seemed quite sincere, she still worked for Whitson. Whom I did not like, and trusted even less. I didn't think she was here because he had sent her on a fishing expedition, but I couldn't rule out that possibility, either.

'Every so often he'd mention how much he admired her,' she said. 'I joked with him one time that he sounded as if he had a crush on her.'

'A lot to admire about Laura Crain.'

'I know I did,' she said, 'just as a woman. She could have just sat back and counted her husband's money when she wasn't off spending it. But she wanted to make a difference, the same as Mr Crain does.'

She folded her hands in her lap. For some reason she suddenly seemed even more nervous than she was when she'd arrived. For the first time I noticed a small tattoo, of three birds, inside her right wrist.

'You don't believe Darius killed himself, do you?' I said.

'One hundred per cent he didn't!'

She seemed embarrassed that the words had come out as heated as they had.

'I tend to get a little worked up when I'm talking about Darius.'

'You *are* aware that somebody removed the hard drive from his work computer, right?' I said.

She nodded. 'You hear things about the fiftieth floor even when you're still just a forty-niner.'

She leaned forward. 'That's why I'm here, Mr Spenser. I did hear about the hard drive. But nobody at Lith seems to be doing anything about that. I finally screwed up my courage and asked Mr Whitson if there was going to be some kind of internal investigation or anything. He just brushed me off. He's good at that, by the way, brushing people off, and not just me. He said they had done an investigation and just concluded that Darius had removed it himself, for some unknown reason, before he died.'

'Can't they find out internally the last time he accessed it?'

'I believe they can.'

'Did they?'

'I believe they did not.'

'Did Whitson have a reason why Darius would have done something like that? Removed his own hard drive?'

'That's the thing,' she said. 'Darius would never have done something like that, unless he had a very good reason. Or was afraid of somebody.'

'Somebody capable of killing him?'

'Yes,' she said without hesitation.

She crossed her legs. It was impossible not to notice that they were very good legs, despite all of my best intentions about being evolved, and even if I felt like her lecherous old uncle looking at them. My rationalization was that if she weren't proud of those legs herself, she would have worn a longer skirt.

Or pants.

Weak, I knew.

All I had.

I forced myself to stop looking at her legs.

'Nobody seems to care about Darius over there, that's the bottom line,' she said. 'It's like he's been gone a few years and not just a few weeks. Like everybody has moved on, and just accepts that he threw himself off his balcony, without leaving a note or showing any signs of depression. Anyone who had ever been around him for five minutes would have known he wasn't depressed.'

'You know that doesn't mean he *wasn't* depressed.'

'I know,' she said. 'But he wasn't.'

'So how can I help you, really?'

'My boss can't know I'm here,' she said. 'He can't *ever* know I was here.'

'Okay,' I said.

'O*kay?*' she said. 'That's it?'

'I can tell you my word is my bond, if that will make you feel any better,' I said.

'Sorry,' she said. 'I didn't come over here to insult you.'

'Easier for a camel to pass through the eye of a needle than to insult me,' I said. 'And all the other stuff that came after the needle part about the Kingdom of God.'

'The truth is, I came here to help *you*, Mr Spenser.'

'And how exactly do you plan to do that?' I said.

She smiled. It was a very good smile to go with the very good rest of Ms Cindy Patton.

'By getting my head in a cloud,' she said. 'Specifically, Darius's cloud.'

65

Cindy Patton didn't have time to explain all of what she planned to do, or at least wanted to do, before she had to leave my office for her own. But she said she was hopeful that this was going to be the beginning of a longer conversation, which she hoped would be a fruitful one.

'By the way?' she said. 'Fruitful to me means I don't get fired at the end of this.'

'You won't get fired,' I said.

'How can you sound so sure?'

'Because if anybody over there tries to do that,' I said, 'I will beat them up.'

'You don't know Mr Whitson,' she said.

'The first one I beat up would be him,' I said.

'Do you have a general knowledge of how data is stored?' she said.

'I do,' I said. 'But it's my understanding there was no way to get at Darius's personal data once the hard drive was gone, at least not the way things work at Lith.'

'See, that's where you're wrong,' she said. 'There's always a way in.' Now she grinned. 'Either through a side door or a back door. Or maybe a window somebody left open.'

'Do tell,' I said, and she did, quickly, explaining about bonded software companies and corporate accounts and the ability for the bonded company to back up a firm's information in case of cyberattacks.

'What software companies are basically saying is that nothing is foolproof,' she said, 'no matter how hard they make it to find a way in.'

'Are you talking about Darius's office computer or his personal one?' I said.

'He worked on both at the office,' she said. 'A lot of people bring laptops from home at Lith. I'd come up to visit him on the fiftieth floor and he'd have his MacBook Air set up right next to the beast that Lith set him up with. Like he was trying to see which one could come up with information he needed the fastest.'

'You know that the police couldn't find a laptop at his apartment and neither could I,' I said.

'I didn't know that,' she said. 'But I'm not surprised. If somebody would take his hard drive, why wouldn't they take his laptop, too?'

'Listen, I can't be sure that the killer, or killers, took it,' I said. 'There's no proof of that, at least not yet. But if it wasn't in his desk at the office and wasn't at his home, where was it?'

'The same person who has his hard drive took it,' she said. 'I'd bet anything on that.'

'So how are you going to find a way into his information?' I said.

'I know someone at Proscape,' she said. 'That's the name of the software company that has the Lith account. It's a guy I used to date. And if he'll help me, which I think he will, I can get to somebody with the key – and the code – to Darius's personal accounts.'

'I heard you need a fingerprint,' I said.

She smiled more fully. 'Not if you find a side door.'

'Or back door,' I said.

'I am going to need a little time and probably a lot of conniving. And perhaps some flirtatiousness thrown in. But I think I can get us to where we want to go.'

'You really think you can pull this off?' I said.

'You think I'm only counting on luck to get me to the fiftieth floor someday?'

She and her smile and her legs left my office then. She actually had made me feel hopeful, even if she'd made me feel older than Paul Revere's House at the same time.

66

Hawk and I were in my office. Me behind my desk. Him on the couch. Our default positions. He said that if it was true that drugs were being dealt at Joe Marino's bar, even in a small-time way, it might be worthwhile to talk to Tony Marcus about that.

'I'm trying to limit my interactions with Tony to one a year,' I said. 'And I already had mine for this year, as well as it worked out for me.'

'Well, it got to be you and not me,' Hawk said.

'You can't make me.'

'Got to,' Hawk said. 'Tony even still got a hard-on for me about a thing happened between the two of us year *before* this one. And you know how the man is when it comes to grudges.'

'He stores them up like squirrels store nuts,' I said.

'Till he sees a chance to grab you by yours,' Hawk said.

'Not so easy to do with you,' I said. 'Or me, for that matter.'

'Tony don't think so.'

'So you think he may have had a hand in over at Marino's?'

'Nothing's changed,' Hawk said. 'Dope or girls, he wants both hands in. Sometimes he don't even care about the amount of money involved. His mind, it's the principle of the damn thing, not having nobody put nothing over on him.'

'You think it's worth it for me to talk to him?'

Hawk smiled. 'Ask yourself what you got to lose at this point.'

'You think I should call him first, or just surprise him?'

'Tony never much for surprises,' Hawk said, 'unless you looking for Ty-Bop to shoot you.'

Ty-Bop, who was Tony's gunnie, had been with Tony Marcus for as long as I'd known him. Junior was Tony's body man. Except that in Junior's case, it appeared to be a lot more than just one body. He was built like half of the Patriots' offensive line. Or all of it.

'Admit it,' I said when Tony Marcus answered his phone. 'You missed me.'

'Like missing the clap,' he said.

'You speaking from experience?' I said.

'Heard you might call,' he said. 'My lucky damn day.'

I offered to meet him at Buddy's Fox, the restaurant where he still kept his office.

'Like I was going to come to you,' he said.

'I was just being polite.'

'And don't bring Hawk,' Tony said.

I said, 'He told me the two of you were having relationship issues.'

'Fuck Hawk,' Tony said, and told me when to stop by, and to leave my piece in the car, it annoyed Junior when he had to pat me down.

There was a decent lunchtime crowd at Buddy's Fox. Tony had once renamed it Ebony and Ivory, which is what he used to call Hawk and me when it was a far more topical musical reference.

But now it was back to being Buddy's Fox. When I came through the door I noticed that the clientele was exclusively black, as it usually was, and that all conversation stopped, as if a pink flamingo had just come walking into the place.

Junior was waiting for me at the other end of the room, at the hallway that led back to Tony's office.

'Junior,' I said. 'You're looking well.'

He gave me a bored shake of the head. 'You know the drill,' he said.

'I was told by the owner to leave my piece in the car and did,' I said.

'Boss don't trust you for shit.'

'I'm not going to lie, Junior,' I said. 'That hurts.'

But raised my hands above my head.

'No inappropriate touching,' I said. 'And no tickling, I mean it.'

Tony was behind his desk. Ty-Bop leaned against the wall next to the door, wearing a white Celtics jersey with Jayson Tatum's number 0 in front and a knit stocking cap on his head despite unseasonably warm weather outside. He nodded to a beat only he could hear, whether he had buds in his ears or not.

Tony was wearing what I thought was a very sporty jacket of charcoal gray with a purple plaid to it, which I was sure was part of a suit, mostly because I had rarely ever seen Tony Marcus, gentleman gangster, not wearing a suit. There was a tea setup in front of him.

''Sup, mother*fucker*,' he said, putting all his weight on the second half of the word, like he usually did.

I nodded at him. 'Are you wearing your hair that short as a fashion statement, or because you're starting to lose it?'

He nodded at Ty-Bop. 'Go ahead and shoot him, Ty. You know you always wanted to.'

I sat down.

'I hear you been looking for intel on Joe Marino's old place,' Tony said.

'And where did you hear something like that?'

He closed his eyes and sighed. 'You really want us to do it like that?' he said. 'You got to know by now I hear everything, and see everything and pretty much know everything, leastways most of the time. Why I'm still me, talking like this here to you.'

'I'm looking for someone who tended bar there about twenty years ago,' I said. 'All I got is the name Rob.'

He frowned. 'Don't think I ever had the pleasure.'

'Of meeting that particular bartender, or gracing Marino's with your presence?'

'Neither nor,' Tony said.

'How much do you remember about the place?' I said.

'What's in it for me, something comes up if it turns out you goosed up my memory?'

I smiled, as I often did at Tony's distinctive use of the language.

'My undying gratitude?' I said.

He sipped some tea. 'Lot of college kids back in the day,' he said. 'Weed being dealt, way, *way* before the shit was legal. Some coke. No heavy shit. Compared to what else I had going, nickel-and-dime stuff. Like a mom-pop.'

He shrugged. 'I got a piece of the action anyways, Joe got a bigger one, it being his place and all. What I recall, more girls in there than boys, Joe was smart enough to hire some pretty boys to work the bar. The movie business started to pick up in Boston 'round that time, and he'd get guys happy to work cheap between, ah, engagements.'

I turned to look at Ty-Bop. Head still bopping. It looked as if his eyes were closed. I knew better. Hawk said that of everybody we'd ever known, the only better shooter than him was Vinnie. I didn't know how old Ty-Bop was, or even what his real name

213

was. But considering his profession, he was older than he should have been.

'I think the guy I'm looking for might have been one of the pretty boys,' I said, 'whether he was in the movies or not.'

'I do something for you, you know how this-all works, you got to do more for me in return.'

'You have something in mind?'

'Let you know when it pops in my mind,' Tony said.

He poured more tea then. The porcelain pot matched his cup and looked expensive. Tony liked nice things and could afford them.

'Why you need to find him?'

'He might help me solve something I'm in on.'

'The Crain woman,' he said.

'It turns out she used to go around with this Rob guy who worked there,' I said. 'And he used to hit her.'

'She sure traded up after that,' Tony said.

'Didn't help her at the end.'

'I got no use for that, man taking a hand to a woman.'

'At last,' I said, 'some common ground.'

Now Tony smiled. 'Now get the fuck out my office.'

As I passed Ty-Bop I said, 'We should double-date at a Celts game one of these days.'

His lizard eyes opened, but just briefly.

I put my hand to my ear as if I had a phone in it, mouthed 'Call me,' and left. There were even more people in the front room than there had been before. Oh, the places I'd go.

67

Cindy Patton called the next morning and told me she was going to need a few more days, her contact at Proscape was out of the country.

I just reminded her to be careful, knowing she really didn't need reminding after what had happened to her friend Darius.

'You wouldn't have come to me if you didn't think that Darius had found out something that got him killed,' I said. 'And if that's true, the threat might be one floor above you.'

'I'm being careful, I promise,' she said. 'I'm not trusting anybody except you right now.'

'Words to live by,' I said. 'And quite literally, by the way.'

'This place is starting to scare me,' she said.

'*Starting* to scare you?' I said.

I hadn't heard back from Tony Marcus but wasn't expecting to, certainly not right away. As fluid as our relationship truly was, he had never forgotten that I had once been responsible for putting him in jail, though I had done favors for him since, including one involving his daughter and the meathead she had married.

I knew he might make me wait, even if he did get the information I needed, just because he was Tony.

Hawk and I had taken a late-afternoon walk along the river after my visit to Buddy's Fox. 'Tony's just another old dog licks himself on account of he can,' Hawk said.

I asked him what he'd done this time to get himself sideways with Tony.

'Some shit he thought I did that I didn't,' Hawk said. 'He'll get himself over it.'

'You sure about that?'

'Yeah,' Hawk said. 'Because if he don't, he'll be the one got himself sideways. With *me*.'

'And who in his right mind would ever want that?'

'Tony knows enough to take his dickery with me just so far,' Hawk said. 'And not one damn step past that.'

We were nearing the end of the path when Hawk told me he had another date with the new woman. I told him I was always excited to get relationship intel from him.

'Is this the second or third?' I said.

'Don't worry about it.'

'You know you're not always the giver you say you are,' I said.

'Not what she says,' he said.

Susan was having dinner in Swampscott with an old high school friend. After Hawk was gone, I stayed in my office, telling myself I would order takeout at some point, but not until I read up on Ethan Lowe's participation in the Aahil project before it went belly-up.

When I finally couldn't wait, and had gotten lost in *Wall Street Journal* stories about Aahil that made as much sense to me as reading about cricket, I ordered a large pizza, green peppers and onions, from Upper Crust.

Before it arrived, I forced myself to read one more story from the *Financial Times*, one that recounted all the fanfare that had accompanied the announcement of the Aahil project, and quoted Lowe proclaiming how expansion like this could only enhance Lith's global brand.

And corporate autonomy.

They were bears for corporate autonomy in the world of big money, something else I had discovered in my reading.

It turned out there was far less fanfare when the project was abandoned. Both sides combined to issue a press release, proclaiming their undying love for each other. There was nothing in the story to indicate that Lith's viability had been compromised in any way, or diminished.

But it *was* a private company, I kept reminding myself.

After that was a long stretch when the only coverage of Lith involved Andrew Crain's charity work around the world. Some of it was in Africa. He had invested a ton of money in various human rights issues, and seemed more passionate about the plight of oppressed women, no matter where he found them.

My pizza was eventually delivered. I ate all of it and drank two beers. When I finished eating I put the empty Upper Crust box into a tall kitchen garbage bag and brought it downstairs to the trash area in the basement, just as a way of getting the smell of peppers and onions out of my office, as pleasant as the smell had been about a half-hour before.

Just to make sure, I lit a jar candle that Susan had bought me, partially, I was sure, because of its name:

Last Call.

Susan said the scent was sandalwood. But she knew better than anyone that you could stump me on most fragrances, and she could easily have told me it was something else and gotten by with it.

'Pretty sure Sam Spade didn't have a scented candle,' I had said after she had given it to me.

'He probably could have used one,' she said. 'I'll bet he opened his window and let fresh air in even less often than you do.'

I had to admit the smell, whatever it was, wasn't displeasing. The candle was still lit when there was a single rap on my door and Martin Quirk walked in.

'How'd you know I was here?' I said.

'Had 'em ping your phone,' he said.

'Isn't that an invasion of my privacy?'

'Hell, yes,' Quirk said.

'I should call the cops,' I said.

'Whiskey?' Quirk said.

We both knew he wasn't asking if I had any, because he knew I did. I went and got out my bottle of Midleton Very Rare. The good stuff. I had been spoiling myself a lot lately. Johnny Walker Blue and now Midleton. But Martin Quirk was well worth it the same as I was.

He nodded at the candle.

'We going to meditate?' he said.

He held up his glass. I held up mine. We drank. The first taste of it, the feeling as it went down, made me want to burst into song.

'Maybe meditating would be helpful,' I said.

'Or maybe we just drink,' he said. 'But first, blow out the fucking candle.'

I did. Now the only light in the room came from my small desk lamp.

'You ever feel as if you stayed at this too long?' Quirk said.

I knew him well enough to know it was not a frivolous question. Quirk was not now, nor ever had been, a frivolous man.

'When I get that feeling,' I said, 'I usually just lie down until it passes.'

'Laura Crain was like royalty in this city,' he said. He took another sip of whiskey. The highball glass looked like a shot glass in his big hand.

'I can't let whoever did it get away with murder,' he said. 'And I know you feel the same way.'

'Goes without saying.'

'Problem is, I got no evidence,' he said. 'And no motive.'

'I assume you are speaking for both you and Frank,' I said.

'The literary *we* can be used with *I* in narration,' he said. 'I assumed you knew that.'

'Why, you literate bastard, you.'

'Goddamn right,' he said.

Somehow the dim light of the office made the hour seem later than it was.

'Frank thinks you might have a thought or two you haven't shared about a possible motive,' he said.

'I'm aware that he thinks that, mostly because he continues to remind me every few days.'

'Do you?' Quirk said.

'There may have been some bad business going on with the big business of Lith, Inc.,' I said. 'But if there is, I haven't found it yet.'

'Because of this merger,' Quirk said.

'Or something else going on over there,' I said. 'Just because there always seems to be something going on over there, hardly ever good.'

'But what would Crain's wife have to do with any of that?'

'She never came right out and told me,' I said, 'but I think she might have taken more of an interest in her husband's company than most people knew. Including him. He has a history of his head being in the clouds.'

I thought of Cindy Patton, her talking about a different kind of cloud.

'And that might have gotten her killed?' Quirk said.

'I'm not sure it even rises to the level of working theory,' I said. 'But what I am sure of is that nobody ever compared any business as big as Lith to church.'

'I'm Catholic,' Quirk said. 'Even church isn't church anymore. Probably never was.'

I got up and refilled his glass. I knew he had a driver downstairs waiting for him. And I knew I was walking home from here.

'I'm working close with Frank on this,' he said. 'You need to know that.'

'The bosses still up your ass?'

'They are,' he said. 'But it's not just that. I'm not going out with one last goddamn case I couldn't close.'

The Midleton was going down easier, for both of us, I assumed.

'You tried to retire before,' I said. 'You were no good at it.'

'I'm putting in my papers at the end of the year,' he said. 'And I'm fuckin' ay going out with a win, and you're gonna help me. Or else.'

'You ever wonder what "or else" might actually entail?' I said.

'All the time.' He grinned. 'Still sounds good.'

'You know I'll help any way I can.'

'Where is Crain on this merger?' he said.

'He was against it before he was for it.'

'But his wife might have died still being against it,' Quirk said.

'The way to bet,' I said.

Quirk nodded. 'You probably have noticed that money, especially a lot of money, can make normally sane people lose their freaking minds. So let me ask you something: Can you see the other partner killing his best friend's wife, or having it done, over money?'

'He could,' I said. 'I just don't see it.'

'And maybe that guy in Charlestown jumped.'

'Don't see that, either.'

'You're still dug in on that?'

'Yes, sir.'

Quirk smiled then. 'I'm off-duty,' he said. 'You can call me Martin.'

I smiled back at him. 'Too soon in our relationship for me to be that informal.'

We sat in silence. I heard a siren, coming either up Boylston or across Berkeley, before it was gone.

'You think the wife's death and the jumper's death are connected,' Quirk said.

'Yeah,' I said. 'I do. I just can't prove it, at least not yet.'

'Have you had a case of your own lately felt like this much of a shitshow?'

'It's not like you didn't warn me.'

He finished his drink. I pointed to his glass. He shook his head.

'I need this,' he said.

I knew he wasn't talking about the whiskey.

There was a longer quiet between us then, before I reached into the middle drawer of my desk and pulled out Laura Crain's note to Darius Baker, the one I'd found in his jacket, and slid it across the desk to Quirk.

He held it close to the desk lamp as he read it, then slid it back to me.

'Now you give this up?'

'Maybe my own Catholic guilt?'

'You're not Catholic,' Quirk said.

'Imagine my surprise at the guilt, then.'

'This all you got that we don't?'

I nodded.

'Not much to go on,' he said.

'Not yet, anyway,' I said.

'You got a much better chance to get inside this thing than we do,' he said. 'So maybe going forward you can act like a team player.'

'No *i* in *team*,' I said.

'But two in Martin Quirk, hotshot,' he said.

When he was gone I stood in my window and saw him standing next to the unmarked on the street, its motor running. Before he got in, Quirk looked up at my window and nodded. There was no way for him to see me nod back.

The car pulled away. I rinsed our glasses and put them away and then I walked home, thinking about what Quirk had said about needing the win.

Maybe I needed a win even more than he did, whether he was really moving toward the door or not. It wasn't my fault that Laura and Baker were dead. I still felt guilt about both of them, Catholic or otherwise.

I had walked along Arlington Street even though it was slightly out of my way. I liked walking past the park, even at night. Especially at night sometimes.

Reggie Smythe was waiting for me outside my building again, leaning against the Navigator.

'Mr Lowe says I should suggest you stop talking to his people without his permission,' Smythe said.

'I don't need his permission to talk to his people,' I said. 'That's one thing. And as I recall, it was Mr Lowe who came to me asking for help.'

'I watch over Mr Lowe,' Reggie Smythe said. 'He doesn't watch over me.'

He casually moved away from the car, as if he were about to walk me to my door.

'So you, as one of his people, have still taken it upon yourself to tell me to stop talking to *other* of his people?'

'Your grasp of the obvious,' Smythe said, 'continues to be almost breathtaking.'

'And if I don't, ah, accede to your wishes?' I said. 'Or his?'

'Cindy Patton is a very nice young woman,' he said.

He was smiling as he said it.

'Blimey, Reg,' I said. 'Was that a threat?'

'Perhaps think of it more as an observation,' he said.

He was still smiling.

'You bring anybody with you?' I said, looking around. There could have been someone in the Navigator, but somehow I doubted it. He wasn't the type.

'What in the world for?' he said.

He was probably good. Just not as good as me, even if he had size on me, and probably reach, or not. I smiled back at him then, before I took a quick first step toward him with my right leg and hit him with a short left hook whose force, even in close quarters, surprised even me. He had a hard body, as I expected him to. I could feel it when the punch landed, but I still could hear air come out of him before following up with the straight overhand right I'd been working on lately at Henry's and of which I was now pretty proud. It didn't put Reggie Smythe down, but nearly did, knocking him back a couple steps before he managed to gather himself.

He didn't swing back, taking a couple more steps backward instead, reaching inside his jacket as he did. But I was on him before he could come out with the gun for which he had to be reaching. Then I pressed the .38 I was carrying tonight right above his nose. It all happened to Smythe with the speed of the combination with which he'd just been hit.

The right hand I'd thrown already had his left eye starting to close. But he was trying to remain cool, even now. Hard to do with a gun between your eyes. But he had forgotten the first rule of being a tough guy, the one about never letting the other guy get the first punch in.

'Nothing is going to happen to Cindy Patton, now or ever,' I said softly. 'Nod your head if you understand me, so I don't have to blow it off.'

He hesitated, but then complied.

Then I was behind him, my gun in his back, shoving him hard toward his Navigator with it, then opening the driver's-side door with my free hand.

'*Now* buzz off,' I said.

I had the gun pointed at his window until the Navigator slowly pulled onto Marlborough. I watched until its taillights were gone into the night.

Martin Quirk might be worried about the game passing him by.

I was not.

68

I called Cindy Patton and she answered right away.

'Are you okay?' I said.

'I'm fine,' she said. 'Eating Skinny Pop and watching *White Lotus* again. Why?'

I didn't know what *White Lotus* was, but chose to move on, telling her that Reggie Smythe had just paid me a visit that had not ended well.

'For him, I hope,' she said. 'That man scares me. I don't know why they keep him around.'

'I'm starting to get the idea that it actually takes more than Reggie Smythe to make you want to hide under your desk,' I said.

I told her then what he said about her and what I'd proceeded to do about it.

'You pulled your gun?' she said. 'On *Marlborough* Street?'

'It was just the two of us at the moment,' I said, 'so as not to scare any of my neighbors.'

'It's creepy that he mentioned my name,' Cindy said.

'Just another way of calling him a creep,' I said.

'What should I do?'

I was resting my right hand, which had started to throb and swell slightly, in a bowl of ice and water. I tried to remember if I used this much ice when I was still boxing.

'Somehow Smythe knew you had come to see me,' I said, 'or there would have been no reason for him to bring up your name.'

'He was having me followed,' she said, and I could hear the ripple of alarm in her voice.

'Maybe by tracking your phone.'

'You're making me feel like I'm in some sort of spy movie.'

I took my hand out of the ice and dried it on my jeans.

'Starting to think even bad spy movies make more sense than ours.'

'Maybe ours will turn out to make more sense than we think.'

'Listen, Cindy,' I said. 'You can walk away from this right now. Go in to the office in the morning and tell your boss that you only came to see me because Darius had been your friend, and you wanted to help me in any way you could.'

She didn't answer right away. Maybe she was considering her options.

Finally she said, 'No.'

'Are you sure?'

'I *am* scared, Mr Spenser. But I'm not going to let that creep make me quit. If I can help you find out what might have happened to my friend, I'm going to.'

'You could be putting yourself into even more danger going forward,' I said. 'And you're talking to somebody who didn't do much of a job keeping your friend safe.'

'You didn't know that you had to,' she said.

I asked for her address and she gave it to me, North Washington Street in Brighton. I asked her what kind of building it was. She said it was a doorman building, her parents had insisted on one when she'd moved from Ohio. Then I told her to go out in the morning when the stores opened and buy herself a burner phone she was to use only when she was contacting me or I was contacting her.

'Wow,' she said, 'this is a spy movie.'

I told her that if Clay Whitson did ask her about coming to see me, to tell him the story I'd just given her, that she'd simply acted

224

out of loyalty and friendship and didn't think she was doing anything wrong.

Before I ended the call, I told her I would protect her, no matter how we moved forward.

Then I called Hawk.

'Middle of something here,' he said, though he did answer his phone, maybe because he'd seen it was me.

'It's important,' I said.

'So is what I'm in the middle of,' he said.

I told him, as succinctly as I could, about Smythe and Cindy Patton and that I needed him to watch her for a couple days.

Hawk said he would, and then told me he'd try to wrap things up in his present circumstances much sooner than he'd planned.

'See,' he said, 'I am a damn giver after all.'

69

I knew from Claire Megill that Ethan Lowe owned a town house of his own on Beacon Hill, even bigger and more lavish than Andrew Crain's, with a tonier address at Louisburg Square. His weekend place, she had also informed me, was in Marblehead.

I was up at seven the next morning and walked over to the address she'd given me for Lowe, stopping along the way at the Starbucks on Charles Street. The largest size coffee they had was a 'trenta.' I asked the kid serving me if he knew that meant thirty.

'Yeah,' he said, running my credit card. 'My parents are pretty proud that I majored in speaking barista at UMass.'

I made my way over to Revere and then W Cedar and then Mount Vernon after that, before hanging a left at Louisburg Square. The red-brick homes here, set back from fences and small, well-kept lawns, always made me feel as if I should be looking at them in black-and-white, imagining that they had looked largely the same a hundred and fifty years ago.

I knew better than to loiter in front of Lowe's building and risk being executed on the spot by someone behind the wheel of a private security vehicle.

So I walked around the small park across the street from where Lowe lived, and then did that again, as if part of my morning routine, finishing my trenta and regretting that I hadn't brought a couple blueberry scones with me. But then I told myself, thinking ahead, that I had something to look forward to on the walk home.

There was no black Navigator in sight, at least not yet. Maybe Lowe walked to work from here, I knew it could be only a mile or so, if that, to the Hancock. Maybe he was less and less afraid of the bogeyman, for reasons known only to him. I was hoping he would walk to work, having no enthusiasm for Round 2 with Reggie Smythe if he happened to show up, not in Louisburg Square, it would have been an insult to everything good and holy about old Boston.

Lowe came out of his front door about fifteen minutes after eight o'clock. Khakis, white T-shirt showing over the top of a dark v-neck sweater. I saw him put his earbuds in, and then check his phone before putting it away.

He was making his way toward Mount Vernon when I fell into step alongside him. If I'd startled him, it had been only slightly.

He sighed and took the bud out of his left ear.

'You don't need to call security,' I said.

'It wouldn't do me much good, from what I heard happened to my security last evening,' he said.

He took out the other earbud and stuffed them both into his pocket.

'I thought I'd made it clear that I'm not trying to make trouble with you,' Ethan Lowe said. 'And that we ought to be on the same side here.'

'Then why'd you send your guy Reggie after me?'

It hadn't taken us long to get to Mount Vernon. Lowe was walking briskly and I was gamely keeping up, even on a sore knee. I assumed we were headed for the Public Garden.

'I didn't send Reggie.'

'Gonna need to call bullshit on that one,' I said.

'Clay sent him,' Lowe said. 'I didn't find out until afterward. He wanted to know why his assistant had come to see you.'

'And how did Clay know that she had?' I said.

I wondered if he and Smythe had their stories straight. If necessary, I knew I could brace Whitson at a later date, just for the sheer joy of it.

'Reggie likes to keep track of people.'

'Big Brother watching?' I said. 'I mean, he *is* a big brother, after all.'

'Clever,' Lowe said.

'It's both my blessing and my curse.'

We had made our way to Charles.

'During the course of my conversation with Reggie,' I said, 'he threatened a young woman who'd only come to me because she'd cared as much as she had for Darius Baker.'

'Reggie's version is that all he'd said was what a nice person she was,' Lowe said. 'And that you then overreacted and sucker-punched him.'

'Twice,' I said. 'But who's really counting?'

'Then pulled a gun on him.'

'Not to make too fine a point of things,' I said, 'but he was reaching for his own at the time.'

'Well, after you'd sucker-punched him twice.'

The conversation was as casual as if he were discussing how the Japanese markets had opened.

'Let's not chase each other around more bullshit,' I said. 'His threat to Cindy Patton was implied, and overt, at the same goddamn time. But here's a threat that's neither: If he goes anywhere near her again, I will be coming for you first, then Whitson, then him.'

'And beat me up, too? I'm sure that you could.'

'Nah,' I said. 'But I will find a way to beat up your company.'

'Don't flatter yourself.'

We'd crossed Beacon and were in the park, angling toward either Newbury or Boylston. It was already an almost perfect autumn morning in the city. I was spending it with Ethan Lowe, who had now officially annoyed me. I found as I grew older it took less and less.

'I have a dear old friend named Wayne Cosgrove, who is a bigger deal than ever at *The Globe*,' I said. 'And I'm thinking that if he suddenly had people from that *Globe* Spotlight team they made that movie about attach themselves to you like deer ticks, there might be an interesting tale to be told about events that led to this merger being so important to you. And even about how you came up with the capital you needed after that Aahil deal turned into this year's Red Sox.'

He stopped walking then. We were in front of the duckling statues inspired by *Make Way for Ducklings*, but whose beauty seemed completely lost on Ethan Lowe at the moment.

He stared at me, but said nothing, as if a bogeyman finally had just jumped out in front of him.

'I know,' I said. 'The story almost takes my breath away, too.'

'You don't know what you don't know, Mr Spenser,' he said. 'We should just leave it at that, and go our separate ways.'

'No,' I said.

'To which part?'

'We have no separate ways now,' I said. 'We just have me wanting to know if Darius Baker's hard drive having gone missing has something to do with your merger, and his death.'

'You're obviously a very smart guy,' Lowe said. 'And a very persistent guy. And you seem to be loyal as hell. But you're out of your depth here. And it's not just going to be one person who gets hurt if you don't leave my company alone, it will be a lot of people.'

I was going to point out that it was really Andrew Crain's company, but didn't. And likewise didn't tell him that I was having a difficult time deciding whether it was him or Darius, when he was still with us, who was trying to hide something. Instead I told him that I'd be in touch, and then the two of us did go our separate ways, at least for the time being.

I was on my way to my office with a box full of Dunkin' donuts, just in case I had guests, when I received the following heartfelt text from Tony Marcus:

Maybe got a name for you, bitch.

70

He followed it up with a phone call, telling me he happened to be in my hood, and would come to me this time.

'"Hood," Tony?' I said.

'Cultural expression,' he said, 'from bygone days, even though I took this boy out the hood a long time ago.'

'To what do I owe the honor?'

'Got a girl I put up at the Newbury,' he said. 'She's not my primary, understand, my primary is the one I got living with me presently. But the one at the hotel, she's worked her way up through the farm system. I'm right around the corner, is my point.'

'I was starting to worry there might not be a point coming along anytime soon. Or ever.'

'You want my fucking help or not?' he said.

I asked what kind of tea he liked. He said he didn't need any damn tea, but if a woman identifying herself as Shirelle happened to check in with me later, I was to tell her that Tony and I had been working together on something all night and into this morning.

'You do that, we square.'

'Seriously?'

'I still got a lot to live for,' he said. 'And Shirelle can be a bad sport.'

He came into the office without either Junior or Ty-Bop. I assumed that Junior had driven and Ty-Bop had walked Tony from the car into my building. Now the two of them were probably downstairs arguing about the president's tax plan.

I would have thought Tony would be once again dressed to the nines, but with him the number always seemed on the low side. Navy suit today, perfectly tailored, a big-knotted tie whose brand I knew I should know but didn't. Whatever had happened last night with the woman at the Ritz who wasn't his primary, Tony still looked as fresh as freshly cut flowers. There was suddenly a scent in the room that reminded me of my candle.

'Troy Robinson,' Tony said when he was seated.

'Tell me more,' I said.

'Ain't much more to tell,' he said. 'Worked part-time at the bar. Did some TV and movie work on the side, couple movies shooting here, and some lawyer show. Or maybe was a cop show. Pretty-boy background actor, or so I was told.'

'Told by whom?'

'Don't ask, don't tell,' Tony said.

'Pretty sure you stole that,' I said.

'We done?' Tony said. 'Other than you handling that business with Shirelle, it ever comes up.'

'The person with whom you spoke,' I said. 'Did they have any idea whatever happened to Robinson? I heard he left town suddenly when he left.'

'Catch me up on this here,' Tony said. 'Who's the damn detective here, me or you?'

He stood up. His way of telling me we were done.

'What if Shirelle doesn't call?' I said.

Tony was looking at his reflection in my window, frowning, leaning slightly forward. I saw him square himself up then, adjusting a knot in his tie that really was as big as my fist. When he was satisfied, he walked over to the door, put his hand on the knob, and stopped.

'Oh, she'll call, sooner or later,' Tony said. 'Girl got herself some serious trust issues.'

'I can't imagine why,' I said.

When he was gone, I called Zebulon Sixkill in Los Angeles and asked him how good his contacts were in the world of TV and movies.

'Let me count the ways, paleface,' Z said.

71

Z informed me, rather proudly, I thought, that he'd already been to the gym and had just finished an energy shake he'd made for himself, from scratch.

'What color?' I said.

'You don't want to know. But think mint.'

We got the small talk out of the way both quickly and efficiently, as we usually did. Business for his own private detective agency was good. Things were also good with Jen Yoon, a computer savant who'd become his partner both in business and in life, the longest relationship he'd had with anybody except me since we'd met.

'She's not sick of you yet?' I said.

'Susan's not sick of you yet?' he said.

I asked about Mattie. He said she kept tabling the discussion of becoming a cop, mostly because she was having too much of a blast, he said, working with him and Jen.

'She's got nearly enough hours with us to get her PI license,' Z said.

'She got any plans to get a place of her own?'

'Not unless she moves in with this new guy she's been seeing.'

231

'I thought there was a new guy the last time I spoke with her.'

'That was a new guy right before this one,' Z said. 'He's like the third lead in some zombie cop show on Hulu.'

'You like him?'

'For an actor.'

'Low bar.'

'Tell me about it. I live here, remember?'

'What's his name?'

'Brick something.'

'*Brick?* You're joking.'

'I wish.'

I then told him what I was working on, in as organised a way as I could manage, even knowing as I did that I still sounded as if I were wrestling myself to the ground. But, I told Z, I now had a lead, if you could call it that, on Laura Crain's old boyfriend, who might not figure into the case but might.

'I got the name from Tony Marcus,' I said.

'Always a reliable source.'

'When he wants something from me, he is.'

'What's he want this time?'

'As far as I could tell, for his current love interest not to kill him in his sleep when he's not sleeping around on her.'

I told Z that all I had was that Troy Robinson might have worked in the industry here about twenty years ago, which meant there might be some kind of union record on him out there. Extra or background actor or event stunt man, I really had no idea. Z knew better than I did about the inner workings of Tinsel Town.

'Tinsel Town? You're getting old.'

'I may be, but irony never does,' I said. 'So could you or Jen or even Mattie help me out.'

'If it's important to you, you know I will.'

'He may be important, or somebody I turned into a red herring all by myself,' I said. 'I just want to know one way or another how he might figure into this thing, if he does.'

'Wait,' Z said. '*Now* you're worrying about tying up loose ends.'

232

'You're pretty funny for a Cree.'

'Guy walks into a reservation,' he said.

'The only thing I've got other than a name is that somebody said he might've looked like Brad Pitt.'

'Half the town used to,' Z said. 'No more. Word is that blonde guys aren't dangerous enough.'

'But you are.'

'Hell, yeah. But I was taught by the best.'

He said he'd worked on a case one time that involved an actor who'd started out in the Screen Extras Guild, before it was absorbed into SAG. He would see what history he could find from what had been the Screen Extras Guild, but that if the Robinson guy had worked on independent shoots in Boston, we might be screwed checking back on him, because it was likely a non-union operation. But there might be a chance, if he was trying to get into the business, that he might have worked in Los Angeles before he went east.

'It was probably a long shot from the start,' I said. 'I just had this feeling.'

'Give me a few days,' Z said.

'I'm the one starting to feel like a zombie,' I said.

'Maybe you could find background work with Brick,' Z said.

72

I called Hawk with the good news that I was on my way to relieve him, as I was taking Cindy Patton to dinner.

'I ain't sleeping in my car, in case you were thinking about asking me after you had dinner,' Hawk said. 'Jag's built for a lot of things. Not that.'

'I've got one of the Vinnies covering the overnight shift,' I said.

'You make it sound like a singing group.'

There was a pause. 'What kind of tab you running, even though you no longer have a client?' Hawk said.

'There's a price to pay for speaking the truth,' I said. 'A bigger price for living a lie.'

'I know you want to tell me who said that.'

'Cornel West.'

'Figured it was so smart, had to be a brother.'

When I arrived at Cindy Patton's building, the Jag was parked right in front on North Washington, only standing out in the neighborhood the way an armored tank would have.

'Thank you for your service,' I said to Hawk.

'Gonna be out of pocket the next few hours,' he said, 'now that my evening opened up like this.'

'Don't do anything I wouldn't do.'

'Think you mean to say *couldn't* do.'

Cindy and I walked to the Brighton Bodega and settled into a booth. I asked if she'd ever been here before. She said she had not. I told her she was about to find out what she had been missing, and ordered the equivalent of a tasting menu for both of us.

Tacos carnitas. Peking ravioli pork dumplings. Korean BBQ short ribs. Crispy Sichuan pepper wings. We each had a glass of True North Ale.

While we waited for our food to be delivered, after I'd told the waitress she could bring dishes out whenever they were ready, I asked Cindy how she was doing, really, with all the sudden drama in her life.

'It probably won't surprise you to know I've never required a bodyguard before,' she said. 'But I have to say, the one I have is *very* impressive.'

'All you have to do is ask him,' I said.

I smiled at her and drank some beer. It was local, from Ipswich, and very good.

'He must be the best,' she said.

'Definitely in the top two.'

She said it had been an odd day at work. Clay Whitson had come downstairs and *he'd* asked how she was doing.

'I take it that's not a normal occurrence?'

'Asking me to do extra work, that's a normal occurrence,' Cindy said. 'Acting as if he cares about me as a person happens about as often as a change of seasons.'

'Maybe me kicking Reggie Smythe's ass got his attention.'

'I really wish I'd seen that,' she said.

'Have you had any further conversations with your friend from Proscape?'

'I'm having a drink with him tomorrow night, as a matter of fact,' she said. 'Does Hawk have to be my plus-one?'

'Only from a respectful distance, so as not to cramp your style.'

Vinnie texted me when we were finishing up with our feast to tell me that Ronnie was on his way to Cindy's apartment. I told him we were just about to leave the restaurant and walk back.

'I feel like your dad walking you home,' I said as we made our way back up North Washington.

'But a very cool dad,' she said.

I saw Ronnie had arrived as I walked Cindy to her front door, as any cool dad would have.

'I want this to be over,' she said. 'And when it is finally over, I still want to have my job.'

'You will,' I said.

'I wish I were as confident as you are,' I said.

'Who doesn't?'

She thanked me for dinner then, and got up on her toes and gave me a quick peck on the cheek.

'I'm not as young as you think I am,' she said.

'Yeah, kid,' I said, 'you are.'

'I'll tell you one thing,' she said. 'I'm old enough to remember when I still thought I was working for the good guys.'

73

Susan and I were with Pearl the next day at Raymond Park in Cambridge on a rare afternoon off for her. We had walked there from Linnaean Street.

'I forgot to ask,' she said. 'How was date night?'

'Very funny.'

'The two of you have any common interests besides the case?' she said.

'A quest for justice?'

'Oh,' Susan said. 'That old thing.'

I was throwing a tennis ball and Pearl was retrieving it and seemed, as always, to be willing to do that until the end of days.

We finally found an empty bench and Susan brought out the small plastic dish she had in her Pearl bag and poured water into it. Pearl drank loudly and thirstily and plopped down in the grass at last.

It was my first chance to brief Susan on having spoken to Z, and Mattie's new love interest, and Cindy Patton's conviction that our accessing Darius Baker's information was imminent.

'Believe in yourself and you can achieve,' Susan said.

'Is that from a poem?' I asked.

'If it's not, it should be.'

I leaned over and kissed her. She kissed me back, with vigor, and then asked, in what I felt was a less-than-poetic way, if I would be interested in heading back to her place for a matinee.

She was in bed reading much later and I was watching the Amazon series about Harry Bosch when Claire Megill called.

'You're back,' I said.

'I need to see you,' she said.

There was something wrong with her voice, as if she were afraid to raise it. She said she was at her apartment and asked how long it would take me to get there. I told her I was in Cambridge, which meant not terribly long.

'Claire,' I said. 'What's wrong?'

'Andrew,' she said. 'I'm worried about Andrew.'

So I was all the way back to the beginning.

'Has something happened to him?' I said. 'Has he done something?'

'I'm afraid he might do something,' she said.

She hesitated.

'To Clay,' she said.

Then she was crying.

'Clay hit me,' she said, before adding, 'Again.'

74

The bruise was around her left eye, in the same general area where I had clocked Reggie Smythe.

'I should have called you first and not Andrew,' she said.

I thought she might start crying again, though it looked as if she hadn't really stopped since we'd ended our call. Perhaps she was finally cried out about Clay Whitson. I put an arm around her and walked her to her couch and took a seat across from her.

'Tell me what happened,' I said.

Since returning from California, she said, she had been thinking a lot about her relationship with Clay Whitson, and the choice she'd originally made with him, and the choice to stay with him longer after she knew she shouldn't. And keeping largely silent about the abuse for as long as she had. Eventually she made the decision to tell him that she was stopping her own destructive pattern once and for all.

'I just finally decided I deserved better,' she said. 'That I *am* better.'

She nodded like a child who had been caught misbehaving, even though she had done nothing wrong, the way Laura Crain had not done anything wrong back in college.

'It was always the same,' she said. 'He would hit me, and then be remorseful, and I would take him back.'

'Did you try therapy?'

'Repeatedly.'

'But you'd take him back, anyway.'

'Madness,' she said.

The same word Missy Jones had used about Laura. Maybe the word all abused women used about themselves sooner or later. Just because it was madness that they couldn't see a way out.

'Perhaps what got me across the line at last was seeing my son on this trip, seeing the strong woman he thinks I am. The *person* I want to be. Clay was still calling, and texting, and begging me to give him another chance. But tonight I screwed up stupid courage and decided to tell him in person that I was never going to take him back, and never planned to see his face outside the office ever again.

'And ended up with *this* face,' she said.

She took in a lot of air.

'He snapped,' she said. 'Worse than I'd ever seen him.'

She lightly touched her fingers to the area next to her eye.

'I locked myself in the bathroom and told him I was going to call nine-one-one if he didn't leave,' she said. 'I had the ability to track him on his phone, and finally saw that he had left the building. I just had to talk to someone who I knew did care about me, and called Andrew.' She put her head in her hands. 'God, I have such awful taste in men!'

Her voice broke again. 'Andrew was the one who snapped when he got here,' she said. 'He said he was going after him.'

'Where is he now, and where is Whitson?' I said.

'Andrew is at the Brookline house,' she said. 'I can track him on my phone as well.'

238

'What about Whitson?'

'I'm afraid he's there, too,' she said.

She took more deep breaths then, as if trying to calm herself, even though it was clear that was a lost cause at this point.

'Andrew does care for me, very deeply,' she said. 'Not in the way that Laura thought. But he does.' One more deep breath, deepest yet. 'He just might care too much in this case.'

'What are you saying, Claire?'

'When he left here he said he was going to kill him,' she said.

75

The gate was open when I arrived at his house.

No floodlights came on as I stepped through it. No alarms sounded.

As I made my way along the tree line toward the house, I finally saw a silver Mercedes parked in front.

Perhaps Crain's own car was in the garage next to the house.

I kept waiting for floodlights, or for an alarm, for something, the closer I got to the house, but nothing happened. I pressed myself against the outside walls, ducking down when I came to one of the first-floor windows.

I kept inching along, eventually making my way to the front door.

I reached over and gently tried the knob.

The door, like the gate, was unlocked.

When I silently opened it a crack, I could clearly hear Andrew Crain's voice.

'You really left me no choice,' Crain was saying. 'I had to save Claire from you.'

Then, as if a switch had been thrown, he was shouting, like a different kind of alarm sounding.

'You can only let so much go!' Crain yelled.

When he stopped yelling, I heard Clay Whitson.

'You don't have to do this, Andrew,' he said.

I knew they were in the living room, on the other side of the foyer from the front door. It meant a fair amount of distance between me and them, I just couldn't remember exactly how much.

I had no way of knowing if it was just the two of them.

I had worn sneakers to Claire Megill's, still having them on after Susan and I had been to the park. I opened the door a few inches more and was into the foyer then. The sneakers made no noise. The fog, on little cat's feet. Sandburg. The things in my head.

'Getting you away from her once and for all,' Crain said, 'is the right thing to do. Then you can't hurt her ever again. Or anybody else.'

I pressed myself against the wall to my left, passing in front of art I knew had to be worth millions, and finally got close enough to the living room to see Crain standing in the middle of the room, pointing what I didn't have to get any closer to know was a .357 Magnum.

'It's funny, Clay,' Crain said, lowering his voice. 'I hate guns. But as hard as it might be for you to believe, I've always known how to use them.'

Whitson was on the couch, the Magnum pointed directly at him, the entire left side of his face bloody and swollen, as if Crain had already used his gun on him without firing it.

Yet.

I stuck mine in the back pocket of my jeans and stepped out into the entranceway, my hands in the air, not wanting to spook him.

'Don't shoot, Andrew,' I said quietly, trying to remember the last time I'd said that to anyone.

He turned his head slightly, but kept the gun pointed at Whitson, and remained surprisingly calm in the moment.

240

'You need to leave, Mr Spenser,' he said. 'This doesn't involve you. This is between Clay and me now. It really should have been long before this.'

'I'm not leaving,' I said.

I calculated the distance between us and how quickly I might be able to cover it.

No way to rush him.

And no way of knowing what he might do if I did.

'Then you need to slowly and carefully walk over and take a seat next to him,' Crain said.

'And if I refuse?' I said.

'Then you can just stand there and watch while I shoot him,' Crain said.

He stepped back a few feet, expanding his field of vision as I slowly walked to the couch, keeping my hands in the air.

'He told me he wanted to talk about the merger,' Whitson said. 'That he was officially onboard, he knew how hard I'd worked on it, and he wanted me to know. I was fixing myself a drink when he hit me in the face with his gun and kept hitting me until I finally passed out. When I woke up, I was sitting where I am right now.'

'Stop talking, please,' Crain said. *Both of you.*

'Andrew,' I said. 'I know what Whitson did to Claire. If you hadn't gotten him here, I would have gone looking for him myself. But doing it like this, that's not you.'

Crain's voice was amazingly calm then.

'Actually,' he said, 'it is.'

'You can't throw away everything you've built and everything you've done,' I said. 'You don't want to be remembered for killing a man in cold blood.'

'I'll change,' Whitson said.

'No, you won't,' Crain said. 'That's the problem. Men like you never change.'

'Even Claire isn't worth this,' I said. 'Not *like* this.'

I did not want to set him off further. I did want him to keep talking.

'They're all worth it!' Crain yelled.

There was an antique coffee table between us, looking as old as one of the maple trees outside. I didn't think I could turn it over if I tried to rush him from here. And I knew I didn't want to shoot Andrew Crain, even if he turned his gun on me.

'Laura wouldn't want you to do this,' I said.

He turned slightly, maybe a quarter of a turn, and now the gun was pointed at me. It had been a long time since someone had shot me. I hoped this time it wouldn't be the husband of my former client putting one in me because I made the wrong move, or said the wrong thing.

But Crain was back to focusing on Whitson then. I knew all about the gun in his hand. Knew there was no safety. If the hammer came back, it would mean the balloon had already gone up.

'Did you think treating her like that, *violating her like that*, wouldn't catch up with you eventually?' Crain said to Whitson. 'That someday a bill wouldn't be presented to you?'

'I'll get help,' Whitson said.

His own eyes were fixed on the gun. One of his eyes was already swollen shut. Crain hitting him with the Magnum must have felt as if he was hitting Whitson with a hammer.

'It's too late for that!' Crain said.

Yelling again.

'Claire knew that you and Whitson were here together,' I said. 'She sent me here.'

Crain had said that he knew how to use the gun. I had no way of knowing whether he did or not. And did not want to find out.

'It's the only way,' Crain said, almost as if he were talking to himself, reasoning with himself. 'I should have done this with my father, to save my mother from *him*.'

He cocked the gun then and I shoved Whitson to the side and dove across the table as the first bullet went into the couch where Whitson had been sitting, keeping myself underneath the barrel of the gun, which he fired again, the sound of it like an explosion in the small world that included only Crain and Whitson and me.

I heard something shatter behind me as I drove my shoulder into Crain's midsection, my full force taking him into the chair behind him, and then to the ground.

He still had the gun in his hand.

Even with all of my weight on him, he tried to roll out from underneath me, away from me, before I finally got the gun away from him.

'*I need this to be over!*' he shouted.

'It is,' I said.

I lifted him to his feet with my free hand and shoved him into the chair that was still in place. As I did, I saw Whitson out of the corner of my eye, running for the front door.

'*Whitson!*'

I was the one shouting.

He stopped and turned and saw me pointing Andrew Crain's gun at him.

'Sit the fuck down,' I said, 'before I'm the one who shoots you.'

76

Hawk said, 'Your boy Crain sounds like the damn buffet at the psychiatrists' convention.'

'At least it sounds as if he's going to get that kind of help now,' I said.

'He doesn't need some fancy place in California,' Hawk said. 'All he needs to do is go see Susan.'

'I'm here,' Susan said, smiling at Hawk from the other side of the table.

'Just paying you a compliment, missy,' Hawk said, and smiled back.

The three of us were having dinner a few nights later at the Atlantic Fish Company on Boylston. Before making the reservation I had asked Hawk if he wanted to bring along his current paramour. He had declined, saying she had elected to break things off.

'She told me she wanted to play the long game with me,' Hawk had said. 'And I had to tell her that unfortunately for her, I *got* no long game.'

Andrew Crain had checked into a place in Pacific Palisades called Groves. Claire had flown out there with him on the company jet. They had managed to do this without leaks of any kind. If someone did question where Crain was this close to the merger with the Prise people, the cover story was that he had gone to California for back surgery, not because of the breakdown that had finally culminated with him threatening to shoot Clay Whitson.

Ethan Lowe was now running all facets of the company, the Prise deal scheduled to be officially consummated in a week or so. There had been only one condition from Crain before he left for California: Lowe had finally agreed to terminate Whitson, after nondisclosure agreements on both sides. Claire Megill assured me that they were more comprehensive, and binding, than a nuclear arms treaty.

'So much of this with Clay was my fault,' she told me on the phone.

'Said the victim,' I said.

'Maybe when I'm out there with Andrew I should talk to somebody at Groves myself,' she said.

'Maybe you should,' I said.

I had dragged Whitson to his car when he was leaving Crain's house that night. Before he'd gotten in, I told him that if he ever sent Claire Megill so much as another email, then what had just happened to him inside would seem like something you could set to music.

We were almost finished with our appetisers. Susan had barely touched her wine, but sipped some of it now, as if suddenly remembering it was there.

'Andrew himself was probably abused by his father, too, along with his mother,' she said. 'It's as if he hasn't been able to stop the cycle of abuse since he was a little boy.'

'Don't forget that he told me he thought his wife might have killed her abuser,' I said. 'Maybe in the end he saw Clay Whitson as being all of them.'

'Why he *should've* shot his ass,' Hawk said.

He pointed at Susan's shrimp cocktail with his fork. 'You gonna eat that last one,' he said. 'Or just try to stare it into your stomach?'

Susan forked the shrimp now and put it on Hawk's plate. 'At least *you* ask, Hawk,' she said.

'I only take food off your plate when it's clear it's going to be wasted,' I said. 'I'm actually doing you a favor.'

We were finishing up with dessert later – New York Cheesecake for me, Crème de la Boston for Hawk, decaf cappuccino for Susan – when Hawk said to me, 'We both know what a bear you are for putting a bow on things. But maybe you got to consider that if you and Quirk and Belson can't roll this thing all the way up, maybe this is one *can't* be rolled up.'

Susan put her hand over mine. 'Maybe not even by you.'

Hawk grinned. 'You know what Drake says.'

'As a matter of fact, I don't.'

'Say you're moving on,' Hawk said.

'Screw Drake,' I said.

Now Susan squeezed my hand. 'Thank you for not saying "fuck," dear.'

Hawk went off into the night. Susan and I decided to walk back to my apartment, having Ubered to the restaurant. We were debating whether or not to have a nightcap at The Newbury when Cindy Patton called.

'I think I might have something,' she said. 'My friend from Proscape came through for me. And it looks like my friend

245

Darius knew plenty about getting into other people's clouds, before someone basically tried to steal his.'

'And found what?'

'Company financial records,' she said, lowering her voice as if she had somehow found the holy grail.

'Private records, I take it.'

'And private codes,' she said. 'I don't know how he did it. But he did. Some of it was on his personal computer, some on his one at work.'

She paused. 'But we may need some kind of forensic accountant to sort it all out.'

I told her I happened to know someone who fit that bill, though he would have been resistant to 'forensic,' thinking it redundant.

Then I told her what I wanted her to do.

'Old school,' she said.

'I went to that school before they closed it down,' I said.

77

The press conference that would announce the merger between Lith and the Canadian car company was scheduled for the following morning. Over the weekend, Marty Kaiser had turned my office into his office, and a bit of a war room, his laptop and mine. Marty worked off the old-school thumb drive that I'd had him pick up from Cindy Patton's apartment, not wanting to go anywhere near there myself, just in case she was still being watched, or I was being watched, or both of us were being watched.

'Are we getting near the end of our movie?' she said, still using the burner phone I'd made her buy, and calling me on the landline at my office.

'Jesus,' I said, 'I hope so.'

Now it was Monday night, and I was on my way to Ethan Lowe's waterfront home on Marblehead Neck. I had called to tell him I needed to see him in person. I wanted to apologise to his face for having misjudged him, that it was time for me to man up and admit I'd been wrong about him, and about a lot of things.

He lived on the eastern side of Ocean Ave Parkway. I'd Googled his purchase of the home, and read that he had as much waterfront exposure as any home on the North Shore.

When I arrived, I saw a Tesla parked out front. I hoped his new business partners didn't find out.

It was the only car in front of the main house, whose size and architecture made me wonder where the West Wing was. There was a huge garage to the side, and in the distance, I could make out what looked to be some kind of guesthouse.

Good being Ethan Lowe.

He was waiting for me on his porch when I got out of my car. He stepped back after shaking my hand and made a sweeping gesture with his own that took in his house, the property, maybe the stars in the sky and the waves I could hear in the distance.

'Annoying, isn't it?' he said, and ushered me inside.

There was less art, at least in the living room, than what adorned the walls of his partner's home in Brookline. It was all more modern in here, glass and steel and a lot of white, including a double-sided sofa, one side facing the water, the other facing a flat screen that was as big as any I'd ever seen in my life.

Lowe asked if I wanted a drink. I told him I'd pass, the drive up had taken longer than I'd thought it would. He asked if I minded if he fixed himself one and I told him to have at it, I'd drink vicariously.

When he'd settled into an armchair across from me he said, 'Okay, I'm ready for the big reveal.'

'Let me tell it in the form of a story,' I said.

'Who doesn't like a good story?' Lowe said.

Now we were bonding.

'Claire Megill once told me she hired Darius Baker because he knew more about modern finance than she and Andrew Crain combined,' I said. 'Following the money at Lith wasn't Andrew's primary skill. He was a science guy at heart. Claire said that from the time she'd first gone to work for him he'd talked about his money guys as if they were neuroscientists. And then, as you know, he set out to save the world. So Claire thought it was almost like checks and balances, trying to stay aware of where the checks were going.'

'There was no need,' Lowe said. 'I was always transparent with Andrew about what was coming in and what was going out.'

'Of course you were!' I said, worried that I sounded too enthusiastic, or eager to please.

I had seen him pour himself tequila. He drank some now. I was aware that in a fitness-crazed world, tequila had become a drink of choice because of the low sugar content. I just thought it made grown men and women whoop.

'Anyway,' I continued, 'it turns out that things got complicated when Laura Crain got suspicious about how you'd pulled the rabbit out of the hat during that period when it looked as if Lith might go under.'

'Don't be stupid,' Lowe said. 'That was never going to happen.'

I grinned. 'Be that as it may,' I said. 'But while maybe you had certainty about that, Laura didn't. She didn't like Claire very much, so she couldn't go to her. But her husband must have told her what a sharp kid Darius was. So she trusted him with the task of, well, following the money for real. More Andrew's than yours.'

I was taking some big leaps, at least with some of this. But believed this version of things to be accurate, around what Marty Kaiser had intuited.

'And you think you know all of this… *how*?' Lowe said.

'As it happens,' I said, 'I am now in possession of the information on Darius's cloud, and what a lucky boy am I because of it.'

I didn't tell him that I had also gotten into Laura Crain's personal information, after breaking into the Brookline house

248

and actually finding passwords inside her old-fashioned Filofax. But there was no point. And I really didn't need her information once I had Darius Baker's, thanks to Cindy Patton's friend from Proscape, who had gotten me all the way to this meeting with Ethan Lowe.

'Somehow Darius accessed the "Sources and Users" reports for the two partners. Yours and Andrew's,' I said. 'I guess that's as good a place to pick up as any.'

I could hear Marty Kaiser's voice inside my head, even though he had occasionally lost me talking about superusers and off-site storage and the kind of history on the cloud, because he was a bit of a computer geek himself.

'I frankly don't know how Darius figured out how to access the files from you,' I said. 'But he did, probably because of some inspired hacking on his part. And from his own records, he analyzed money going in and money going out over the past few years, and how it just didn't seem to add up.'

I told him the rest of it then the way Marty had told it to me, just not nearly as well.

'In the last month of his life, Darius Baker somehow managed to access the codes for money coming in from off-site storage of company files, from the period when Lith was in big trouble that you'd frankly created. Only during that period, the money suddenly wasn't coming through JPMorgan the way it usually did. It was coming from a different bank. UBS. Lots and lots of money.' I shrugged again, and smiled, what I hoped was sheepishly. 'But I'm not telling you anything you don't know.'

'It's called diversifying, Mr Spenser,' Lowe said, a bit dismissively, I thought. 'And nothing I did was illegal, though you probably wouldn't know anything about that.'

'What I *do* know,' I said, 'is how strict UBS's policies are about privacy for their clients.'

I actually hadn't known that. But the world's greatest accountant sure had.

'Even Hitler had a Swiss bank account,' I added. 'Did you know that?'

Lowe's tequila had gone untouched now.

'Long story short?' I said. 'What we found in Darius's history, as well as he tried to cover his tracks, was that the money you needed to keep the big wheel turning and maybe even Proud Mary to keep on burning had come from Saudi Arabia. Of all places.' I shook my head slowly from time to time, like I was the one explaining things to a slow kid in class. 'Oh, Ethan,' I said. 'You've been a very bad boy.'

Lowe stared at me, maybe blinking a little more rapidly, the way his partner did under stress.

'Because you went panhandling to the country that is your partner's sworn enemy because of the truly shitty way it treats women,' I said. 'Now Darius knew, and he told Laura what he had. Then she knew. The one thing I'll never know is why she confronted you when she found out. Maybe she wanted to give you the chance to deny it, or at least explain it, before she went to her husband. Maybe she didn't want to believe it was true. Or didn't want to send her husband any further around the bend than he already was. But she knew that if it *was* true, you were fucked, because of language she knew existed in the partners' agreement giving her husband the right to buy your forty per cent, as long as he had cause. And Saudi Arabia sure as shit would have been enough cause for Andrew Crain, whether he was in a diminished mental state at the time or not.'

I breathed in deeply through my nose, out through my mouth, loudly, and largely for effect.

'And all of this, Ethan, just to put a bow on things,' I said, 'is why I believe you had to have Laura and Darius killed.'

I shook my head from side to side, more slowly than before, and more sadly.

'Funny how things turn out, really,' I said. 'Laura Crain came to me because she thought her husband had gone crazy. But the crazy partner turned out to be you.'

78

'No wonder you didn't want a drink,' Lowe finally said. 'Clearly you're already drunk.'

'Only with power,' I said.

He got up now and walked over to his bar and poured more tequila, came back and sat down.

'You've literally taken numbers out of thin air, *out* of the clouds, and convinced yourself that they're facts,' he said.

'Here's a fact,' I said. 'I've got your ass. And as soon as the cops figure out a way to get DNA from your pal Reggie and I match it to what it turns out they ultimately found on Laura Crain's body, I'm going to have his ass, too.' This wasn't entirely true – there had been no DNA on Laura's body – but Ethan didn't have to know that.

It wouldn't have happened without Cindy Patton. Or her friend from Proscape, who had become a superprovider in more ways than one. All because Cindy had convinced him to do the right thing. People still did that, whether there was anything in it for them or not.

Something I was certain Lowe would never understand.

'You need to go now,' Lowe said. 'But before you do, just be aware that if you try to take this fever dream of yours to your friend at *The Globe* or anybody else, I will have *your* ass in litigation when hell freezes over with you in it.'

I stood.

'Take your best shot,' I said. 'Forget about *The Globe* or *The Wall Street Journal* or CNBC. What I'm wondering is how you're going to explain taking that blood money to your partner.'

'Oh, spare me your woke bullshit about blood money, Spenser,' he said. 'Take a look at the real world, and at how much business this country does with the Saudis, and how many other American businesses do the same goddamn thing.'

'I thought you and Andrew were supposed to be brothers,' I said.

'We are,' he said. 'I'm Cain. He's Abel.'

'What *are* you going to tell Andrew?'

'I don't have to tell Andrew shit,' Lowe said. 'Andrew wouldn't still have a company if it wasn't for me. He was more interested in saving whales and women. Fuck him. You can tell him that the next time you see him.'

I walked over to Lowe and moved the pocket square I was wearing to the side, and showed him the tiny camera that my high-tech thief, by the name of Ghost Garrity, had outfitted me with after he'd helped get me into the Crains' house.

Now I was the science guy, helping the science guy.

'You just told him,' I said.

My phone sounded then. I took it out of my pocket and put it on speaker and held it up between Ethan Lowe and me.

The voice was Andrew Crain's.

'Remember that TV show, Ethan?' Crain said, his voice sounding tinny, the way speakerphone calls always did.

Lowe hesitated, then seemed to find his own voice.

'What show is that?' he said.

'The "you're fired" show,' Crain said.

Lowe was staring at the phone in my hand as if it might go off like a grenade.

There was a pause.

'Fuck *me*, Ethan?' Crain said. 'No. Fuck *you*.'

79

I had flown to Los Angeles, but not to visit Andrew Crain and Claire Megill at Groves. Now I was back, and so were the two of them.

'So who's minding the store now that the big boss bought out the weasel boss?' Hawk said.

Maybe it had been the LA weather while I was away. Maybe it had been Z's trainer, and the combination of runs and walks Z and I took along the boardwalk in Santa Monica every morning. But my knee felt as sturdy as it has been since I'd been assaulted that night.

Hawk and I had finished our own morning run, and were walking the last half-mile along the Charles.

'The public version is that Andrew Crain is back in charge,' I said. 'But it is my belief that Claire Megill, who is probably more qualified than Crain or Ethan Lowe at this point, is the real point person.'

We stopped and sat on the bench that was just a few yards past the head statue of Arthur Fiedler. The old boy was still looking good.

'How's it hanging, Pops,' Hawk had said, rubbing the head for luck.

'I see what you did there with Pops,' I said.

''Course you did.'

I leaned back and felt the morning sun on my face.

'So the merger's dead,' Hawk said.

'Deader than the Sox.'

'Where's Lowe at?'

'Claire says the Maldives,' I said.

'No extradition, it ever comes to that. Least the boy did something smart.'

'Just to give you a heads-up?' I said. 'I'm not giving up on tying him to the murders, even if he ends up living on the moon.'

'Murders you believe got committed by the badass Brit brother,' Hawk said. 'And where's the brother at, by the way?'

'Parts unknown,' I said. 'But if I have anything to say about it, not for long. I'll get to him eventually, same as I'm going to get to Lowe.'

'Take me with you,' Hawk said.

'I assumed that was understood.'

'Crain sounds like he's as sure Lowe got Smythe to do it as you are,' Hawk said.

'Which is why Crain wants to hire me now the way his wife did,' I said. 'She wanted to find out what was wrong with him. Now he wants me to find the guy he believes killed her.'

'On account of he can't get to Lowe,' Hawk said.

Hawk leaned his own head back. It was like watching the sun reflect off a smooth black stone gem.

'You think Crain can really put his Humpty Dumpty self back together?' Hawk said.

'Esoteric language like that, I can't believe you weren't the one treating him out there.'

'*Do* you think he can get put back together?' Hawk asked.

'Guy's pretty damaged,' I said. 'But Susan doesn't think beyond repair. And would be ready to help, if he ever asked her for it.'

'Susan gives up on people about as easy as you do,' Hawk said.

Hawk turned his head to admire two young women in impossibly tight running pants and tighter tops, if such a thing were even sartorially possible given the way their pants fit them, until they disappeared up the path. Being a good friend, I joined him with my own laserlike focus just to keep him company.

'Couldn't understand why you went out to LA when you went,' he said.

'But now you do.'

'Uh-huh.'

'I was right, just not the way I thought.'

'No law got passed that you got to tell him,' Hawk said. 'Or tell her.'

'I've given that some consideration,' I said. 'But then decided that I can't help myself, I am just one transparent sonofabitch.'

It had taken a substantial amount of old-fashioned legwork from Zebulon Sixkill and me, around what turned out to be a pleasant visit with him, and Mattie, in our spare time. I had even met Mattie's zombie actor. And while I didn't love the guy, I also didn't feel the urge to rearrange his disgustingly perfect features.

Maybe Cindy Patton had been right.

Maybe I was the cool dad.

'So you gonna tell them what you went and found out?' Hawk said.

I nodded.

'Forthwith?' he said. I nodded again.

'Was gonna go with "anon,"' Hawk said. 'But I decided in this case bigger was better.'

He smiled and further brightened the day,

'Something you wouldn't know nothing about,' Hawk said.

80

Claire Megill was once again conducting regular hours at her office. She'd informed me that Andrew Crain was not, but was at least showing up for a couple hours every day, so that people on the fiftieth floor could see him back at work, and the people down on the forty-ninth would hear about him being back at work.

Claire's office looked the same. But so much had changed, for both of us, since I'd first been inside it.

I previously hadn't taken any notice of the small display of framed photographs near the big window behind her, but did now.

She sat at her desk. I sat across from her, as if I were the one in the client chair now.

'How's he doing?' I said.

'A little better every day,' she said. 'For the time being I've moved into the house on Chestnut with him.' She smiled. 'As a friend.'

'I don't judge,' I said.

'The hell you don't,' she said.

She really did have beautiful eyes.

'So have you decided to come work for Andrew?' she said. 'He continues to be of the belief that only you, and you alone, can prove that Ethan really was behind those murders.'

'If I do decide to stay with it,' I said, 'it would be on the house. I still feel as if I owe it to Laura and to Darius.'

'I doubt Andrew would agree to it.'

'It won't be up to him.'

'You really are exceptionally stubborn.'

I winked at her. 'Don't judge,' I said.

She spoke of the intense treatment he'd gotten in California, and how she'd been a participant in some of it, almost as if it were an Al-Anon meeting for a family member, now that she was all the family he had.

'Such endless abuse in his life,' she said, 'starting with his parents and extending all the way to me.'

'I wouldn't have ever known about his father if he hadn't blurted it out the night he threatened to shoot Whitson,' I said.

She sighed. It was almost a mournful sound. 'His primary doctor believes that what Clay did to me was a trigger for the way he has been acting.' She shook her head. 'It's amazing that he's been able to function as well as he has as an adult, and be as successful. His father treated his mother the way he did. The woman he would marry was abused after that. Then me.'

'But he wasn't the only one in a cycle of abuse, was he?' I said.

Claire Megill looked puzzled. 'I'm not sure I understand.'

'I'm not entirely sure I do, either, to tell you the truth,' I said.

I reached for the inside pocket of my blazer and took out the photograph that Z had come up with, and slid it across the desk to her.

The head shot of a young man who really did look a little like Brad Pitt.

She reacted as if she'd seen a ghost, mostly because she had.

'That's a picture of… That's my husband,' she said.

'Troy Robinson,' I said. 'But Laura called him Rob.'

81

She started to reach for the photo from the Screen Extras Guild that had finally been discovered, though Troy Robinson hadn't joined SAG before he left Claire Megill and left Los Angeles and headed east.

Then it had taken most of the week I was out in LA to finally trace him to the address at which Claire had still been living with her young son when she went to work for Andrew Crain, at one of the businesses that Crain and Ethan Lowe had acquired about five years after the start-up of Lith.

Claire's hand, shaking slightly, hovered over the photograph like a drone, as if she were afraid to touch it.

She looked at me. 'Did you find out… Do you know what happened to him?'

The view behind her was as clear and perfect and every bit as thrilling as it had been the first time I had been on this floor, and in this office. What looked like a graduation picture of her son, either high school or college, was on that table next to her.

He had some of his mother in his face. But even from a few feet away, I could see that he was the spitting image of his father, what his father had looked like at that age. Same dirty blonde hair. If I looked closer, I was sure I would see the same blue eyes.

'No,' I said. 'As a matter of fact, I don't know what happened to him.'

'But I do,' Andrew Crain said from behind me.

I hadn't heard him come into her office. I'm not sure she had even seen him, as fixed as she was on the photograph of Troy Robinson, as clearly knocked back as she was by her husband being in this room with us.

Crain shut the door quietly behind him, came around the desk, stood next to Claire Megill, putting a hand on her shoulder.

She looked up at him. But Crain was looking directly at me.

'I killed him,' he said.

82

He took us down the hall to his own office.

When we arrived there and he'd shut the door he said, 'I'm going to assume you're not wearing another of your recording devices, Mr Spenser.'

'I'm not,' I said. 'And that's not why I'm here, you must know that.'

The office was at least three or four times the size of Claire Megill's. The three of us sat in a corner that was like the small living room of a hotel suite. Crain and Claire were on a small silk sofa. I sat in a matching chair across from them.

The view in here was even better. More windows.

Claire Megill had not spoken since we'd left her office.

Now she did.

'How, Andrew?' she said.

258

He told us both about Troy, who his wife had known as Rob, putting Laura Mason in the hospital, and Missy Jones telling Crain about that, but how Laura was going to be safe after Missy had literally taken matters into her own hands. Or her father had.

'But he didn't leave town the way he said he would,' Crain said. 'He came back. Missy Jones didn't know that. I did.'

He turned to face Claire Megill.

'I went to see Laura one night later that summer,' he said. 'He had beaten her again. Not badly enough to put her in the hospital this time. But badly enough. And Rob told her that if she told anybody this time, if anybody came after him, he was going to kill her.'

I said to Claire Megill, 'Did he hit you? Your husband?'

She shook her head. 'At the end,' she said. Then in a whisper she said, 'Maybe he didn't love me as much as he loved Laura.'

She put quotes around 'loved.'

'He blamed me for the pregnancy,' she said.

Crain said he stayed with Laura that night, taking the couch in her apartment. When she was finally asleep, he snuck in and got her phone and texted the man he knew only as Rob, texting just starting to become popular at the time. Crain told Troy Robinson, using Laura's phone, that she still loved him, and wanted to meet him and just talk.

'Where?' I said.

'It doesn't matter where.'

'How did you kill him?'

'I shot him,' he said. 'I really am a very good shot when someone like you isn't rushing me.'

'What did you do with the body?'

'I disposed of it.' He shrugged. 'I'm a scientist, remember?'

He seemed quite composed, and clear-eyed, in light of the story he was telling.

'Then I went away for a couple years, to deal with what I'd done,' he said. 'Like I was trying to escape myself. When I came back, Laura and I were finally together and Ethan and I hit it big with Lith. And I have been trying to bury what I did ever since underneath good works.' No one spoke. Claire Megill was still turned to him, but staring vacantly past him at the same time, as if in a mild state of shock. I had come here expecting some sort of reaction from her.

Not from him.

And not this.

'For all of these years,' he said, 'it's been like that Poe story, about the telltale heart. No matter what I did and no matter where I went, what I'd done was there. Finally I became obsessed with the man I'd killed, wanting to know more about him other than what he'd done to Laura. I did what Mr Spenser did, and finally traced him back to you. But I had one advantage that Mr Spenser didn't. I'd taken his California driver's license, the night I killed him.'

'You found Claire and her son,' I said.

'She was working at Apple at the time,' Crain said, 'but she and her son were just scraping by.'

'Then one day I got the call from the headhunter,' she said, shifting her head slightly and looking at me, as if picking up the story.

'The headhunter called because I told him to call, and to offer you a much better job, at much higher compensation,' Crain said. 'After that, the law of unintended consequences took over. Because you weren't some charity case, you turned out to be brilliant. And ultimately, for me, indispensable. Now more than ever.'

He took her hands in his now.

'I wanted to save you both,' he said to her. 'That night with Whitson, I was ready to kill again, as much as I'd fought the urge to do that, for as long as I had.'

Claire Megill started to say something, didn't.

'You can't escape your own past forever,' Andrew Crain said. 'I realise that now.'

I didn't have anything to add to that, for either one of them, so I headed for the elevators. Forthwith.

83

'So both the partners at Lith, Inc. get away with murder,' Susan Silverman said.

'I hadn't thought of it precisely that way, but I suppose you're right, Doctor,' I said.

It was Sunday at her house. We were in her kitchen, and I was about to prepare brunch.

'His break with reality obviously came when he wanted to kill again,' she said. 'Whitson, in this case. He had fought the urge as long as he could. To kill Whitson the way he had killed the man he knew as Rob.'

'Claire was being abused the way Laura had been,' I said. 'But he didn't want to kill again.'

'Who does?' Susan said.

'Only then Whitson went after her again, and he went after Whitson, and I stopped him,' I said.

'And my hero became his,' Susan said. 'It is almost a festival of symmetry.'

'And you call me a poet.'

'No,' she said, 'you call yourself a poet.'

I was preparing Belgian waffles, doing them up big, from scratch, flour and sugar and milk and baking powder and too much butter, three large eggs, freshly sliced strawberries on the side, Vermont maple syrup, and, wait for it, even freshly whipped cream. Susan called the whole thing the Triple Bypass. She was still in her favorite white robe. I was in a LARAMIE WYOMING T-shirt she ordered from The Knothole in Laramie, and sweatpants. She sat at the butcher-block table while I cooked. At some point after

261

we ate we would walk Pearl and then, if all went according to plan, be back in her bed for yet another matinee.

I liked Sundays with Susan very much.

I poured more Dunkin' coffee for both of us.

'So in the end we are talking about an otherwise good and moral man committing a terrible and immoral act,' Susan said.

'We are.'

'A terrible and immoral act for which you have given him a full pardon,' she said.

'He'll never fully pardon himself,' I said. 'I think of it more as clemency. For a crime, incidentally, I could never prove.'

She held her mug in elegant fingers and stared at me over it with eyes dark and deep. It was past noon and she had not yet done her face. She was still the most beautiful woman I had ever known. I told her something then I told her often: If she ever left me, she just needed to give me time to pack a bag, because I was going with her.

She got up then and came around the table and got behind me and got up on her toes and kissed me behind my ear.

'I love you,' she said.

'I loved you first.'

'I'm not sure that is verifiable,' Susan said. 'But I'll take it.'

She kept her arms around me.

'Everything you now know,' she said. 'Is it enough?'

'I'm afraid it's going to have to be,' I said. 'In the words of the philosopher Dirty Harry, man's got to know his limitations.'

'As I recall from all the times you made me watch that movie, he said that right before he blew up Hal Holbrook's car.'

'Boy,' I said, 'those were the days.'

I told her to sit down and prepare herself, if she possibly could, for the brunch of her dreams.

'It's funny,' I said. 'I couldn't get it out of my head that Troy Robinson was a part of this. It just wasn't the way I ever could have imagined.'

'Even you're not that smart, big boy,' she said.

We ate. And walked Pearl. And made love in the big bed in the middle of the afternoon. She was leaving in a few hours for New York, a two-day psychotherapy conference. When it was time, I drove her to Logan Airport, Pearl in the backseat. I always hated saying goodbye to Susan, even when she was leaving for just a couple days. A week in Los Angeles had seemed like a couple lifetimes for me.

When she had disappeared into the terminal, Pearl and I drove back to Marlborough Street and I threw one of her old tennis balls until I thought my arm would detach from my shoulder, then let her frolic for a while with a golden retriever, the other dog seeming to have as much energy as my own. We went back to the apartment and I fed her and fed myself with huevos rancheros, which I ate while watching, but paying scant attention to, *Sunday Night Football*.

When the game was over I felt the same sort of restlessness I had been feeling the past few days. Susan had asked if knowing what I knew was enough for me. I had told her it would have to be. But knew in my heart it never would be. Because I would never know for sure exactly how two innocent people had died. Or be able to prove that Ethan Lowe and Reggie Smythe were behind it, though I knew they were.

I had taken Frank Belson to lunch the day before and finally laid out everything I knew, excluding only what Andrew Crain had told me about Troy Robinson, because that got Belson nowhere on either Laura Crain or Darius Baker.

'I did everything I could, Frank,' I told him.

'I'll tell Quirk,' Belson said. 'He'll probably want to give you a participation trophy.'

I stared out my window. The nights were getting longer, and the temperature had dropped, and, combined with the rain that had started to fall when Pearl and I were back in the apartment, blanketed the Back Bay in fog.

'A foggy day...' I crooned.

Pearl was underneath the TV. She briefly picked up her head as I began to sing, but then put it right back down, realising the song wasn't about food.

I had found out more than I had bargained for, a lot more, and it wasn't unreasonable to think of that as a form of closure.

But was closure without justice enough?

Z had joked about me and loose ends, but we both knew loose ends were no joke, not for me.

I put on my leather jacket, the old thing impervious by now to rain, and went outside and walked past the river, the lights of Cambridge on the other side dimmed mightily by the fog.

'Take the damn win,' Hawk had said.

'Even if it feels like a tie?' I said.

I passed Arthur Fiedler and began walking toward Mass Ave. Somehow the fog made the city and the water and even the traffic seem more quiet. I wasn't looking for peace out here. Just less restlessness.

I turned up the collar of my jacket and told myself it would be a short walk tonight because Susan was probably at her hotel in Midtown Manhattan by now and I wanted to call her.

I was the only one out here.

Or thought so.

'Spenser,' I heard from behind me.

I recognised both the voice and the accent.

When I turned I saw only the outline of him, twenty or so yards away.

I could see his arm outstretched.

'Even with you,' Reggie Smythe said, 'I felt it wouldn't be sporting to shoot you in the back. But get those hands nice and high, you darling boy. Because I can guarantee you that I won't miss this time.'

'Not that *you* asked, Reg,' I said, 'but I'm unarmed.'

'I don't care,' he said.

He did miss with the first bullet, as it turned out.

Just not the second, which hit me high up on the left side, just below my shoulder, and spun me half around and staggered me off the path and down toward the water.

84

The feeling of being shot was as I remembered it, because you never forget. I could still vividly and painfully recall being shot by the Gray Man, going into the Charles River by choice that time, my only chance I had at self-preservation, and the Gray Man thinking that he had fired kill shots when he had not.

My left shoulder felt as if someone had set fire to it.

But I was not all the way in the river this time, just in wet grass and mud at the water's edge, turning myself enough to see Smythe jogging to cover the distance between us.

I knew by now he had a suppressor.

He fired again into the fog, this bullet missing me but splattering mud I felt hit me in the face.

I screamed as if the bullet had hit me and thrashed around briefly and then lay still.

'I told our Mr Lowe he couldn't scare you off with a couple of bully boys, you weren't the type,' Smythe said. 'And then I told him to let me finish the job after I missed, but he said he'd thought it was over and he was too close to getting everything he wanted.'

I heard him sigh. He was very close by now.

'You really did kill them both, didn't you?'

He ignored the question.

'Even though everything has now been buggered up beyond belief, I still can't take the chance that what you told him about my DNA was true,' he said softly.

He was down off the walking path then, slipping slightly as he

265

made his way to me, righting himself. The moon was hidden by the night. I couldn't make out his face.

I didn't know how much blood I was losing, but had to assume it was a lot. My left arm had gone numb. He had made his way back to me then, and was raising his gun, for what I knew would be the last time.

'May I say one last thing?' I said.

'I'd make it fast.'

'I lied about the DNA,' I said. 'And I also lied about being unarmed, you dumb bastard.'

Then came up with the gun I'd told him I didn't have and shot him in the chest, center mass, and then again, and saw him stumble and go into the Charles River, facefirst into it, arms and legs extended.

Dead man's float.

85

Somehow it was the week before Thanksgiving.

The stitches underneath the front of my left shoulder had been removed, and I had stopped wearing a sling, but was still in the early stages of rebuilding my left hook at Henry Cimoli's gym. Day at a time.

Claire Megill had stopped by my office, and was seated in the same chair where it had all begun with Laura Crain.

'I don't know if you've heard,' she said. 'But Ethan Lowe seems to have disappeared from the home he was renting in the Maldives.'

'Is that so?' I said.

'He was last seen hiking near Mount Villingili,' she said. 'It's the highest point there, though not all that high.'

'Good to know,' I said.

'Maybe Andrew was right,' I said. 'That day in his office. Maybe in the end you can't escape your past.'

I smiled. She smiled.

'Anyway,' she said, 'I just thought you should know, and wanted to thank you again for caring as much as you did. And do.'

'I'm curious about something,' I said.

'Curious to the end.'

'Do you plan to tell your son about what really happened to his father?' I said. 'Who his father really was.'

She stopped smiling, and shook her head, and looked quite sad. Still beautiful. But sad.

'Some things *should* stay buried,' she said.

Before she left, she told me that Crain had entered into negotiations with the Prise car people, not for a merger this time, but to sell them his company. And that she and Crain were planning a trip around the world once everything was in place, like some sort of tour of his good causes.

'What about Saudi Arabia?' I said.

'It will be our first stop,' she said. She paused and said, 'On our way to wherever the two of us are going to end up, and whatever we're going to be.'

She hugged me before walking out the door. Hawk and I were meeting for a drink at the Rowes Wharf Bar in an hour or so.

It gave me just enough time.

When he opened the door, after I had bluffed my way past his doorman with almost breathtaking ease, and knowing my left was nothing these days, I hit him with the right hand that had only gotten better since I'd used it on Reggie Smythe in front of my building that night.

I was almost certain, just from the sound and the feeling in my knuckles when I connected, that I had broken Clay Whitson's nose.

He was already bleeding all over his white shirt and onto his off-white carpet as he managed to get himself into a sitting position.

But he was still a smart lawyer, even now. It meant smart enough to not even consider getting to his feet, and then trying to come at me.

'What was that for?' he said.

'For every woman who ever got hit by somebody like you,' I said.

Then I went to meet Hawk at the bar.

Acknowledgments

As always, I must first acknowledge David and Daniel Parker, who continue to give me the high honor of continuing their father's characters.

My agent, Esther Newberg, is the one who got me into the game in the first place, telling me one summer day to write a sample chapter in the voice of Sunny Randall, and now here we are.

You simply cannot ask for a better or more supportive boss than I have with Ivan Held, the capo di tutti capi at Putnam.

One final and heartfelt thanks to a wonderful editor named Danielle Dieterich, literally my partner in crime on so many books in the Parker-sphere.

And last, but certainly not least, my gratitude once again to Capt. John Fisher of the Bedford (Mass.) Police Deparment; the great Ziggy Alderman, still giving me the business; and Peter Gethers, spitballer supreme.

THE NEW SUNNY RANDALL MYSTERY

ROBERT B. PARKER'S

BAD INFLUENCE

by ALISON GAYLIN

Sunny Randall's newest client, Blake, seems to have it all: he is an Instagram influencer, with all of the perks that the lifestyle entails – a beautiful girlfriend, wealth, and adoring fans.

But one of those fans has turned ugly, and Sunny is brought on board to protect Blake and to uncover who is out to kill him. In doing so, she investigates a glamorous world rife with lies, schemes and ties to Boston's mob.

Soon the threats against Blake grow to include personal attacks on Sunny.

Sunny must learn new tricks – and call in old friends – to stop a killer.

NOEXIT.CO.UK/BAD-INFLUENCE

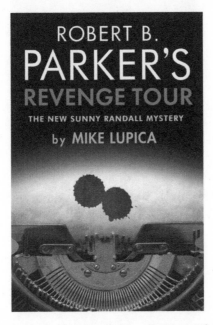

Sunny Randall owes a favour. Her landlord and former client, famous novelist Melanie Joan Hall, is being threatened and blackmailed, and it is up to Sunny and her best friend Spike to ensure her protection. But as Sunny looks into the identity of Melanie Joan's stalker, she learns that much of the author's past is a product of her amazing imagination, and her loyalty to her old friend is challenged as she searches for the truth.

At the same time, Sunny springs into action when her ageing ex-cop father, Phil, is threatened by a shady lawyer with a desire to settle an old score. Fighting crimes on two fronts, Sunny must use all of her savvy, and the help of her friends, in order to protect those she loves.

And one thing is for sure with both of these cases: this time, it's personal.

NOEXIT.CO.UK/REVENGE-TOUR

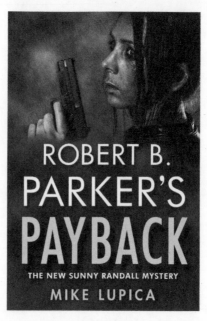

ROBERT B. PARKER'S PAYBACK

THE NEW SUNNY RANDALL MYSTERY

MIKE LUPICA

Sunny Randall has often relied on the help of her best friend Spike in times of need. When Spike's restaurant is taken over under a predatory loan agreement, Sunny has a chance to return the favour. She begins digging into the life of the hedge fund manager who screwed Spike over – surely a guy that smarmy has a skeleton or two in his closet – and soon finds this new enemy may have the backing of even badder criminals.

At the same time, Sunny's cop contact Lee Farrell asks her to intervene with his niece, a college student who reported being the victim of a crime but seems to know more than she's telling police. As the uncooperative young woman becomes outright hostile, Sunny runs up against a wall that she's only more determined to scale.

Then, what appear to be two disparate cases are united by a common factor, and the picture becomes even more muddled. But one thing is clear: Sunny has been poking a hornet's nest from two sides, and all hell is about to break loose.

NOEXIT.CO.UK/PAYBACK